Vengeance Is Mine

What I have given in love I now take with revenge.

By
Hope C. Clarke

Author of Best Seller, Shadow Lover
& Not With My Son

I dedicate this book to my two men Terence Jamal Clarke and Ibraheima Diallo. You two give me every reason to be happy and strong. Against all odds, with you two, I can conquer all.

This book is a work of fiction. Names, characters, places and incidents are products of the author's imagination or are used fictictiously. Any resemblance to actual events or locales or persons, living or dead, is entirely coincidental.

Published by:

P.O. Box 1746, New York, NY, 10017
Phone: 718-498-2408 Fax: 718-498-2408
www.anewhopepublishing.com
email: NewHopePublish@aol.com
email author: HopeClarke@aol.com

Library of Congress Catalog Card Number:

ISBN: 1-929279-03-5

Cover Design:	**Keith Saunders**
	m_asaund@bellsouth.net
Copy Edit:	**Marlon Green**
	Marlonwriter@yahoo.com
Final Proof:	**Deidre Wall**
Printed by:	**FNIS Canada - Publications Solutions**
	Phone: 800-268-4217 Fax: 416-284-5452
	bostrander@fnis.com

Shadow Lover

Abrutal beating and a miraculous surgery leaves behind a trail of bodies as an angry husband goes out on a binge to reclaim his escaped wife.

A surgeon's love and compassion will lead him to risk it all to protect her…maybe even with the lives of his medical staff. But can he protect her when there are no more bodies between them?

Shadow Lover is a riveting tale of passions, fears and choices.

ISBN: 1-929279-00-0 $14.95

Not With My Son
(originally published as Pent Up Passion)

Keesha Smalls has been out of passion's game for a long time until she takes a second look at her best friend's son.

The dashingly gorgeous Chris Walker brings more than flaming romance to Keesha's bedroom. Their secret romance is perfect until Christine, Chris' mother finds out.

A mother's rage can be terrifying but someone's past can be deadly. Keesha learns that sometimes it's better to have never known love than to love the wrong man.

ISBN: 0-9722771-5-3 $14.95

Best Seller

Kurt Daley, an aspiring writer, gets more than she bargains for when her favorite bestselling author, Dean, hands her a possession he is dying to pass on.

Dean's new protégé, Kurt, will fulfill her destiny and write the greatest best-seller ever—a dreadful tale that reaches out and touches everyone close to her. It isn't long before the accomplished writer finds herself living out a perilous tale of her own. Now Kurt Daley will have to find the secrets hidden behind being a best-seller before the clock runs out.

What if you knew that everyone page you wrote brought you closer to your end?

ISBN: 1-929279-02-7   14.95

Deborah Maisonet, you are an absolute God sent. Thank you so much for helping me at signings, designing, maintaining and updating my website. You continuously do a wonderful job at which I am eternally grateful.

~ Website designer
www.webfulyours.com

Duane Saunders, my spirited brother. Book signings wouldn't be the same without you. Thank you so much for all your zeal and energy. Paired with you, I can't fail.

~ Author of forthcoming title
Black Jesus, 120 Degrees of Pain—Heaven or Hell

Keith Saunders, I don't know how to thank you. Our union has only been successful. You have refaced all of my books and they are now flying off the shelves and I can't seem to keep them in print. I am a dedicated patron and you can believe that Marlon Designs will always be my choice. I highly recommend you to any and everyone. You a sistah can be jealous, but I know that I have to share your skill, so do your thing and keep a little space for me.

~ The very best in graphic designs
www.mariondesigns.com
m_asaund@bellsouth.net

Marlon Green, I am so proud of the work you've done on Vengeance is mine. Thank you for taking a personal interest in editing my work and helping me get grammatically correct. You're the best and wonderful to work with.

~ Editorial services & Author of
forthcoming novel *Butter*
marlonwriter@yahoo.com

Erika Alexander, I couldn't have been luckier to find at the Harlem Book Fair just the face I was looking for. Thank you for agreeing to model for my cover. I've got to say that beauty was in Harlem that day and I found it.

Notable People   *iii*

Nancey Flowers and Yvette Hayward, you two are the dynamic duo. Thank you for stepping up to the plate and taking on the responsibility of whipping my marketing plan into shape. I look forward to prosperous years because of you.

Carl Weber, I am grateful to you for helping to fine-tune my way of thinking in publishing and marketing. I have learned a great deal from you. Your friendship and support will forever be appreciated.

~ National Best Selling Author of
Baby Momma Drama, Married Men & Looking For Luv

Special thanks to Tammy Leiva for her encouragement and storage space. Your friendship is long lasting and cherished.

Yolanda Allen, if I didn't know any better, I would think you were my personal publicist. Knowing you have been such a pleasure. I don't know how many Pent Up Passions you have sold for me, but Eden Books will always be number one in my book. Thanks for taking special pride in my work and continuing to put events together on my behalf. You are wonderful in every way.

~Eden Books
Hamden, CT
edenbookks@aol.com

Heather Covington, whew! girl, if I only had your spunk and energy, you are the absolute best friend and supporter. I am so glad that we met , your wealth of knowlege continue to make a sister flourish. Don't ever change.

~ The real Jane of many trade and Persoulnalities
www.Disilgold.com

Gloria Mallette, Michael Pressley, Nikki Turner, Chris Knight, Shanon Holmes, Denise Campbell, C&B Book Distributors, Phil Andrews, Culture Plus, Nubian Heritage, A&B Books, Mark Medley, Gary Williams, Jessica Mclean, I wanted to single each of you out for your encouragement, support and friendships. You have made my literary venture pleasant. Never change who you are.

About The Author

Hope C. Clarke, is the eldest daughter of seven siblings who reside in Brooklyn, New York. She's a single mom who divides her time between being a full-time mom, employee of JP Morgan Chase and a devoted entrepreneur. When she isn't cultivating her nine-year-old son, or playing the role of administrative assistant, she utilizes her extra time writing and self-publishing fiction novels. She considers herself a Jane-of-many-trades as she has acquired education and training in many industries including accounting,. She is a licensed financial planner, multitasking in software operations, etc. Publishing, writing, promoting and marketing has now been added to her list as she introduces to the public her movie-style writing.

Hope Clarke has always been an advid reader of fiction novels. It was during her high school years at Norman Thomas, her English teacher noticed her skill in abstract writing. The annual Transcript published by Norman Thomas hosted a short story authored by her entitled 'The Day When The Big It Happened.' He also incorporated this story as part of the literary abstract writing for his English classes. This encouragement sparked the desire to continue writing. She has written more than fifty poems and short stories.Through her college years, Dean Koontz and Robin Cook are among her favorites.

Today, Hope Clarke encourages the development of talent whether it's writing, singing, speaking, dancing or whatever it may be. She is a firm believer that everyone has a talent and that it should never be wasted.

Spread the word and not the book!

Chapter One

"04673, you got a visitor."

Michelle dismounted her cot and moved towards the cell bars and faced the correction officer.

"Who is it?" she questioned with a slightly raspy tone. She stared at the officer while waiting for a response. His lips twisted into a half-cocked smile exposing an exaggerated overbite.

"Chris Walker."

The mention of his name brought pause. And why shouldn't it? She's been in this cage for ten years and it's been just that long since she's seen her daughter—their daughter. Chris vowed to her moments after her delivery that she would never see Ashley again. She held her daughter only moments before she was taken away from her for what would be forever.

"Yes or no, 04673?" he insisted, snapping her out of her trance.

"Yes. I'll see him."

"Let's go," he instructed manually opening her cell door. He escorted her to the awaiting female officer and she was taken to the shower to clean up. After a thorough search, Michelle quickly dressed and followed her escort to the visitor's room. This would be Michelle's first time having a visitor and she didn't know what to expect. When the doors were opened, the desk officer went over the rules and then directed her to her seat. This was better than she expected as she thought that she would have a Plexiglas between them and a telephone. She was seated at a table with four seats to it. Surrounding her was approximately a hundred other female inmates with their guests. Some were at vending machines buying prepackaged food while others were using the microwave. Officers were stationed throughout the cafeteria with direct eyeshot of everything.

After Michelle sat there by herself for more than twenty minutes, Chris walked in with a group of other people. They handed a form to the officer at the door and were then instructed to their party. Michelle could feel her heart racing as Chris closed the distance between them. He was as handsome as ever. Time had matured him well. She could also see that he had put on a little weight, but in a good way. His muscles were bigger as well as his chest. He wore a grey, short-sleeve, nylon shirt that clung to every ripple of his tight stomach. The black, Italian cut pants fell seductively over his perfectly firm ass.

He stopped as he reached the table while taking in a full view of Michelle. Although ten years had passed, ten hard years, she still maintained her beauty. Of course, with the exception of the scar that lingered just above her right eyebrow, he could see that she had been working out on a regular and her body was a bit less feminine, but attractive nonetheless. She wore her hair in long braids that fell down her back and rested probably six or seven inches above her butt.

"Are you going to sit down or are you going to stand there and observe me all day?" A grin spilled across her face as she noted his embarrassment.

"Sorry. I'm going to sit down."

"You look well," she stated as he got comfortable.

He cleared his throat.

"So do you."

Chris looked around observing all the women in the facility. He then focused his attention on the officers holding the guns at the doors.

"Not really a friendly place, is it?"

"It's a prison, Chris. Did you think I was on vacation here?" she remarked no longer yielding her sarcasm and annoyance. "Why are you here? And where is my daughter?"

"Ashley is fine. She's a beautiful young girl."

"I'm sure. But that doesn't answer my first question." Her eyes never left his.

Chris shifted in his seat, leaned forward and rested his clasped hands on the table.

"Ashley has been asking about her mother lately. She wants to meet you."

His words were labored since the thought went against his wishes. But his love for Ashley was enough to make him go against his promise. He would give her anything she asked for to make her happy. Things were so simple when she was an infant growing into a toddler, but now that she is among older children and they talk about their parents, Ashley has become obsessed with knowing her mother.

Michelle narrowed her eyes at Chris. He was still that selfish bastard he was ten years ago when he disregarded her feelings for him.

"Did you think that you could take my daughter and turn her against me? No State paper can break the bond a mother has with her child. She was with me in the beginning and so shall she be in the end. That bond can not be broken, Chris. Maybe from your perspective it could be broken; I mean you did abandon yours."

Chris' first instinct was to punch her lights out, but being surrounded by shotguns wouldn't make that choice prudent. He shifted back in his seat glaring at her. Michelle could see the tension building between them. Chris' once relaxed muscles became taut, making the vessels more pronounce including the ones in his neck.

"You know that look isn't appealing," she added to his fury. "By the way, did you ever make partner? You know, at Goldman, Thurman & Sacs? You look like you're pretty well off."

Chris didn't respond. He couldn't believe how cold and vicious Michelle had become. Did she feel any remorse for what she'd done? Or over the life she'd taken? How many years would it take for her to realize that what she did was wrong? She's got some nerve asking about his daughter, his Ashley, when she was so willing to let her be raised by the State. When the Social Worker called him and told him that his daughter would be turned over to the State, Chris immediately hurried to the hospital awaiting the arrival of his daughter. Shortly after she was born, Chris began the paperwork to get full custody of his daughter and remove any possibility of Michelle ever seeing her.

"Michelle to Chris. Are you there? It's not even fun talking to you. You're like a zombie. Well, since you didn't bring my daughter,

I think you should be leaving now."

Chris stood from his seat and casually returned it beneath the table.

"I can't say that seeing you again was a pleasure."

"Don't worry. You'll see a lot of me soon. My appeal is just around the corner."

"I look forward to the battle. You will never have my daughter. And you will pay for your transgressions."

"I've spent ten years here. I have paid for my transgressions."

"No. I mean your transgression against me and my mother."

"You have no proof that I killed your mother."

"You did it. I know you did it."

"Well, the court system found me innocent on that charge."

"But I find you guilty."

"Thanks for taking care of my daughter for me. I'll see you two soon," she called out to him.

He turned and walked away. He returned to the officer at the door and retrieved his pass. After a few moments, he disappeared through the steel door where they checked for a stamp on his hand.

When Chris returned to the waiting area, his girlfriend Simone, and his daughter Ashley stood to greet him. Her hair was curly like her fathers and pulled into two ponytails that bounced at the sides of her head. Ashley was excited because she knew that her daddy would be bringing her in to meet her mother. He told her to wait with Simone until he spoke with her first and then he would return to get her.

Chris took a seat and caught hold of Ashley's hands. He kissed both of them and told her how much he loved her and would do anything in this world for her. All of his emotions surged forward and his tears exposed the hurt he felt. He continued to hold her hands, never letting his eyes meet hers.

"What happened, Dad? Why are you crying?"

"Honey. Your mom…" he stammered.

Simone could see that something went wrong. Chris never told her the whole story about Michelle and how Ashley came about. He only told her that her mother was locked up and that she was sentenced to ten to twenty years. Simone worked as a Social Worker and was the one who contacted Chris about his daughter. She helped him gain legal custody of Ashley. Chris was surprised at how easy the process had been for him to get Ashley. Simone was somehow able to get Michelle to sign the papers giving Chris sole custody of their daughter. Not long after, Chris and Simone began seeing each other. She reminded Chris so much of his ex-lover Keesha; sweet, gentle, caring and so desperately in need of love. Her companionship was so timely as Chris had no idea how he was going to raise Ashley by himself. Simone took to Ashley as if she was her own daughter. Strangely though, Simone never mentioned marriage after being together for seven years; they still maintained their separate places. Simone would spend some weekends with Chris and Ashley, and other times Ashley would stay with Simone for weekends. This was their bonding time to do their girl thing.

She rested her hands gently on Ashley's shoulders.

"Come on, sweetheart, let's wait for your dad in the car. We'll come out another day to see your mom. She wasn't feeling well today."

Ashley hesitated for a moment then followed Simone outside to the car.

While Simone escorted Ashley out, Chris could hear their conversation.

"Simone, how do you know that my mom is sick?" Simone responded by saying that Chris told her that she wasn't feeling well before they left, but he didn't know how sick she was. "Don't worry, your dad said hello to your mom for you and she knows that you love her."

Chris pulled himself together before getting into the car.

"How are my two angels doing?" he said forcing a big smile.

"Will mom be okay, Dad?"

"Sure, honey. She's just got a really bad cold and she told me to give you a big hug for her and tell you that she will see you soon."

Chris pulled Ashley into his arms and squeezed her tight.

"Mom's coming home soon? She's going to live with us?"

Instinctively, Chris' eyes met Simone's then he looked back at his daughter.

"Honey, your mom and I will have separate homes. She won't live with us, but you can see her from time to time."

He started the car and they were on their way home. The ride was quiet. Chris asked Simone if it would be okay if he took her home because he needed some time alone to talk with Ashley. She didn't feel his request to be prudent, but she reluctantly nodded her head and focused her attention out the window until Chris entered her driveway.

"Ashley, sweetheart, come give me a kiss."

Ashley sat up in her seat, puckered her lips and gave Simone a big kiss.

"I'll see you tomorrow or over the weekend, okay?"

"Dad, why isn't Simone coming to the house? I don't want her to go home."

"I know, honey, but your dad wants to spend time with you and talk to you about some really important stuff that can't wait. Simone will come over tomorrow and she will be around for a very long time. How is that?" he asked while winking at Simone in an effort to make light of a very tense situation.

"Okay, Dad. See you tomorrow, Simone. Love you." she called out to her as she closed the door and stepped out of the way of the car.

"You want to sit up front with your dad?"

"Sure."

Chris waited for Ashley to come to the front seat. When she had buckled herself in, Chris waved to Simone then started toward home.

He pulled into the driveway of his mother's home. After all that had happened, it became his sanctuary. Although Christine was gone, he could still feel her presence upon entering what was once her home, his home. He did, of course, modernize some things Christine neglected to repair or update. It made a suitable home for him and Ashley. So many memories remained that he wanted to share about his mother, her grandmother.

Upon entering, Ashley raced upstairs to her bedroom. Chris had decorated it with pink wallpaper with tiny pastel hearts on it. The square room was filled with teddy bears, Barbie dolls, and a canopy bed with Barbie accessories. She also had Barbie furniture, including a vanity, where she often sat and imagined growing up to look like her mother. Chris didn't talk much about her mother and neither did he want to. He only told her that her mother had gone away and would be gone for a very long time.

She sat at her vanity looking at herself in the mirror while clutching a teddy bear her dad had given her on her third birthday. The fur was so soft and plush. Today was disappointing. She had told her classmates that she was going to see her mother this weekend and that she was going to live with her and her father. Why didn't mommy want to see me? she wondered. Why would Dad not let me see her?

Ashley felt empty inside. Although Chris went over and beyond to make her happy, and Simone was like a mother to her, the desire to be with her real mother still existed. She thought of Simone as a really cool person. She was fun to be with, but she was not her mother. She found that out on her seventh birthday during an argument she had with her father. A lot changed between them since that argument. Simone didn't keep Ashley overnight as often as she had in the past, but she did come over on a regular and they still enjoyed the mall during the day. Chris was overprotective of Ashley and he seemed to be afraid of losing her.

Chris climbed the stairs quietly. He knew that Ashley was upset and that now was the time to explain to her where her mother is and why. He looked into her room and remembered the day he brought her home from the hospital. As much as he hated Michelle, he could not live with himself if he let his daughter be placed in a foster home for ten years until her mother was released from jail and able to care for her. She was adorable the moment he laid eyes on her. She had a head full of dark curly hair that seemed overwhelming for her tiny face, but nothing that a brush couldn't tame.

He silently walked over to her and knelt by her side. When she lifted her head, her eyes were soaked with tears. The sight melted his heart. What am I going to tell her to help her understand? I can't tell her that her mother is a crazed killer or that the grandmother she never had is dead because her mother ended her life. I also can't tell her that I want to kill her for ruining my life.

"Hey, what are all the tears about?"

"The kids at school won't believe me if I tell them that I have a mother."

"Of course you have a mother. How do you think you got here? Huh? Come here."

Chris cuddled her for a moment and then walked her over to her bed. He sat her down beside him then turned her chin to face him. It was like looking into a mirror. She was a total replica of him. She had his eyes, his nose, his complexion, his hair, his lips, everything.

"Honey, there are some things that I need to tell you. I don't want to because it is something that I wanted to protect you from, but I'm afraid that if I don't tell you, I may lose you."

"You can never lose me, Daddy," she comforted him.

Chris was the only thing real to her. He was the only true family she had. Without him she would have no life. Ashley was quite perceptive and her reasoning skills were advanced for a child her age. He found it difficult sheltering her from things. She understood his relationships, especially the one he had with Simone, and she knew that there was something he was hiding about her mother because he avoided talking about her.

"And I don't want to, but honey, you're growing so fast. Everyday when I look at you I can't believe how fast time flies." He paused for a moment. Acid scorched his stomach as he sifted through the things he held inside for so long. He glanced around the room at the décor. How innocent and free she was. What he needed to tell her would take that innocence away and probably make her now hate. It could potentially make her hate him or even hate herself. He squeezed her hands.

"Dad, that hurts."

"Honey, I'm sorry," he said rubbing her hands. This was all too difficult for him. There had to be some other way around this, some way to avoid speaking this ugly truth.

"Honey, I want you to know that I love every ounce of you and I wouldn't trade you for anything in the world."

"Are you my real dad? I know that Simone isn't my mother."

"God, yes. You are my daughter and I couldn't deny you if I wanted to. Have you looked into the mirror lately?"

She laughed for a second then her face turned serious again.

"Then what is it?"

"Your grandma would have really loved you if she were still here. She would say that you remind her so much of her Chris. But she's gone forever." Chris' eyes began to bulge as they fought to hide his pain. "Your mother took her from me. She took her from you. She killed her. She tried to kill the only woman that made me feel complete and I ended up losing that woman to another man. Honey, your mom is in prison. She isn't in a hospital as I've always told you. She did a really terrible thing and she is being punished for it." Without knowing it, all of the anxiety and the pain he harbored was finally being released. Chris could feel her tensing up, but he continued.

"Your mom had become jealous of my relationship with Keesha."

"You mean Aunt Keesha and Uncle Jamal?"

"Yes. She tried to hurt Keesha and punish me for loving her. The police realized that she was bad and put her away. That's when I met Simone. She called me up and told me that you were about to be born. I stopped everything I was doing and raced to the hospital. You were so beautiful. I loved you so much. I knew that moment that I had to do whatever it took to make you all mine. I would never let anyone come between us or hurt you. Not even your mother."

"Mommy would hurt me?"

"She would hurt you to hurt me by trying to take you away."

"Why can't you share me with mommy?"

"Because your mommy doesn't want to share. She wants to use you as a weapon to hurt me. If your mommy takes you from me, I will die."

Ashley grabbed him tightly by the waist as if to never let him go. Her little arms trembled as she clung to him.

"I won't ever leave you, Daddy. I won't ever let mommy take me away from you. You are my daddy and my best friend."

She pulled away from him and looked at him sincerely. Her big, brown eyes looked deep into his for truth. Chris could see that worry and concern were written all over her face.

"What's wrong?"

"Does that mean that I won't ever have a mommy? I mean a real mommy that lives with me like the other kids in my class?"

Chris grabbed Ashley by the face and placed a big kiss on her lips. He caught hold of her hands and led her out of her room and into the hallway. He took her to his bedroom and told her to close her eyes and she did as he said. She could hear him shuffling around and shortly after he returned to her side. He stooped in front of her and began to whisper.

"Remember the story of Prince Christopher and Princess Kiana?"

Her face lit up with a big broad smile as she remembered the story her father used to tell her before she went to sleep.

It was about a beautiful woman who fell in love with a very handsome prince. They loved each other so much that the thought of not being together forever made them sick. Unfortunately for them, the queen wouldn't hear of their relationship and they soon parted. The prince was very sad until one day, another beautiful princess came along. She was as beautiful as the first princess. Prince Christopher couldn't believe it so he waited seven long years before he realized that she was the one. One day, when the new princess came over, the prince went into his closet and pulled from it something that he cherished more than anything in the world.

Chris opened Ashley's hand and placed the cold, shiny ring into her palm. She opened her eyes and beheld the beauty of the twinkling diamond solitaire. Ashley began reciting the remainder of the story.

"A diamond ring. Not just any diamond ring, but one that she would wear forever and ever. That princess would become the mother of all of his children and they loved each other forever and ever."

"That's right, honey, so you don't have to worry about having a mommy. Daddy is going to give you the perfect mommy and she will love you just like a real mommy."

"And make babies?"

"And make babies," he emphasized.

She held him tightly around the neck.

"So, are you going to help me find our princess?"

"I know who would make a great princess?"

"Who?"

"We could give it to Simone. She would make a great mommy."

"You think so?"

"I do. I like her a lot and she likes me too."

"Well then, let's go ask her."

Chris and Ashley went downstairs, got the car keys, and went outside to the car.

Chapter Two

───────────⧓───────────

After a twenty-minute drive, Chris stopped in Simone's drive-way. He drew in a deep breath and stared out through the front window. His eyes dropped to the clock in his dashboard. It read eight forty-six. Only the bedroom light was on in Simone's house. He watched as she moved back and forth past the curtains. Her silhouette was very sensual. The few minutes Chris watched her, he soon realized that she was upset.

Ashley took notice of her dad's hesitance.

"What are we waiting for? Look, she's home," she told him pointing to the shadow that again crossed the view of the window.

"Nothing, honey. I was just wondering if maybe we should wait until tomorrow or the weekend to stop by. It's pretty late."

"She won't mind. Come on, let's go. Are you scared?"

Chris looked at Ashley in amazement. He couldn't believe that she actually challenged him. She was goading him to make a move.

"Okay. You think I'm not going to do it, don't you?" he teased and shut off the car. "So let's go."

Ashley sprung from the car without a second thought. She followed suit and closed her door quietly. She made a quick shuffle and caught up to Chris who was waiting for her by the door. He tried turning the knob, and to his surprise, the door was unlocked so he opened it and walked in. He then called her so that their presence wouldn't frighten her in the event she didn't hear their entrance.

"Simone! Ashley and I are down here to see you. Did you know that you left your door unlocked?"

"Hey, guys!" Simone called from the top of the stairs. "No, I must have forgotten to lock it. I had some things on my mind." She leaned over the banister to catch a glimpse of them before frolicking down the stairs. She was happy to see them. She had felt so out of place when Chris dropped her home earlier. It was a definite setback in what she thought she had developed between them.

"You two look happy. What are you doing here?"

"We thought you could use some company," Chris stated as she descended the last step.

He placed a warm kiss on her lips and encircled her waist. Ashley watched as her dad set the stage for what he was going to do. They rehearsed the whole scenario before they got there, but she was already familiar with the plan as he told her the story many times before. She fanticized the fairytale in what her tiny mind could reason.

Ashley caught hold of their hands and led them into the living room. She turned on the portable fireplace then patted the carpet for them to sit down and they did as instructed. Simone snuggled against Chris and rested her head on his shoulder. Simone couldn't believe how romantic Ashley was. She seemed to be totally in tune with her father. Although he didn't utter a word, she knew exactly what to do next.

While Ashley was in the kitchen searching and putting together the next step to their plan, Chris turned Simone's chin to face him. The flame's light twinkled seductively in her eyes. He let his fingers trace her manicured brows, the bridge of her nose, and the curve of her lips while absorbing each and every detail of her beautiful features.

She trembled with expectancy. What was he saying to me? Where is this line of affection going? she wondered.

He lifted her chin, tilting her head back, and observed the rise and fall of her neck as she swallowed. His fingers traced its delicate form until it rested above her heart. He lingered there counting the beats. The rapid drumming played a tune of anticipated passion. Chris brought his head down and rested his ear above her breast, listening to the sweet sound of her existence. She was soft like the petals of a well-cultivated rose. This tenderness reminded him of his once loved Keesha; so beautiful, so smart, and so lovely. Chris feared that history would repeat itself, but he warded off the butterflies fluttering in his stomach. His eyes closed as he listened, drinking in the beauty of her body. A fragrance he so greatly remembered filled his nostrils, Jessica McClintock; just a light powder dusted over her skin, emanating a gentle scent.

Ashley returned holding two crystal flutes carefully between her fingers and a bottle of Tropicana apple juice in her other hand. She placed everything on the coffee table. She reached into her pocket and pulled out a tiny, velvet pouch and sat it between the two glasses. Without saying a word, she headed upstairs to what has become her room whenever she visited.

When Chris realized that Ashley was safely upstairs and out of view, he moved his hand down over the fullness of her bosom. He cupped one into his hand and lightly squeezed it. The sound of Simone's sigh aroused him. Her lips were met with a deep kiss, probably deeper than ever before. Chris penetrated her lips with his tongue and motioned it as though it was his organ inside of her. She welcomed such a lustful kiss. This enflamed expression of passion could only be extinguished with a woman's inner essence.

The two-piece, burgundy, satin chemise and pant set she wore contrasted beautifully with her skin. It reminded Chris of fine wine waiting to be sipped slowly until every drop has been consumed. He gently slid his hand down between the satiny material and through the coiled hair that covered her precious mound and into the moist, beseeching tunnel. It crackled as he toyed with it. When his fingers were wet with her natural juices, he strummed her swelling pearl like the strings of a guitar.

Simone's ache was great. She squeezed and pulled at the solid appendage that was buried beneath the smooth, Italian fabric. After fumbling with his unrelenting zipper she managed to extract, with great effort, his immense dick. She couldn't count how many times she had held it before, but just as the first time, it excited her. Her hand massaged from the lowest of his shaft all the way to the pulsating tip and each time her hand obliged his awaiting head, anxious semen spewed onto her fingers. How lovely she thought of his excitement as she used his liquid as lotion. While relishing the strumming of his fingers and anticipating the rapture that neared like soldiers at the enemy's gate, she quickened her manipulation. Blood rumbled beneath his flesh and Chris caught hold of her hand and returned her tempo to a slow, manageable speed.

"Not yet," he whispered.

He could feel her tremble from her readiness to go further. Her body began to writhe and gyrate. He muffled her cries with his mouth and allowed her to collapse into the cradle of his arms. She released his member and fought to catch her breath, but Chris was not finished. There was so much pleasure to give. He slid her satin pants over her butt while lifting her legs up into his chest. After pulling them over her feet, he tossed them to the side. He caught hold of her ankles and let his hands move up to the back of her knees. He massaged her legs then lowered himself to face her nature. Without warning, he forced his tongue into her and she cried like a baby whimpering with uncontrolled sobs. His tongue spread out like a carpet over an open sea and with it he mopped up and ingested her love. He made mental note, That's two. This time, he lifted himself up, pressed her legs against his chest and made one deep plunge into her.

"Chris," she pleaded, "I love you. Oh, God, I love you."

With each thrust he gave all of him, all that she could stand, and this time her passion was met with his own.

"You love me?" he asked while fighting to hold the erection that so rapidly began to diminish.

"I do, Chris. I love you so much," she replied enjoying her climatic throb.

Although he continued to move within her snapping cave, his iron skin returned to its mushy normality.

Simone motioned to pull her legs down and Chris lifted momentarily to let them find a comfortable place beneath him.

They shared a quiet moment while relishing the aftermath of their lovemaking.

"Simone," Chris spoke gently to her, "I can't tell you how much you really mean to me and Ashley. You have been like a mother to her."

"Chris. I only…"

"Shhh!" he quieted her. "Your being a part of our lives, my life, has brought me through a time that I don't think I could have made it through on my own. You were there when I needed someone." Chris struggled to control his emotions. "I didn't think that after my last girlfriend I would be able to feel…" he paused searching for the words, "love for a woman to that degree again. I wanted so much to have a family, a healthy family where we all cared for each other. She broke that dream, my mother broke that dream and Ashley's mother broke that dream."

Simone listened intently. His labored words were heartfelt and deep. This unity meant so much to him and she felt at a loss for words.

Chris continued. "My sleeping with Michelle was wrong. She got pregnant and it was an error I was not able to recover from. When she realized that her being pregnant wasn't going to win my heart, she murdered my mother in retaliation."

Simone gasped at such a horrific tale. How could someone be so cruel and mean? she wondered. "Is that why she's in prison?"

"No. She tried to kill my girlfriend Keesha by poisoning her. And somehow she was able to set the stage to look like I had done it."

"God, I can't believe this. She's really evil."

"I know. During the trial she was found innocent on the murder charges. We couldn't find enough evidence to prove that she had done it or had probable cause. As long as she is not punished for her crimes against my mother, her spirit can not rest."

All this information was too shocking for Simone. She noticed a change in Chris' eyes, a look that she hadn't noticed before. It was cold with malice. He was bent on revenge.

"Chris, that's all in the past now. Your mother's vindication will come. You have a beautiful daughter who loves you and you love her. Don't let the past cloud your mind. Don't let hatred overshadow the good that has come out of it. You wanted a family and you got it, maybe not the way you wanted it, but you are still blessed. You have had ten wonderful years raising your daughter and I know that she appreciates everything that you've done for her."

"I know she does, but this isn't about Ashley, it's about me. It's about my obligation to my mother."

"Well, what will you do? Not kill her I hope."

His eyes met hers again and the fact that it had been a consideration was evident. A smile overshadowed the intent look and he held her hand. "You're right. I have so much to be grateful for. I have Ashley and I have you." His look showed that it was more of a question than a statement.

"Yes, Chris. You do have me. I'm right here for you and Ashley. I love her just as much as you do."

"Then marry me," he said taking the ring from the table and holding it purposefully between his fingers. He looked at the brilliant stone and could see the flames from the fireplace dancing through it. This hurled him to a place that was quite familiar. He remembered the green plant, the note 'Green outlives any other'. He thought of Keesha wearing the ring he gave her and then her returning it to him. Jamal's words then flashed through his head, This ends your pursuit of her, right? His mind returned to the present. He presented the ring to her, holding its opening toward her so that she could insert her finger. She didn't.

"It's beautiful, Chris." Her reply was not what he was looking for.

"Do you accept?"

"Chris, I can't tell you how I feel right now. If only you could hear this beating that's in my heart right now. It's as though it could jump right out of my chest. You don't owe me anything."

"But I do. I owe you more than this and I want to give you more than this."

"Chris, I can't. Not now. You have so much rage in you and I'm not ready to take that on. Let's work on that healing first."

"I am not in a rage, Simone. You have pacified that. Can't you see that? I tried to make things right for Ashley by taking her to see her mother, but her mother is unwilling to cooperate. That does not stop us from loving each other."

"I'm not saying that. All I'm saying is that we should work on that first then see where it goes. Relationships aren't built overnight."

"We've been together for seven years, it's hardly overnight."

"I know, but I need time. Just give me a little more time, not much, just a little. Can you do that?"

This was all too familiar. To Chris, time had been his enemy. Everything he waited for had come to a crashing end, one disappointment after another. But what could he do? It wasn't as if he could force her to accept his proposal. What will I tell Ashley? That I couldn't give her a full-time mother? he thought. Chris settled in his place, letting his hands fall to the side. When he had presented the ring, his dick had already rose to the occasion ready to please, but this head understood all too well the disappointment the bigger one felt. It wilted like the unnourished leaves on a once pampered flower and tucked its head shamefully within the crevice of his thighs.

This moment brought an uncomfortable silence between them. Chris no longer felt the urge to spend the night. He wanted to fall back to his home and wallow in the hurt he felt. Loneliness seemed to be his curse. No one would ever make him complete. He thought about the story he had told his daughter earlier and all the extra effort she put in to make this moment special. Why couldn't Simone see how important this was to me? How important it was to Ashley. She claimed that she loved us, he reasoned, but her actions did not convince him. Was she too seeing someone else? Did she slip around those nights when I left her alone at home?

"Chris, talk to me. Please don't be angry." Her petition oozed like old honey, stiff, because Chris had already put up his wall the moment she rejected him.

"I'm not angry, Simone," he lied. But what could he say, that he was experiencing adult tantrums? Or that he refused to wait? That his high opinion of her had diminished and the only thing that kept him from walking out on her this minute was his sleeping daughter upstairs? He would not hurt Ashley with this news tonight.

"Look at me. Why are you behaving this way? I thought that you would understand."

His true emotions had now become apparent.

"You know, I came here tonight expecting to complete and legitimize our relationship. I felt that if you stuck by me all these years that there was no way this could be a mistake. I didn't realize that you had reservations about me. I love you, Simone, and so does Ashley."

"And I don't want you to stop loving me and I will never stop loving Ashley, but this is about cleaning out closets. You have a lot of baggage, Chris, and I am afraid that if you don't get that all settled, what happened before will happen again. I don't want to be a part of that."

"I will protect you. You don't have to worry about that at all. Michelle won't harm you."

"How do you know that? You were supposed to protect Keesha and you were supposed to protect your mom. Where are they now?"

"I can't believe you said that."

Chris grabbed his pants and began pulling them on. His eyes fixated on Simone while he picked up the flute of apple juice. In one gulp it was gone. He wiped his lips and told Simone good night. When he stood up Simone tried to catch hold of his arm.

"Chris, wait."

She was too late. Chris was already to his feet and made quick strides toward the stairs. He mounted the steps, two at a time, until he had reached the top and then disappeared out of sight. Ten minutes later he was bringing Ashley down the steps and making his way to the door.

"Chris," she called his name again. "Wait a minute. I didn't mean to say that. You didn't give me a chance to finish."

"Then in the future you should choose your words more wisely. Have a good night, Simone."

He held onto Ashley's shoulders, sheltering her until she was outside and securely into his car. Ashley watched Simone at her door looking on as Chris put distance between them. She didn't say a word, only watched out the window wondering what went wrong. I guess fairytales don't come true, she thought.

Chapter Three

It was the weekend, two days since the fight between Chris and Simone. Ashley was sitting outside on the steps reading Ms. Rumphius, a book her teacher had assigned for their next book report. She had not heard from Simone since that day and didn't imagine that she would ever again. Chris didn't talk about her either, but she knew that Simone had hurt him. The house was really quiet and for the first time since she could remember, her father didn't tell her a bedtime story. She longed to hear one of her dad's stories. As much as she wanted to ask him to tell one, she just accepted her goodnight kiss and being tucked securely into her bed. He would kiss her forehead and tell her how much he cared for her.

***

Chris was in the kitchen fixing dinner. He pulled the steak from the refrigerator that he had prepared last night and placed it on the counter. He spread homemade stuffing across the length of the steak, then a row of spinach, and began rolling it until the steak was completely wrapped around itself. He tied it together and placed it into a small roasting pan. He then pulled from the vegetable rack four, big, baking potatoes, washed them and placed them individually into aluminum foil and sat them on the lower grate in the oven. Inside another pot that was already on the stove was boiling water seasoned with smoked meat, awaiting the cabbage that he would soon submerge into it.

He wiped his head while suddenly realizing that the kitchen was pretty hot this Friday afternoon. This drew his attention to the clock, which read twenty minutes after four. Today was going to be a tough day to get through since Ashley was looking forward to going with Simone and it didn't look promising since he hadn't talked to her since the other night. From the kitchen, Chris couldn't see Ashley, but he knew that she was right outside. He had not been fair to his daughter by coming between her and Simone. Now that he had time to think about it, he realized that he hadn't told Ashley a story nor did he help her work on her Science project as he had promised. He sauntered over to the window and quietly peeked out at his daughter. She was sitting on the steps reading. This was one of her favorite pastimes. Ashley loved to read anything. He enrolled her into the Science club at her school because she was so curious about life and how things worked. She was a wonderful daughter and he refused to let her fall between the cracks.

"Hey, sweetie," he said as he opened the door.

She looked up at him and instantly a welcoming smile spilled across her face. She hadn't seen him look so happy since he thought Simone would marry him.

"Dad, how are you? Finished making dinner?"

"No, that won't be ready for a couple of hours." He emerged from the house and took a seat next to her, turning the book to face him. "Ms. Rumphius, huh?"

"Yeah, my teacher assigned it to us. The report is due on Wednesday."

"That sounds good," Chris said while admiring her beauty. He could never imagine someone so precious coming from anyone as evil as Michelle. She made him so proud to be a father. "I am really sorry about not giving you the attention you deserved these past two days. I was in my own mess and I forgot that someone more important was right in front of me."

She nodded as he spoke. He didn't need to explain the hurt he felt. She understood because she too wanted Simone to marry him and become her mother.

"Will you and Simone be friends again? Will I see her again?"

"I don't know, honey. I overreacted the other day and she may not want to see me again, but that has nothing to do with you. I think that when she remembers how wonderful you are she will be over to see you."

"When will that be?"

"I don't know, but she will."

"Why don't you call her and tell her that you're sorry?"

He squeezed her. God, is this child smart, he told himself.

"You're right. I should call her, but I can't right now."

"Why not?"

"Because I don't know what to say to her. Honey, sometimes people react to things the wrong way and feelings get hurt. When this happens, it's hard to say 'I'm sorry.'"

Chris reflected on the other day. In his mind he recounted the events that forged distance between he and Simone. Mirroring that thought, he remembered the encounter he had with Keesha. These women had scarred him. One would never think that finding love was so difficult. With all things considered, Chris realized that he had to start paying attention before Ashley inherited his burden.

She sat quietly next to him, peering into his face and absorbing his handsome features. Her dad was the most caring man she had known, but behind the scenes he was tormented. In a way, she resented Simone for not accepting her father's proposal of marriage, but what did she know? She was only ten-years-old. The complications of relationships were beyond her limited knowledge.

"Honey, why don't we go inside and get a game of Scrabble going?" Chris offered trying to lighten a heavy situation.

Ashley smiled up at him. She didn't want to play Scrabble or any other game for that matter. She had fixed her heart on spending the weekend with Simone. Although her dad was really great and she did enjoy the time she spent with him, Simone was far cooler. Not only that, but she knew that Simone would not disappoint her as her dad had made habit of doing lately.

A horn tooted and Chris and Ashley looked up to see Simone in her purple Dodge Caravan. She rolled down her window.

"Hey, kiddo. Are we still on?"

Ashley looked to Chris and, without a word, she knew that it was alright for her to get her bags. She jumped up, hurtled the steps in a single effort and dashed into the house not realizing that she had stepped on her dad's fingers.

"Jesus!" he swore, massaging his fingers. "Slow down, honey, before you kill somebody...like me," he uttered. He heard Ashley upstairs in her room scrambling around. He shook his head at his anxious daughter. He turned his attention to Simone who waited patiently for Ashley to come out with her bag. Their eyes locked on each other and neither said a word. Shortly after, Ashley emerged from the house and was about to dash toward the van when Chris caught hold of her arm.

"Hey. Don't act like you're dying to leave me."

"Sorry, Dad," she told him. Her embarrassment quickly diminished as she shuffled on to the van. Chris rounded the van behind her. He opened the side door and put Ashley's bag on the floor. He knelt in front of her and told her to enjoy herself and not to forget that he loves her more than anything in the world. He hugged her as though she was leaving him forever.

"Okay, Dad. I'll be back Sunday so don't worry. No one's going to steal me away." She gave him a quick squeeze and a peck on the cheek. He opened the door and helped her into the van.

"See you, honey. You know if you need me-"

"I know, you'll be there."

"Right. Take care, honey."

Chris moved around the front of the van and stopped by Simone's window. She froze when he touched her arm. Their argument the other day was pretty silly and it shouldn't have come to this. She wanted to call him, but was afraid that he would reject her.

"I missed you, Simone. I overreacted and things really got out of hand. Can you forgive me? I just want to start over."

A heavy ball formed in her chest and seemed to drop down to the pit of her stomach. It rested there like a sack of bricks.

"I've missed you too," she managed as she fought to keep her tone even. But her voice crackled and revealed the hurt and relief she felt.

"You guys go ahead and enjoy the weekend. We can talk on Sunday when you return."

He leaned in and kissed her and, to his delight, she returned the kiss. While their lips were locked, Chris winked at Ashley who was looking on with pride.

Chris stepped back out of the way and allowed Simone to pull the Caravan from the curb and continue up the street. After watching the Caravan disappear around the corner, he returned to his house and planned on completing his dinner. He was so happy that Simone hadn't disappointed his daughter. She had far too many disappointments in her life and one more was far too many.

***

Simone got Ashley up early Saturday morning. She had already prepared breakfast and put together something to snack on. Today was going to be a full day and she wanted to make so much of it. She calculated hitting the mall at ten o'clock, get their hair done, and browse the shops until noon or one o'clock. They could then check out a movie and have dinner at about five.

On the way to the mall, Ashley sat quietly while Simone burned the pavement with her Caravan. Her thoughts were deep and she so desperately wanted to confide in Simone, but she feared that Simone would discuss it with her dad.

"Simone, if I told you something, would you tell my dad?"

"Not unless you wanted me to." Simone pulled the car over and shut off the engine. "Is something wrong?"

"No."

She looked at Ashley's reflection in the window. She could see that Ashley was pensive.

"I'm listening. What's on your mind? You know women have a special bond between them? There are some things that we only share with other women. I want you to think of me as your best friend."

Ashley let out a deep sigh and Simone listened for what was to come.

"I want you to do something for me. It's real important, but I don't want you to tell my dad about it."

Simone became apprehensive, but she maintained a straight face. She didn't want Ashley to close up as she could see that her secret was very important. She nodded her head.

"I want you to take me to see my mother today. I know that she isn't sick and that my dad was trying not to hurt me, but I really need to see her."

She now turned to face Simone, searching for understanding or anything that said that she would grant her wish. One thing she noticed is that Simone didn't seem surprised or concerned about her request.

"Why do you feel the need to see your mother? You know this will hurt your father?"

"I know, but I can't feel complete unless I see her. The kids at school tell me that I'm a bastard and that I don't have a mother."

"That's terrible, Ashley. Did you tell your father about it?"

"I did, but he doesn't want me to see my mother. He's still angry with her because she did some really bad things before, but she is still my mother."

"Are you sure? I mean, I don't know what will happen when we get there, but if you really want to see her I will take you there."

"You know her. She'll talk to you."

"Okay. I guess the mall is out of the question."

She pulled away from the curb and started toward the Long Island Expressway. Traffic wasn't too bad and Simone maneuvered through traffic with efficiency. After a two and a half-hour drive, they were at Sing Sing Correctional Facility. After parking the car, they walked down the narrow stairway that lined the mountain the facility was situated on. When they reached the foot of the steps they returned to the familiar visiting area. This was as far as Ashley had gotten to see her mother. There were other people waiting to get passes to visit their loved ones. Simone filled out the visitor's pass and included Ashley's name. This wasn't a problem since Chris had completed a form for her before.

After being scanned, Simone and Ashley followed a line of other visitors into a room with awaiting inmates. The officer looked at the pass then directed them to Michelle. When Ashley looked in the direction the officer indicated her eyes locked with Michelle's and Ashley knew for sure that it was her mother. Her heart raced with anticipation. A lovely smile welcomed her as she followed Simone's lead. When they arrived at the table, Michelle drank Ashley in from head to toe. All of her delicate features she took in as if uploading it into memory.

"You must be Ashley," she broke the silence. Her tone was very calm. "You are a beautiful young lady."

"Thank you," Ashley managed. Earlier she was anxious to meet her mother, but now she felt trepidation slipping in. "People say I look like my dad." She then paused while taking in her mother's features. "But now that I see you, I think I look more like you."

Michelle's delight became quite evident. She closed the space between them and held her daughter close. So much time had passed and she hardly knew her daughter. She believed that their birth connection attributed to the comfortable atmosphere.

"I can't tell you how much I have dreamed about holding you again."

Ashley, unable to hold in her emotions, began to cry.

"Honey, what's wrong?" She looked to Simone who nodded and walked toward the vending machines and searched for something good to nibble on while she waited.

"Mom, why did you kill my grandmother?"

Michelle had to put a maximum effort into maintaining her composure. The last thing she wanted to do was scare her daughter because that would ruin her plan. She sat down and asked Ashley to have a seat as well. She softened her eyes and summoned up the tender-most element of her being.

"Ashley, honey, did your dad tell you that?"

She nodded, never removing her stare. Chris told her that the window to anyone's soul is through their eyes and she was determined to find the truth. She let out an arduous sigh.

"I didn't kill your grandmother," Michelle finally revealed. "I only heard about your grandmother's death at my trial."

"My dad wouldn't lie," she challenged. She was not going to let her mother weasel her way out of this. She was going to give her the truth and an explanation.

"Honey, your dad blamed me for what happened to his mother, but the truth is he doesn't know what happened to her. Everything that has gone wrong in Chris' life he has blamed on me. During my trial, I admitted poisoning Keesha, that's why I'm here. I loved your dad so much that I couldn't take the thought of anyone else being with him. I had you to think about. I didn't want my baby to grow up without a father. Keesha was trying to steal my baby's daddy. I couldn't let that happen. You understand?"

Ashley nodded her head. The information her mother revealed to her was shocking because it was very different from what her father had explained. All this time, Ashley thought of her mother as a monster, but she wasn't. She was a strong woman fighting to protect the circumstances of her unborn child. The hatred she felt for her began to crumble. She had rehearsed in her mind for two years what she would say to her mother when she came face to face with her. Now she only felt shame and hurt; hurt that her father could lie to her and hurt that he would tell her all those awful things about her mother.

"Your father was selfish, Ashley. He never cared about you. He never cared about me. The only reason he came to the hospital when you were born was to torment me. He told me the moment you were born that I would never see you again. Do you know how much that hurt me? Can you imagine knowing that your only child will never know that you exist or that you love her? Your father says that I'm the bad guy, but he's worse than I am."

"Mommy, I'm so sorry," Ashley cried. She sprung from her seat and wrapped her arms tightly around her mother's neck. Her tears flowed, emptying her angered soul and those cumbersome feelings of hatred were absorbed into the blue cotton fabric her mother wore.

"I love you so much and I wish you were home with me. I'll love you and I'll take care of you."

This was exactly what Michelle wanted to hear. She held on to her daughter until her grasp loosened. Michelle extended her arms and held on to Ashley's shoulders while looking at her. She had grown so much. So much time had passed. Wasted time, she thought.

"I've got something really important to ask you, but I need you to keep it between you and me."

"I promise," Ashley answered sniffling and wiping her eyes. She would do anything her mother asked of her. She felt as though she owed her the world. Her own mother she betrayed and condemned. Not any longer, she would stick by her till the end and no one would come between them.

"What would you say if I told you that there is a chance that you and I can be together forever, would you like that?"

Ashley lit up, that beautiful smile parted her perfectly formed lips and her well-maintained teeth shone brilliantly. Chris did an excellent job, Michelle thought. Not that she expected any different. That's why she chose him to father her child.

"Mom, that would be wonderful. You mean you will be coming home with me and my dad?"

Michelle shrugged. "That will be the tough part and I doubt that your father and I will be getting back together."

"Then what do you mean?" she asked with a genuine air of concern.

"You can come and stay with me."

"I don't want to live in jail."

Michelle laughed. Her daughter was too cute to handle, but her sentiment was sincere.

"Oh, honey, I will be getting out soon. I have a house that you and I can work together to paint and decorate. We can go shopping and find you some furniture. It will be great. We'll be like best friends."

"What about my daddy? I promised him that I would never leave him."

"Your dad has had you for ten years. Don't you think that your mommy should have a turn?"

Her request seemed reasonable. Ashley always dreamed about being with her mother.

"Okay," she answered after taking a moment to consider her mother's request.

"Now remember, you can't tell Chris, okay?"

Michelle held out her pinky and waited for Ashley to lock fingers with her. When she did, she pushed off with her thumb and sealed their secret promise. At this time, Simone had returned with some snacks. She had been fiddling with the vending machines, waiting on a long line to heat up the burgers and purchased the overpriced sodas. She placed identical meals in front of Michelle and Ashley then one for herself.

Remaining quiet, she opened her meal and took a bite. Her distaste was evident and she used a napkin to discreetly empty the vile contents from her mouth.

"So, how is this place treating you?" she asked, now focusing her attention on Michelle. She also noted that Ashley didn't like her sandwich either.

"The sodas are pretty good."

They laughed then opened the cans of orange soda.

"I've managed. It won't be long now," Michelle answered Simone's question.

The three of them talked for another hour. It was now two o'clock. Ashley asked to go to the bathroom. Michelle pointed to where the restroom was and Ashley went on her own, leaving Simone and Michelle in conversation.

"So how's Chris?" Michelle asked now free to say what she wanted.

"What do you mean?"

"I mean, can he still fuck or did he forget everything I taught him?"

"You are so bitter and arrogant. He asked me to marry him?"

Michelle was heated. She tensed up and glared at Simone. This was like the ultimate betrayal. All her coaxing and preaching was for her own selfish benefit. She didn't care about her or Ashley. She wanted to win her Chris.

"I told him no. You can take that ugly look off your face now and stop cutting me with that stare."

Michelle smiled. "You didn't answer my question."

"Yes, he can fuck. I love fucking him. He's good. His dick is big and he knows exactly how to break a sister off a piece. The man had me screaming my head off. Is that what you wanted to hear?"

"Yeah. I want to know what I've got to look forward to when I get out of here."

Simone frowned. "I thought your interest was Ashley. You mean to tell me that all this time you've been wasting away in prison, all you can think about is Chris, how big his dick is and whether or not he can still fuck?"

"No. I've also considered how I can torment him and make him feel like he's the one who spent ten years in the can."

Ashley returned. As she was about to take a seat at the table, Simone stood up.

"Well, Ashley, you should tell your mother bye for now. We've got a bit of driving to do and I don't want to get home too late."

She looked to her mother. She drank in her features and embedded them into her memory. Until she was home, that's all she had to hold on to.

"Wait," Michelle told them. She noticed one of the inmates taking pictures with a Polaroid camera. "Find out how much those pictures are."

Simone did as instructed. She returned and told her that they were five dollars each. The three of them walked over and joined the line and there were only two other people in front of them. When it was their turn, Michelle took three pictures with Ashley. She held her face close to hers and their resemblance was so striking. Everyone thought that Ashley looked like her father, but to see her side by side with her mother let everyone know that she resembled her mother more. She pressed her cheek next to Ashley's and the camera flashed and captured all the tell tale signs that Chris tried too hard to hide.

"Now when you get home, you put these pictures in your secret place. Don't let your father see them otherwise I won't get to see you again. Okay?" Michelle asked her.

Ashley nodded in agreement. She caught hold of Simone's hand and they walked back to the exit where they were allowed to leave.

Michelle watched as Simone played the maternal role with her daughter. She may be fucking Chris now, but all that is going to come to an end soon. Very soon, she told herself.

Chapter Four

Ashley returned home with Simone on Sunday. When she hopped from Simone's van, she bolted to the house, past her father up the stairs, and into her room. She haphazardly emptied the contents of her bag onto her bed and found the two pictures she took with her mother and Simone and placed them securely under her mattress. When she heard her father come into her room, she spun around and her eyes met his.

"Hello, Daddy," she quickly muttered.

"Did you miss me even a little bit?" he asked. "I know that Simone is great, but we do have a little fun together, don't we?"

"I'm sorry, Dad. Of course I missed you."

He walked over to her and looked at the mess she made on her bed with her clothes. This was such unusual behavior for her. Ashley was meticulously neat and Simone would definitely not leave her clothes rumpled up in her bag.

"What's with the mess?"

"Oh, I wanted to put my things away before dinner and when I tried to shake them out neatly they spilled over. I'll get them straightened out," she assured him.

He moved closer to her. Ashley wondered if he saw her reaching under her mattress.

"Give me a hug. Show your dad some love."

She reached around his neck and hugged him. She didn't squeeze him as she usually did. Her peck was done halfway as well. The thing that surprised Chris the most was that his usual embrace was abruptly broken as Ashley pulled away from him and started mustering through her clothes.

"What did the two of you do this weekend?"

"Nothing. We went to the mall and got our hair done. You know, girl things. You're not supposed to ask about girls' weekend out," she reminded him.

"I know. I was just curious. Did you enjoy yourself?"

"Simone is the best. I love her so much."

"That's great, honey, but you still love me, don't you?"

"Of course, Dad," she responded, but her attention never detached itself from the task of folding and putting away her clothes.

"Dinner is ready. Do you want something to eat?"

"Nah, Simone and I stopped and grabbed something on the way."

"Well, I didn't eat. How about you come downstairs and sit with me? I've missed you."

"Okay. I'll be down in a minute," she told him.

Chris waited around another minute, shrugged, turned and returned downstairs to the kitchen. Simone was peering into the pots. That Chris can burn, she told herself. She hadn't noticed him standing there as she took a fork and plucked out a piece of smoked meat from the cabbage. Just as she popped it into her mouth and confirmed that it was good, he reached around her waist and pressed his groin against her. He traced the curves of her hips with his hands.

"Ooh! You scared me."

"I didn't mean to. Does it taste good?"

"Yeah. It does."

"What's up with Ashley? What did you guys talk about? What did you do this weekend?"

"Our usual girl thing. You've never inquired before, why are you so inquisitive now? Is it because of our last episode?"

"She just seems so distant. It's like she's going out of her way to avoid talking to me."

Simone turned around. She couldn't believe how good his body felt against hers and that cologne he wore was making her crazy. This was hardly the time to talk about Ashley and his trepidation. How could he come in here and press his body against me like that then expect me to ignore my womanhood?

"Ashley loves you, Chris. Why do you feel the need to control everyone? Let the child breathe. If you want to suffocate someone, suffocate me," she told him covering his mouth with hers. She grabbed two handfuls of his firm ass and, although she knew that it was not pliable, she still made an effort to squeeze it. Her hands hungrily groped at his body and massaged his muscles beginning with his strong shoulders and descending down to his waist. Her fingers then crept around and bounced over his rippled stomach and rested on his firm dick.

Chris was all too familiar with this routine. Women loved his body and the way he made love, but they never wanted the full commitment that came with it. What is it about women that made them play these games? Is sex my only real attribute? Is that all I have to offer women?

Simone was on fire. She squeezed and pulled at his erection as though she wanted to rip it off. The only thing that prevented her from doing that was the tight jeans he wore. Although Chris was harder than an iron pipe, he still resisted her lustful display.

"I'm starving. I feel like my stomach is going to eat me if I don't put something in there. Do you still want some food or did you and Ashley get enough before you got here?"

Simone backed away and straightened out her clothes, but composing herself was a little more difficult. Her panties were soaked and he never touched her. She wondered if he could hear her pussy crackle when she walked. Why is he resisting me? she wondered. Is he still upset about the other night? She looked at him surprised by his statement and display of self-control.

"Yeah. I'm fine. I took Ashley to Applebees before we came in. She said that she was hungry. I didn't know that you had cooked. You're not offended are you?"

"No. Not at all, I was just hoping that I could share dinner with her, that's all. Don't mind me. I'm just hungry and a little disappointed, but whatever."

He pulled a plate from the cabinet and fixed himself something to eat. Simone lusted over the erection that lingered in his pants. Those jeans couldn't hold his member down, she could see its entire imprint through his jeans. Chris pretended not to notice Simone's lust.

He was determined to ignore the ache he felt. This was the last time he would be manipulated sexually by a woman. If Simone wanted him she would have to give him everything.

He placed his plate on the table and took a seat behind it. He picked up his fork, pierced the steak and placed it into his mouth. Simone watched as his lips motioned while he chewed.

"Are you sure you don't want any?"

She smiled weakly. "I'm sure," she responded. If he wanted to play that game she would play it with him. Chris finished his dinner and Ashley never made it downstairs. He looked at the clock on the microwave and noted that it was eight forty-eight. He could hear his daughter upstairs shuffling around. She had taken a bath and was putting on her pajamas. Chris washed the dishes while Simone put away the food.

Every so often, she would glance at Chris to see if he even showed the slightest interest in her sexually. To her disappointment, he hadn't. While he continued to work on cleaning up, Simone mounted the stairs and entered Ashley's room. She had already gotten into bed. Her covers were pulled tightly around her shoulders and she was shocked to see Simone standing there.

"Hi, Simone."

"Hey, kiddo. What's up?"

"Nothing. I'm tired. I want to get some rest for school tomorrow."

"You know your dad was hoping that you would join him for dinner. Are you angry with him or something?"

"No. I just miss my mother and wish that I could be with her."

By this time Chris was outside her door. He didn't show himself, but he listened. He needed to know why his daughter seemed to distance herself from him.

"I know how you feel, but you don't want to hurt your father, do you?"

"No!" she said excitedly. "I love my daddy. He's really sweet, but I know that he lied about my mom and he's using me to hurt her."

"Ashley, don't say that. Your father is only trying to protect you. He only wants to make you happy. If you treat him this way he won't let me spend time with you because he will think that I'm turning you against him."

She sat up. "I don't want you to go, Simone. Will you stay tonight? You know you really hurt my dad the last time. You hurt me too."

Simone held her tightly. She didn't have any children, but she regarded Ashley as her own. Life would be strange without her…without Chris.

"Listen. I will stay, but you've got to do something for me."

"What is it?"

"I think you already know."

She kissed Simone on the cheek and held her tightly. "I love you, Simone."

"I love you too, baby. Goodnight."

Simone got up, leaving Ashley sitting up on the bed. She knew that Ashley would do the right thing and see her father before she went to bed. If she wanted to get laid tonight she had to bring ease to Chris. When she emerged from the room, Chris was standing there. His eyes were slightly red with traces of moisture that made it evident that he had cried. She started to say something, but he stopped her, squeezed her hand and entered Ashley's room.

Simone waited outside the room with her back pressed against the wall. She was so glad that Ashley didn't mention their going to see Michelle during their conversation. Ashley was a really smart girl and she never would break her promise.

Chris knelt at Ashley's bedside. He didn't say anything he only looked at her. His warm brown eyes beseeched understanding. He securely clasped her hand between his hands, holding on to it lovingly. His eyes never left her. She was his daughter and never would he let her go, not for anyone. She had become his life support and without her he would stop breathing. He wished that she could hear his inner soul as he opened his windows to her. He gently pressed her hand against his cheek then kissed it gingerly.

"Ashley," he began, "You are my daughter, the only thing that exists in this world that is a true part of me. The only thing I know to say to you to express how I feel is to say that I'd die for you. I don't want to live without you, Ashley," he emphasized, "No one else can ever or will ever take your place."

Ashley listened. She was absorbed into the brown clouds that looked at her. He had heard her. Every word she said to Simone, he had heard her and she hurt him. Chris never looked at her the way he now did. His feelings toward her were undeniable.

"Honey, everything that I have told you about your mother is true. I don't know why you chose to not believe me, but I promise you."

She turned away from him, but he caught her chin and gently brought her face back to face him. "I promise you that I have never lied to you. Sweetie, my mother is gone. I have no reason to lie about it. My mother never liked your mother. She told me that she was not good for me. I used to date your mother when I was younger and we became very close, but after I moved away, I realized that I liked her for all the wrong reasons. Your mother would do anything to get me back. When I first heard about her being pregnant I was so angry. I didn't know what I was going to do."

"You didn't want me?"

"Honey, at the time I didn't know you. You were with your mother in prison. Because of her pregnancy, you were condemned to her crime. My mother came to me in a dream and told me not to leave you there. She told me that her grandchild should never become a product of the system. I fought so hard to get you. I wanted to protect you from your mother's wrongdoing. I was there when you were born. I didn't know what a blessing you would turn out to be, but when you came out everything changed for me. My life would be yours forever. I live for you, sweetie, and no one else so if you leave me it will kill me. For you, I will forgive your mother. I will do anything to make you happy and for you, I will live or die."

She held her father longer than ever. Her mother told her that he never loved her and that the only reason he took her in was to punish her. None of this was true. He did love her and he did a very

unselfish thing by taking her in. He protected her. She remembered
the movie South Central and how hard life had been for the little boy
whose father was imprisoned for murder. She too would have been in
foster care living with strangers if he didn't love her enough to protect her from that.

She didn't have to say a word because her tears and warmth
said it all. Chris felt renewed. Anything else could be taken away
from him, but not his daughter. He kissed her and said good night. He
stood up and left her bedroom, but not before turning out the light.

When he emerged from Ashley's room, he expected to see
Simone, but didn't. He went to his room and saw her sprawled across
the bed. She was completely nude and the dancing flames on the
scented candles played on her caramel skin. Chris felt an erection
coming on as he watched her legs open and close before him, beck-
oning him to enter. Without haste, Chris tore out of his clothes and
obliged her before she changed her mind.

***

Monday morning came and things were back to normal.
Ashley got dressed while Chris and Simone waited for her to come
downstairs for breakfast. When she did the three of them ate together.

Simone volunteered to drop Ashley off to school. Chris needed to get to work and it also gave Simone time alone with Ashley.
Chris agreed and gave his two girls a kiss before leaving.

Ashley and Simone got into the Caravan and started toward her
school. When they arrived, there were a few kids standing at the gate
and they noticed Ashley when she emerged from the van. Simone
stepped from the van and rounded it to the front passenger door. She
opened it for Ashley and told her that she would pick her up after
school. Ashley kissed her and hopped onto the sidewalk. Two girls
watched as Simone got back into the van. Once Simone left, they
turned to Ashley.

"That's not your mom," they told her. The two girls began teasing Ashley telling her that she had brought a stranger to school pre-

tending that she was her mother.

"Let's jump her. She's bad. Her mother doesn't even want her." The girls charged her along with two other girls. Ashley started running toward the school doors, but they had caught up to her. One of them grabbed hold of her hair and pulled it while another clawed at her. Suddenly, Ashley's rage came out and she began striking the girls back. She grabbed Tiffany by the hair and snatched her backward. Her fists pounded into Tiffany's face. When Joanne noticed Tiffany's nose bleeding, she let go of Ashley and hurried to the school and got one of the teachers.

Mrs. Howard came out to see what was going on. Upon arriving, she caught sight of Ashley kicking Tiffany on the ground. Ironically, Tiffany, whose mouth was bigger than her size, was now towered by Ashley. This led the teacher to believe that Ashley started the whole thing. Letting out a gasp, the teacher snatched Ashley by the arm and separated her from the other girl. At this point, Ashley was still angry and made her best effort to show Tiffany a lesson that she would never forget. This would be the last time she decided to pick on her. She was tired of her teasing her and making her feel bad about her mother. While the teacher lifted her from the ground to keep her from striking the girl, her feet continued to lash out at Tiffany.

"Ashley Walker! That's enough!" Mrs. Howard screamed. She shook Ashley forcefully and finally caught her attention. "Do you want to go to jail, little girl?" she asked her. "What is this all about?"

Ashley started to explain, but the other girls who were with Tiffany began their fabricated side of the story.

"Ashley started it. She said that she was going to kill Tiffany."

"You're a liar!" Ashley screamed. "They were picking on me."

"Well, it didn't look like that to me," Mrs. Howard concluded.

She helped Tiffany up from the ground. Her face was scraped up from the kicking. Her nose continued to bleed and her clothing and hair were in a complete mess.

"Look at what you've done. I've got to take you to the office and have Principal Carmine contact your father. He is not going to be happy about this."

"The teacher took the two girls into the school. She proceeded to nurse Tiffany's bruises and clear the blood from her nose. Thankfully, her nose wasn't broken, but with all the abuse it took, Mrs. Howard expected that it would hurt for a few days. She'll probably have a black eye too with her fair complexion.

Principal Carmine was a tall man with very dark features. His stance was intimidating to say the least. Ashley's dad had a deep voice, but he always made it soft when he spoke to her. She had no reason to shudder when he called her name. But when Principal Carmine called her into his office, it was like rolling thunder. Ashley looked around to see if lightening would flash and to her surprise it didn't. She slowly peeled herself from the wooden seat and slinked into his office. There was no doubt that she was in trouble. His call let her know that he was furious with her. This was Ashley's first time in Principal Carmine's office, but other kids talked about him as if he was a real life monster.

When she entered, he was seated behind his huge desk with his large hands resting palms down over her file, she presumed. His fingers alternated as he tapped on the desk. He looked as annoyed as he was.

"Have a seat, Ashley," he said. His eyebrows were tattered and disarranged. They were also pushed together with a show of frustration.

"Can you tell me what happened this morning in my yard?" he asked.

Ashley cleared her throat. It really didn't matter what she said because she didn't expect him to believe her anyway. Her head dropped and she hesitated for more than twenty-two seconds from the moment he asked her to explain. Being the type of man Principal Carmine was, twenty-two seconds was more like twenty-two minutes because it was longer than he wanted to wait for any answer.

"Ashley, did you hear me? I asked you a question and I expect that you will give me an answer this instance." His large hands pounded on the desk.

Ashley could hear some of the other kids waiting to see him outside his office shuffle in their seats and gasp. They could only imagine what was going on in the office.

When Ashley continued to remain silent he opened her file and started dialing. She knew that he was calling her father. The two of them challenged each other with their stares. Ashley was quite vigilant at this moment and would not back down. She waited to hear his description of the events.

The phone rang and after a few moments her father had apparently answered the phone.

"Hello. Can I speak with Mr. Chris Walker?"

"This is Chris Walker," he responded, not recognizing the voice on the other end. "Who's speaking?"

"This is the Principal at your daughter's school."

Immediately, Chris became worried. He could only imagine the worse.

"Is Ashley hurt?" His heart seemed to be at a standstill as he waited for the principal to respond.

"Well, Mr. Walker, she is all right, but unfortunately, she was involved in a fight today. She hurt one of the other students whose one of her classmates. This, Mr. Walker, is unacceptable in our school and won't be tolerated."

This surprise was more than Chris could handle. He neither responded nor interrupted. He only listened and let the principal finish what he had to say.

"I don't know what is going on at home, Mr. Walker, but this is the first time that Ashley has been in my office and with the attitude she has I can see this becoming a real problem in the future. Are you there, Mr. Walker?"

"Yes, I'm here. This must be some kind of mistake. My Ashley is a very gentle and loving child and she never fights. Something must have happened for her to react violently."

"Well, again, Mr. Walker, there were several witnesses that confirmed that your daughter started the fight including one of the teachers that brought her to the office. She said that your daughter was still kicking and screaming and it took a real shaking to settle her down.

Chris couldn't believe what he was hearing. What in the world was going on with his Ashley? First the attitude she had last night and now this. He was going to get to the bottom of this. He needed to find out what happened between her and Simone Saturday before things really get out of hand.

"Because of the school's policy, I will have to ask you to come and pick up Ashley right away. She won't be able to return to school for a week. The other child's parent has been contacted as well and she will be taken to the doctor to make sure that she is alright. You will be notified if the parent wants to press charges."

"I'll be there in about an hour. Where is my daughter now?"

"She's right in front of me. She hasn't said a word since she's been in here. I have questioned her about the events and she refuses to answer me. Perhaps you should consider having her evaluated."

"Evaluated for what?" Chris retorted, resenting the principal's suggestion of his daughter's sanity. "There is nothing wrong with my daughter. Like I said, I will be there in an hour. Please don't question her anymore until I get there. I will talk to her."

"Fair enough, Mr. Walker. I didn't mean to offend you, I was only suggesting that -"

"Thank you, Mr. Carmine," Chris cut him off. "That will be all for now."

***

Chris hung up the phone, pulled his suit jacket from the closet and told his assistant that he would be out for the rest of the week. He didn't give any other explanations. Without hesitating, he left the building and got into his car. He sped onto the expressway like a mad-man. Just as promised, Chris arrived at Ashley's school in an hour. He parked right out front and sprinted up the stairs two at a time until he had entered the building.

Security directed him to the office. When he entered, he was just in time to see the child his daughter had been fighting with. By now, her right eye was swollen shut and her nose still had traces of blood. There were raw scars that traced the delicate side of her cheek. It was more than he could bear. An angry parent screamed at the principal about what should be done about the matter. Of course, Chris understood his rage, but he needed to talk to Ashley to hear her side of the story. He couldn't imagine what must have happened to make her react in such a way. This was worse than he imagined. He expected to see her hair pulled and maybe some scratches, but this was terrible.

"Mr. Walker, please join me and Mr. Connor in my office. Mr. Connor is Tiffany's father." Chris reached out to shake the man's hand, but he did not return the courtesy.

"Where is my daughter?"

"Ashley has been taken to the counselor's office. She'll be joining us shortly."

"I want her here now…right now!" His usual calm tone disappeared and the strong baritone took over.

Principal Carmine instructed his secretary to contact Mr. Sherman's office, one of the school's counselors, to bring Ashley to his office.

"Mr. Walker, we can wait in my office. Your daughter will be with us in a moment as you requested."

"I'll wait right her until she gets here. We will join you and Mr. Connor in a moment." He couldn't believe that the principal had disregarded his wishes.

Chris stepped into the corridor and waited for his daughter. He saw her emerge from one of the rooms at the other end of the hall with the counselor. Although it was quite a distance away, he could see that his daughter was crying. Chris became enraged. He started toward them. He couldn't stand still another moment waiting for her.

"Ashley!" he called out to her as he closed the distance between them.

The principal called out to him to wait. One of the security guards hurried toward him.

Just as Chris reached them, the security guard caught hold of his arm. Chris immediately snatched it away and looked at the little man that stood at least eight inches shorter.

"You only get to do that once," Chris threatened then returned his attention to his daughter. "Honey, what's wrong?"

She pulled away from the man and melted into her father's arms. He was there to protect her. Everyone treated her like a criminal and no one wanted to hear her side of the story. This is probably how her mother felt when they put her away. No one listened. No one believed her. No one understood her. Ashley continued to hold on to her father sobbing.

"Honey, what's going on? Why were you fighting?"

By now, Principal Charmine had reached them. He was all out of breath.

"When Simone dropped me off today, Tiffany and her friends were picking on me. They were teasing me about my mother. I tried to ignore them, but they grabbed me and started hitting and kicking me."

"That's not true!" Tiffany's father shouted. "My daughter is no liar and she is definitely not a troublemaker."

"Well, neither is mine," Chris challenged. "If Ashley says that's what happened, I believe her. Ashley never lies to me."

"I'm pressing charges," Mr. Connor insisted.

Chris turned to him.

"Bring your best. I promise you that when I finish with you, you will wish that you never made that challenge." He put his arm around his daughter and started toward the exit.

"You'll be hearing from my attorney!" Mr. Connor called behind them.

Chris continued walking with Ashley safely tucked beneath his arm. He knew that his daughter could not have started a fight. He heard the principal telling Tiffany's father to calm down and that a case against Ashley would be hard to prove since this is her first time being in trouble after being in the school for six years. His daughter was a regular to be in trouble. Mr. Connor's roaring fell silent as they watched Chris and Ashley leave the school.

Outside, Chris helped Ashley into his car. When he entered on the driver's side, she broke into hysterical crying. He reached into the glove compartment and handed her tissue. She took it and wiped at her eyes and nose. She clasped the tissues in her fist and sat quietly. Chris started the car and reached over and held her hand. They were going to get through whatever was happening between them. He believed that Ashley didn't start that fight, but he knew that for her to attack that girl the way she did that something else had to be bothering her. She took something deeper than criticism out on poor little Tiffany.

Chris parked the car. This was going to be a long night. Ashley was a very cleaver girl and was not going to make this task easy. He rounded the car and opened her door. She emerged from the car and started toward the house. She didn't say anything, but Chris could tell that she was thinking and planning. He locked the doors with his remote and followed her to the house. Once at the door, he unlocked it and Ashley went upstairs to her room.

Chris went to the kitchen and sat at the table. He took a moment to calm down. The security guard grabbing his arm really upset him. That guy was lucky he didn't put his lights out. Chris wondered what he was thinking putting his hands on him like that. He called Ashley to come down.

He heard her descending the steps and making her way to the kitchen. She entered and took a seat across from him. The table was round with four chairs to it. Chris softened his expression because he didn't want to be confrontational, but communicate with Ashley in a manner that would make her feel free to discuss all that was in her mind. As he could see, she wasn't going to open up on her own so he began with what he thought made sense.

"Honey, I first want to say I'm sorry about what happened to you today. I believe that Tiffany and the other girls provoked you this morning and that you were retaliating. But, I also think that you went to school with a chip on your shoulder and that's what I want to talk about."

He couldn't believe he came out like that. Ashley couldn't believe it either. Her mouth fell open and he could see that a wall had already gone up; a wall that he knew that before they left the table would be back down again.

"I didn't have a chip on my shoulder, Dad. It happened just as I said. My classmates were picking on me. I didn't want to fight them, but they were hurting me. I had no choice but to fight."

"You had already beaten her, why did you continue to fight her after the teacher tried to break you up?"

"I don't know. I was just so angry and I wanted her to remember for the next time. The teacher didn't see that there were two other girls fighting me at the same time. I was trying to keep her off of me so that I could get to the other girls that were kicking me."

"Ashley, what did Tiffany say to you to make you so angry?"

"She told me that I didn't have a mother and that I was pretending that Simone was my mother."

"Well, you know that you have a mother and Simone isn't pretending to be your mother so why did that bother you so much?"

"I don't know. I don't want anyone talking about me and my mother that way."

"You know I didn't send you to martial arts school so that you could beat up people."

She made a quick chuckle. His statement struck her funny.

"Honey, this is not a joke. You could have killed that girl. Do you want to go to jail?"

"You mean like Mom? Maybe I am bad like her."

Chris became angered. Ashley was challenging him and her attitude wasn't necessary. He couldn't understand why she was so hostile and sensitive about her mother. It's not like she ever met her. Maybe Michelle did have a mental connection with her as she told him during his visit. Ashley didn't cease her tormenting.

"No one gave my mother a chance. No one believed her. Now she's in jail and I'm without a mother. It's your fault. You took her away from me."

He couldn't believe it. What have I done wrong to make her feel that way? he wondered. Who was feeding her ill information?

"Did Simone tell you that? Is that what you two have been

talking about on your weekend visits? Well if it is, it's going to stop."

"Now you want to blame Simone. This has nothing to do with Simone, Daddy. Stop blaming people for things you can't understand. Now you want to take Simone from me?"

"Stop talking like that, Ashley!" his voice raised. "I have given you everything. Why are you being so mean?"

She didn't respond, only looked at him. She seemed so angry and hateful. This was not his daughter. This was not the daughter he fought for and would do anything to protect. This was someone who was malicious and wanted to punish someone, anyone. It seemed that she wanted to punish him.

"Have I ever lied to you, Ashley? Can you think of one time when I didn't tell you the truth about something?"

"You didn't tell me the truth about my mother. You wanted me to believe that my mother is a criminal and a murderer, but she isn't and she does love me."

She broke into a sob. Chris hurried over to her and held her.

"Honey, what your mother did has no bearing on you. You are my perfect angel. I love you more than anything and so does your mother. I never meant to make you feel like your mother didn't love you. She does, sweetie. Your mother would not get rid of you for anything in the world. That's one of my greatest fears. I am so afraid that when your mother is released that she will try to take you away from me.

"If Mommy is bad then so am I," she said between snivels.

"Why, honey? Why do you insist that this is true when I have told you different?"

"My science teacher told me that whatever is in your parent's genes are also in the children's jeans. I am half her and if you say she is bad then half of me is bad too. I'm going to go to jail just like mom. I wanted Tiffany to die."

"No, baby. You don't mean that. You were just angry."

"Dad, I want to go to Simone's house. Can you take me there?"

Things were getting out of control by the minute. Chris realized for the first time how apart he and Ashley had become. They used to talk about everything and now she was calling on Simone. How did I let this happen? he wondered. When did it happen? Was it the weekends they spent together?

"Ashley, why do you need to go to Simone's house? What is it that you feel you can say to her that you can not say to me?"

Ashley broke into a full bawl. The screeching sound of her voice pierced straight through him. Chris couldn't understand where he went wrong. He watched as his daughter displayed her act of defiance. Habitually, it was Chris' custom to give in to Ashley's display of insolence, but if he didn't stop it now, he was going to lose her completely. His mother would never have stood for that and he wouldn't have even tried it. Maybe he allowed it because he felt guilty for not providing her with a mother or because he wanted to make up for the soft side that was missing, but this had gotten too out of hand.

"Ashley, I want you to stop that crying this instance. You will talk to me and tell me what this is all about."

Her crying had gotten louder and more unbearable. Not being able to take it anymore, Chris grabbed her by the shoulders and held them firmly. His eyes glared as he looked deep into her eyes. He repeated his request. In shock Ashley stifled her bawl. She saw something new in her father's eyes and heard something different in his voice. He was not sympathetic, but angry. For the first time that she could ever account for, her father had actually gotten angry with her. There were red vessels chiseled into the whites of his eyes and the light brown hues within them were masked by widened pupils that warned her not to test his patience.

Once Chris realized that her screaming had stopped he loosened his vice. Ashley sat frozen in her seat, eyes glued to her father's own. She had a frightful gape that broke Chris' heart. She was afraid of him. She was afraid that he would hurt her. He would never hurt her, but she had hurt him. He backed away returning to his seat. Just as he was about to sit, Ashley dashed from her seat and bolted upstairs and into her room. Chris heard the door slam shut and the lock engaged. He started behind her, but as he reached the foot of the steps, the doorbell rang. He looked out and it was Simone.

He quickly opened the door. She was in tears.

"Where is Ashley? Is she all right?" She was looking frantically around him trying to get a glimpse of her. "The school told me that you had picked her up and that she was in a fight."

"Everything is fine. Calm down. Ashley is in her room."

"Oh, God, I've got to see her."

"No. Ashley needs to be alone for a while."

"Chris, what do you mean? What are you saying? You didn't punish her, did you?"

"No, I'm not punishing her. She's just got a lot to think about. I need to spend time with Ashley alone."

"What have you done?" Simone started toward the steps and Chris caught hold of her arm.

"Simone, why would you try to go against my wishes when I just clearly stated that Ashley needed to be alone? I think you and I need to talk and get a few things straight."

He held on to her arm and led her to the living room where they could talk. Simone had no idea what he was talking about. She feared that Ashley might have told him about their visit to see Michelle. Fearing the worst, she had begun sorting through excuses in her mind. Chris moved a pillow over, making a comfortable spot for Simone to sit. Everyone had become so sensitive and this was definitely one of those touchy issues.

"Simone, I don't even know where to begin," he said taking a seat next to her. He had turned to face her and if only she looked into his eyes, she would know that he meant no harm, although what needed to be said was strong.

"You should say what's on your mind. That's a beginning."

"I feel like I'm losing my daughter. That's one of the things I have always feared since the day I brought her home. Everything has been so perfect between us up to this point. I find that the more time she spends with you alone, the more distant she becomes." He paused, waiting for a reaction.

Simone felt the blow of his words and even though he said

them softly, it was like a knife being forced slowly into her heart. *What is he saying, that he doesn't want me to see Ashley anymore? That I can't take her home with me on weekends? That he doesn't trust me?* This was all too confusing for Simone.

"Yesterday when you brought Ashley home, she ran right past me. It's like she was rushing to her room to hide some secret. Her whole attitude has changed. I don't know if I'm just being over possessive, but since she has been staying with you weekends she has become preoccupied with her mother. She has even come short of calling me a liar about her mother and today she got into a fight at school. None of this makes sense. She should be getting better, but the more she spends with you, the worse she seems to be. I tried talking to her today and she became hostile. She even seemed to hate me. She asked me to take her to you. Since when have you become her savior?"

"Chris, wait a minute. Ashley is just a young girl growing up. It's natural for her to desire to be with her mother. You didn't think that the issue would come up? It would be the same if it were the other way around. No matter how you slice it, children will always yearn for completeness. You've got to let her see her mother. If you don't, you're going to lose her."

"Is that what you have been telling her? That she needs to build a relationship with that evil woman? That it's okay to want to be with her mother even though she's a murderer?"

"Listen to yourself. You're so hung up on what you think her mother did to you that you haven't thought about Ashley. Chris, she is a child yearning for that completeness. I am no replacement for her mother. Even if we were married, I still would never be a mother to Ashley. I will always be Simone. So this problem has nothing to do with me. It's got to do with you and the issues you are having with dealing with your past."

"What do you know about my past? You weren't there. What do you know about her mother more than what you saw in the file given by the State? Michelle is dangerous. I spent an entire day in jail because of her. My first true love could have died because of her. My mother is gone because of her. What could she possibly teach my daughter? Kill anything that gets in your way? Listen to what you're saying. Does this assessment sound prudent to you, Miss Counselor?"

That last statement angered Simone. She threw her hands up and Chris knew it was on, but she surprised him by pulling herself from her seat and starting towards the door. As she reached to leave, she noticed Ashley sitting on the steps. She had been listening to their conversation. Her eyes were so puffy and red that they stung when she blinked. Her voice was feeble and weak as she pleaded with her.

"Simone, please don't go. Don't leave me here." She reached for Simone, but Chris stepped between them.

"Chris, this is crazy. We shouldn't be fighting against each other, we're supposed to be helping each other. Let Ashley come with me. Let me talk to her. I promise things are going to work out. This is not the way to do it."

Chris didn't move. He still kept himself wedged between them.

"Chris, I love you and I love Ashley. I don't want to split you two up. I want to become a part of you. Let me help us."

She gently touched his arm and moved him aside. "Come, Ashley," she called.

Simone caught hold of Ashley's hand and pulled her to her feet. Her little hand trembled in her grasp. She slowly moved past her father and over to Simone. Chris gently touched his daughter's cheeks. Her tears cascaded along his finger. He no longer fought his own tears. He let them fall because he wanted her to know just how much all of this was hurting him. He wanted her to know that he too felt pain.

"Ashley, I love you. You may not believe that right now, but you are more special to me than life itself. I will be here waiting for you to come back. I will be waiting for my little girl; the one with the bright smile and eyes that twinkle when they look at me."

He kissed her, although she never looked at him. He nodded to Simone to let her know that it was okay. She leaned back and kissed him as she ushered Ashley out the door.

Chapter Five

Today was the day, April 25th, ten years exactly since she was sent to this forsaken place. Michelle waited for her escort to take her to the meeting with the parole board. It's probably been three days since she has been able to sleep. Seeing Ashley was an incentive that things were going to turn out right.

"Okay, 04673, it's that time," the officer said as he opened her cell. "This is the moment of truth. You think you're a reformed woman ready to rejoin society?"

Normally, Michelle would answer him with a rude remark, but today was special and, although that lisp created by his overbite irritated her, she refused to let him ruin her day. She and Officer Brown became quite close, as one might say when they've shared a connection, intimately that is. Officer Brown had a habit of creeping during the night with a fetish for grazing through dark pastures. Michelle guessed that because his last name was Brown, that meant he was supposed to mess with brown women. Of course, she didn't mind. That job kept her going all these years. She imagined getting arthritis in her derrière from pressing it against the bars for so long to get her nightly lick.

He escorted her down the corridor past fifty cells that harbored one hundred of some of the sickest personalities one could ever want to come across. Michelle didn't even look at them as she feared some bad Karma. She thought about Lot's wife turning into a pillar of salt when she turned to witness the doom of those behind her. Not Michelle, she moved forward and never once desired the things of the past, at least not from this place.

She entered a room with four people sitting at a long table. There was a chair waiting for her in the center of the floor. Nervously, she sat down placing her hands gingerly onto her lap. Her fingers remained outstretched. Her feet planted themselves together on the floor. Her back and shoulders squared taking on a position of poise. She waited.

"Michelle Tanner," they addressed her after a long silence. "You were sentenced to Sing Sing Correctional Facility ten years ago. You were charged with possession of an illegal drug and attempted murder against Keesha Smalls. Having spent ten consecutive years in a correctional facility, why do you feel that you are ready to return to society?"

Michelle thought about it. She summoned up her speech that she rehearsed again and again until it was ingrained into her memory.

"I have learned a lot while being in here," she started. "So much time wasted over something so foolish." Her candor was felt. They nodded as she spoke, absorbing her words.

"Being here helped me to understand that there are rules to be followed and human respect should always be present when making decisions. I made a mistake and I allowed jealously and anger to take control of my sound judgment. I wish that I could wipe that day, that moment away, but I can't. I know that what's done is done, I can never go back there or make it right. But today, I am sorry for my past transgressions and wish a thousand times that I could do something with my life that would make up for that wrong." Michelle fought to control her emotions.

The parole board listened intently, being caught up in her heart-felt sentiment. It was quite obvious that this woman had remorse over her wrongdoings and was ready to start her life new. She spoke with sincerity and there was no way they could deny her request for parole.

"Michelle, we believe that you have been rehabilitated. We will grant your request."

Without further comment, the papers were stamped "Approved" and Michelle watched as the four of them exited the room. When they were completely out of the room, Michelle let her stiff stature go limp. She exhaled deeply, emptying her lungs. Her nightmare was over and she could now begin to put her pieces back together.

Once the official papers had been put through, Michelle was released. A familiar face met her.

"Hey. So how does it feel to be a free woman?"

"Righteous." Michelle stood outside in the parking lot. She looked out at the dark waters that surrounded her. "I can't say that I'm going to miss this little island."

"I can imagine. You ready to go home?"

She shrugged, turning away from her ten-year grave. "Yeah. There's no point standing here. I have no lingering desires for this place."

Michelle got into her Silver Mercedes and stared out the window. Her thoughts drifted to her plans. There was so much to make up for and she would begin that task today. Ashley was her first priority. Halfway into the drive she redirected her destination.

"I want to stop by my attorney's office," she said, never once looking to the person she spoke to. His head nodded in agreement. The car sped across the black highway and the harmonious tune played by the tires sent her twirling into slumber.

Two hours later they were sitting outside of two-ninety-five Madison Avenue in New York. The driver lightly tapped her letting her know that they had arrived. She opened her eyes and looked out the window. When she gathered her thoughts, she straightened herself and left the car to enter the building.

"I'll be around. Here is my cell number. You can call me and let me know when you are ready to be picked up. It should only take me ten minutes to get back."

Michelle nodded as she stepped from the car. The jeans she wore clung to her perfectly revealing her taut body. She wore a soft yellow top that exposed her smooth brown skin and flat belly. She had Chris and Ashley's names tattooed onto her belly above and below her navel. Her long hair was pulled back from her face and wrapped into a tight ball. She was beautiful. The smell of feminine soap emanated from her as she entered the building. The security guard that sat at the desk looked up from his paper and rested his eyes on her braless breasts. Her prominent nipples saluted him. She smiled as her eyes met his.

"Can you remind me where Simon Walsh's office is?"

"How can someone as pretty as yourself need an attorney?" he flirted.

She leaned into the desk further exposing her cleavage. "You'd be surprised how dangerous a beautiful woman can be," she teased. "I was just released from a ten-year sentence and I haven't felt the thrust of a man in a long time. Interested?"

He shuttered. "What were you in for?"

"Attempted murder," she said casually.

"Whose office did you say you were looking for?"

"Simon Walsh," she repeated.

"Suite 1503. Take the elevator in bank three to the 15th floor," he told her.

"I guess that means you'll pass," she said as she turned and walked toward the third elevator bank. He watched as she worked her tight rear until she disappeared through the hallway. He shook his head and returned to reading his paper. This was not the kind of drama he needed.

Michelle pressed the button for the elevator. It lit up and shortly after the doors opened for her to enter. She stepped inside and pressed the fifteenth floor. The doors closed and she waited as the elevator ascended to the fifteenth floor. The doors opened and to her surprise Simon was standing there waiting for the elevator. He instantly recognized her.

"Ms. Tanner, you look good. When did you get out?"

"Why so formal?" she said stepping from the elevator. If he was going somewhere that idea went straight out the window. Michelle interlaced her arm in his and he escorted her back to his office.

Michelle was one of his rare clients. When she contacted him, he feared that she wanted him to get her off the attempted murder charges she faced. That was impossible, but he soon realized that Michelle was a planner. She wanted something far greater from him…redemption. Michelle knew that she would have to relinquish her daughter to either the State or her father and requested Simon to act as the mediator between she and Chris. Simon made everything look smooth on the surface with Simone as the go between. He need-ed her to make certain that Chris showed up at the hospital during delivery and signed the papers for custody of Ashley and kept her away from the State.

They entered his office. Michelle sauntered over to one of the leather seats that were situated in front of his desk. Simon went to his filing cabinet and looked up Michelle Tanner's file. When he retrieved it he sat in the seat next to her.

"I trust that everything is in order?"

He opened the file and handed it to her, indicating with his fin-ger the third paragraph from the end. Michelle ran her eyes over the text, absorbing the content of that paragraph. A wide grin spread across her face as her eyes filled with tears.

"You don't know how happy you have made me."

Although this moment marked a joyous occasion and he had kept his end of the contract, he worried about the lingering damage. What about Ashley? Is this what she wants?

Michelle returned the papers to Simon. "When can we begin?" she asked him.

"We can start the process whenever you are ready. But what if Ashley doesn't want this? Will you force her?"

"That's been taken care of. Ashley wants this as much as I do. This isn't going to be a problem, is it?"

"No. All is in order. You don't have to worry about a thing."

Michelle stood from her seat with an outstretched hand. Her gesture was met with a handshake. Now for part two, she thought.

"Care for a drink before you leave?" Simon offered, appraising her feminine assets.

"No. I think I will be going. I just want to go home and make myself a hot, bubble bath and begin feeling like a lady again. Prison has a way of taking away the softer side." She picked up the receiv-er from his desk and dialed the number on the paper given to her. She told her driver that she would be down in a few minutes. She was relieved to hear that he had already returned and was waiting for her right outside.

"Well, Simon, it's been nice. We'll be in touch. You get your end rolling and let me know when you need me."

"It's your turn to reign."

"I know. Now he will know that vengeance is mine."

She turned and left his office. Simon listened as her heels made music on the marble floors and he thought, That's a nasty piece of work.

Michelle boarded the elevator and took it to the first floor. The same guy from earlier met her. He didn't say anything this time. She continued on her way, but could feel his lustful stare. She exited the building and found her car waiting there for her as stated. She got in and they continued to her home in Long Island.

When they arrived, Michelle paid her friend for picking her up and bringing her car. He had parked his Accord on the street in front of her house then went into her house. Everything was still in order. She made a mental note to give Tanya, her housekeeper, a bonus for keeping up the place. Michelle moved through her home slowly, taking in the remaining ghosts from the past. Pictures of Chris rested on her counter. He was so young then, she thought tracing the details of his handsome, developing features. She carried the pictures over to the couch, continuing to be absorbed in the memory. She sat back, melting into the sofa's cushions. It felt good, nothing like the hard cot she had become so accustomed to. You'd be surprised what a person could adapt to after so many years. Her eyes closed and she remembered.

***

"Everything is going to be alright, Michelle. Just breathe, keep breathing," the female officer told me as they hurried me to the hospital. There were several people in the room including Simone, who was anxiously waiting in the corner. Chris was there and he looked so worn and tired. He had not been taking care of himself. He stood nearby waiting for our child. The pain was so intense and I reached for him hoping that he would hold my hand while I go through this miracle. He didn't. His eyes were cold with hatred. He had not forgiven himself or me. He stood so far…too far. I realized that not even this child would bring us together. So much had happened between us, so much hurt, so much pain. Everything had diminished to animosity.

Birthing Ashley was tough, especially since she didn't want to leave my body. She had become so comfortable there. I fought so hard to endure the pain but something went wrong. Blood began to spread and the doctor's fear became evident. I wondered if I was going to die right there. I was in a grave situation and was not going to be able to deliver this child. I was given a spinal injection and soon after, Ashley was pulled from my belly through an opening made by the surgeon.

Ashley was placed on my stomach for a few seconds as I was told to confirm her gender. The nurse then took her to be cleaned up. When they returned with her, they handed her over to Chris. His eyes met mine then he turned the child to me and told me to look at her good because this would be the last time I saw her. My finger was pressed onto a card with the prints of her tiny,little feet. This was the only thing I had to remind me of my daughter.

I watched as Chris disappeared with my little girl. He kept his word as best he could. Two weeks before my meeting with the Board he shows up without my daughter. What did he expect? That I was going to tell my daughter not to love me, or to hate her mother for breaking his heart and for taking his mother's life? It took a long time for me to realize it, but Chris was a fool and he would always be that fool for me. I will now show him why I have always had a hand up on him and the grave he dug for me will be his own.

***

Simone and Ashley arrived at her house. By now, Ashley had calmed from her crying and was ready to talk. She followed behind

Simone as she unlocked the door and held it open for her. As if it was expected, she went into the living room and sat on the sofa. Simone went into the kitchen and fixed two glasses of water and joined Ashley on the sofa. She didn't say anything, only handed her the glass and started sipping her own. She seemed too defenseless as she held her little face down and studied her lap. Her body was frozen in the same spot. Simone felt so bad for her. This whole situation was taking its toll and was certainly too much for any young child to bear.

Simone patted her on the lap and left her there on the sofa. She climbed the stairs and went into the bathroom and ran some water in the tub with a capful of floral bubble bath. Ashley always enjoyed that one. When it had filled, she went into the room she reserved for Ashley when she visited and pulled a lavender nightgown from the drawer.

She looked from the top of the landing and called Ashley upstairs. Ashley acknowledged her petition and climbed the steps leaving her glass on the table. Realizing that Simone held her hand out for her own, she caught hold of it and followed Simone to the bathroom.

"You know, whenever I felt down I would take a warm bath and soak away my troubles. Maybe it will do the same for you," Simone told her.

Ashley nodded her head. Simone caught her chin and faced her eyes to meet hers.

"Your daddy loves you, Ashley. You shouldn't be so hard on him you know. He only wants the best for you. I'm going to leave you to get undressed and into the tub. I will come back in a little while and scrub your back."

Before leaving the bathroom she noticed that Ashley's hair was on her shoulders. She removed her clamp from her hair and used it to hold up Ashley's hair. She held her tightly then left her to get undressed.

Simone went into her room, closed her door, and sat on her bedside. Things had really gotten out of hand with Chris and Ashley. This was definitely not what she had intended. All she wanted to do was give Ashley a fair chance to get to know her mother. Although she knew that Chris would not agree, she thought about how she felt not knowing her parents - her real parents. Her real mom and dad abandoned her at a very early age, long before a real connection could be made. Right around Ashley's age now, Simone started her quest to know her real parents. Her foster parents weren't pleased about it and were not supportive of her choice. It was also because of this quest that they never opted to adopt her. A distance formed between them and it wasn't long before the schools started calling and her foster parents grew tired of hearing her excuses about children picking on her. They told her that according to her, everything that happened to her was always someone else's fault. If she didn't talk to Ashley, she would soon go down that same path. Chris may tire of her hostility. Not having a real mother can be difficult for a child and Simone knew it very well. Ashley was not her daughter, but she couldn't bear to see her become another product of a dysfunctional home. She had to reunite Ashley with her mother, Every child has a right to know their mother, she reasoned with herself. Don't they? she wondered, second guessing her assessment.

She returned to the bathroom to see how Ashley was doing. Her little shoulders were hidden behind a thick mass of pallid bubbles. Such a beautiful little girl, she thought as she observed her features and perfectly tanned skin. Ashley was like the daughter she always wanted, but as long as she harbored the desire to be with her mother, she would never be able to fit completely in her world.

"Hey there, kiddo, feeling any better? Bubbles always made me feel better whenever I was down."

Ashley shook her head no. Her eyes never met Simone's. She captured mountains of suds in her hands and blew them.

"Where's your cloth?" Simone asked feeling the water to see if it had run cold.

Ashley handed her the cloth and then the soap. She remained quiet, listening as Simone vigorously rubbed soap onto the cloth. She then felt soothed as she washed her neck, shoulders and back. This was something she looked forward to when with Simone. Chris used to wash her back too, but he told her that she was becoming a young lady and that he shouldn't bathe her anymore. It felt good being cared for. If her mother was around she would always have someone to wash her shoulders. He doesn't even smooth lotion on her skin anymore.

"Sweetie, I would love to know what's going on in your mind. What are you thinking about so hard?"

"Simone, why does my father hate my mother so much?" she asked immediately placing her hands over her mouth.

Simone caught hold of her hand and removed it from her face. She held it and peered into her eyes. So much hurt and pain were there. She had no idea where to begin; not because explaining it was difficult, but because she felt as though she was intruding by telling her about her mother.

"Your mom and dad went through a very difficult time before she was arrested. Your mom did some really horrible things to your dad and people he loved and he hasn't been able to forgive her for it."

"But you would if it were you, right? The Bible says that we should forgive everyone. My dad taught me that and yet he can not forgive my mother."

"I know that the Bible says we should forgive everyone, but honey, sometimes it is difficult for us as humans to forgive people when they do certain things to us. Your daddy wants to forgive your mom, but the hurt he feels is still there. You shouldn't hold that against him."

"I know, but I hate the things he says about my mother. It's not right and I love her no matter what he says."

"Come on, I should get you out of the tub now. I wouldn't want you to melt away," Simone told her chucking her under the chin. Ashley laughed and allowed Simone to help her from the tub.

Simone cloaked Ashley in body spray and lotion then pulled a lavender nightgown over her head. She combed and brushed her hair into a single ponytail with bouncy curls. Ashley slid her feet into the plush, pink slippers that awaited her. She then followed Simone down the short hallway to her bedroom. They sat on the bed and Ashley cuddled up with Simone, resting her head in her lap. She looked up at Simone and wished so much that she could have been her real mother. Everything would have been so perfect if things were different. She wondered why she told her father no if she loved him so much. Maybe her dad was the real bad guy and not her mother.

"What did you and Michelle talk about? Did she tell you anything about your dad?"

Ashley hesitated. For the first time her eyes met with Simone's and she wondered what that had to do with anything. Her mother wasn't the one trying to keep her away from her father. Besides, she promised that she wouldn't tell anyone about their discussion.

"That's a simple question, Ashley. I thought we were friends."

"We are friends," she defended right away.

They both fell silent, looking away from each other. Simone didn't want to push too hard and make Ashley close up completely.

"Why did you say no when my father asked you to marry him?"

Her question took her by surprise. How did she know that I had told him no? Chris must have told her that, she imagined.

"Don't you love my dad? Don't you love me?"

Simone melted inside. Things were about to become very complicated for all of them. Michelle's release was today and that is only the beginning of the problem. Simone was never supposed to fall in love with him, but only to keep tabs on him and Ashley. Their bond is so strong and now she would have to give it all up.

"Of course I love you, Ashley. You know that's a silly question."

"Do you love my daddy?"

She swallowed then answered. "I love your daddy too. You should get some sleep."

Simone slid from under Ashley's head and placed a pillow there. She leaned down and kissed her on her forehead. She walked to the door and cut off the light.

"See you in the morning."

"Simone. My dad loves you too and you really hurt him."

"I know, sweetheart. Sometimes we hurt the ones we love by accident."

"That's true because I hurt my dad too."

Simone could hear her soft cry in the dark. The pillow's cushions could not muffle the sounds of her pain.

"Can I call my dad and tell him good night?"

"Sure, baby, he would really appreciate that."

Ashley got up from the bed and went to the telephone that was on the dresser in her room.

Chapter Six

Chris got up bright and early. He felt a whole lot better after having talked with Ashley last night. He made a mental note to do something special for Simone to make up for the way he treated her yesterday. He went downstairs to the kitchen and put on some water for some tea. He then took out two slices of bread, sliced six strips of extra sharp cheddar cheese, placed it on the bread and then placed it onto a cookie sheet. In a skillet, he cooked two lean beef sausages then duo eggs over easy. While that was working, he heated a small pot of grits. When everything seemed to be just about ready, he toasted his bread with cheese. He placed the plate on the table with his complete breakfast. He opened his paper and started sifting through the news. There was nothing interesting going on.

He turned his attention to the mail that he had placed on the table last night. He opened his checks first and confirmed that they were in order, and then he noticed a letter from the correctional facility where Michelle was serving time. Without hesitation, he opened it and began skimming through it. The letter stated that Michelle Tanner had been released yesterday after serving ten of her twenty-year sentence by the parole board. Upon reading it, Chris spewed out his breakfast. Not being able to control the wrenching in his stomach, he dashed to the first floor bathroom that was just outside the kitchen. Everything that he had eaten had all came out. Starting his day with Michelle on his mind was the last thing he wanted to do. Things were about to become more complicated than ever. With Ashley feeling the way she is, Chris definitely has his work cut out for him. Now his stomach was empty and he had to be off to work.

When he arrived, his boss told him that there was a client waiting to see him. Chris went into his office and took a seat behind his desk. He sifted through his messages and jotted down some notes. He buzzed his assistant to come in. When she arrived, he handed her some client information and asked her to pull their files and keep them at her desk until after he saw the client. After reviewing his calendar, he couldn't imagine what client was dropping in on him. He opened his pad to a fresh page and placed his pen next to it.

Mr. Thurman was on his line probably to let him know that he was sending the client over. He watched as his assistant Danielle nodded her head while talking to his boss. She hung up the phone without transferring the call. Seconds later she buzzed him to let him know that Ms. Tanner was coming in.

"Who did you say?" he asked feeling perplexed. He could feel that earlier sickness returning.

"Ms. Tanner. Does she have a file you need me to pull?"

"No. Just send her in."

Michelle appeared through the entryway of his office. She wasn't wearing the prison attire he thought fitted her so well. She was cloaked in a long fitted white and navy blue pinstriped dress with white and navy shoes that complimented her attire perfectly. There was a high split up the front of the dress that revealed a very shapely, toned leg. Her stockings were completely sheer with a light shimmer. Her hair was pulled back away from her face in a bun with fine curls nestled at the top. Two deliberate curls framed her face on either side as well as at the nape of her neck. It made her appear soft and sensuous, a look Chris was unaccustomed.

"Are you going to offer me a seat or am I going to have to stand here all day?" she asked moving toward the seat facing his desk. Not bothering to wait for his response, she sat down.

"I was actually going to tell you to stand there all day, but since you're already sitting, don't get too comfortable."

"You're charming as ever. It must be parenting that's taught you such manners."

"Why are you here, Michelle?" he snapped while getting up to close the door. He pushed it shut and returned to his desk then took a seat. His eyes never left hers.

Michelle observed the pictures of him and Ashley on his desk. Most of them were of Ashley alone. He had a picture of her when she was first born and four other pictures of her seemingly a year difference between each. There was one recent picture of the three of them together like one big happy family. She reached out to pick it up, but Chris stopped her.

"Michelle, cut the bullshit. I asked you a question. Why are you here?"

"I came to let you know that I was out. Aren't you happy to hear that?"

"I got the letter and I can't say that I am."

She laughed then shifted her hip in the seat, revealing her long leg. His eyes followed her every movement.

"You know if you keep watching me like that I'm liable to think you want me."

"Well, I don't. I have no interest in your wiles and I'm definitely not interested in rekindling anything. So again, why are you here?"

"I'm here for my daughter, of course. I appreciate you keeping her for me."

Chris' eyebrows furrowed into a frown. He knew that Michelle was serious, but this wasn't the time or place for confrontation.

"Ashley is staying with me. I have full custody of her and I'm not going to let you ruin her life with this crap."

"She's our daughter, Chris. Did you forget that it was my body that she came out of? Or does Christine's prodigy think he could deliver a baby too?"

The mention of his mother's name angered him. Chris maintained his cool. It took a maximum effort and Michelle didn't make that task easy.

"Like I said before, you will not get my daughter and I'm not going to allow you to see her."

"I see you and Ms. Social Worker have been getting along very well. Can I safely assume that this is Keesha's new replacement?"

"You better not even think about hurting her."

"I wouldn't dare think about hurting her. I should thank her. I mean, look how well she's taken care of you for me. She deserves a medal." Her eyes traced his body, deliciously taking in every firm cut of his muscles. "You know I'd kill to ride you again," she smiled showing her perfect teeth.

"Well, you've done all the riding you're going to do as far as I'm concerned unless you mean a ride back to prison," he grinned sarcastically back at her.

Chris was going to be more entertaining than she'd imagined. For a few minutes they watched each other. Neither Chris nor Michelle said a word to the other but only calculating the next move. They were like pawns in a game of chess and no one wanted to make the first move. Chris broke the silence.

"Unless there is something particular you want to discuss, you should be going."

"Oh, I have plenty to discuss. But before we get on a bad note, I was wondering if you wanted to see if we still had that insatiable inferno we once shared."

Chris laughed. He couldn't believe that Michelle hadn't changed a bit. He would never let her touch his body again. Not even his hand. He hated the very fabric of her existence. She must have feared him to some degree, which is why she would use his boss to facilitate this meeting. It was totally unlike Michelle to visit him in a public place. His cynical stare penetrated her facade.

"I guess I should get right down to business then," Michelle said breaking his gaze. As always, Chris thought he had everything under control. Not this time, she thought. He doesn't know who he's dealing with, at least not yet. I will show him that the rules have changed and he's not the one in control, but I am.

Chris nodded in agreement that Michelle should get down to business. He had no desire to play this game with her and definitely didn't want her to waste another minute of his time.

"I want my daughter," Michelle stated.

"That's not happening."

"Not permanently, we can share her and have equal time with her."

"Ashley doesn't need to know you. You're a monster, Michelle, and I wouldn't dare let you weasel your way into her life."

"In case you've forgotten, she's already a part of my life. I gave birth to her."

"And that's it. But I have been the only mother and father she's known."

"Well, that's not true. You have the social worker playing mommy to her, but every child wants to know their real mother. If you think I'm lying just wait and see."

"See what?"

"Everything comes in time, Chris. Everything comes in time. So, before I leave, are you sure you don't want me to saddle that ride for old time's sake?"

She stood revealing a "V" print in her dress contouring her sex. Chris shook the image from his mind. Her dress fell out of its tuck and the seductive imprint disappeared. As Michelle strolled toward the door her hips twisted with every motion. When she reached the door, she turned to face Chris who was still seated behind his desk watching her.

"The fun is only beginning, darling. If you think for a moment that you have gotten rid of me, you are sadly mistaken."

Chris waved her out with the back of his hand, unmoved by her statement. As Michelle opened the door, Mr. Thurman was standing there ready to join the meeting.

"So," he started jovially, "I trust that Mr. Walker has tended to your needs, Ms. Tanner."

Michelle accepted his hand and he planted a kiss on the back of it.

"Yes. Everything is in order. You will hear from me in a couple of days. Mr. Walker and I have some things we should go over first to make sure that we need to do business."

She gave him a reassuring smile then turned back to Chris.

"It was a pleasure meeting you, Mr. Walker. I look forward to seeing you again."

Mr. Thurman released her hand and Michelle left the office. Mr. Thurman watched her leave, lusting at every move she made.

When the outside door closed behind her he turned to face Chris.

"You will take good care of that client. She has more than three million dollars of liquid cash. I'm giving you the account because she requested you. She only wants to work with you. I don't know how you work those serious referrals, son, but your name really travels. How's Ashley?"

The mention of Ashley's name brought a pleasant smile to Chris' face.

"Ashley is a handful. She is such a wonderful daughter. I can't imagine ever being without her."

"I know how that is. I have four daughters and two sons. Daughters are the best. They pamper their dads. It's a shame her mother died during delivery."

Chris swallowed at the lie he told being thrown back at him. He was grateful that Michelle hadn't mentioned their relationship with his boss.

"I know. Sometimes the dead doesn't stay dead."

"Tell me about it. My wife has been gone for five years and it still seems like yesterday that she was in my arms. I commend you for stepping to the plate. That took a lot of courage. Anything you need, I want you to know that I'm here."

"Thanks, Mr. Thurman."

They went over a few other accounts that Chris had been working on. When Mr. Thurman was pleased with the progress, he dismissed himself and returned to his office.

Chris opened a letter on his desk. It was a letter from Keesha. It had been a long time since he had any communication from her. In fact, the last time he received a letter from her it had actually came from Michelle. The memory made a sore spot in his heart open. It took him ten years to close that wound and now the current events had found an opening and started picking at his scabs.

He read the letter.

Hello Chris,

So much time has passed since we've talked. I don't know where to even begin. I thank you so much for the pictures of Ashley.

She is a lovely little girl. I know that you are taking good care of her because her smile radiates off the picture. It's been so long since I've seen you and I guess it was best that you didn't send me a picture of yourself.

Chris, we don't have to be enemies. As you know, I have two children, fraternal twins, a boy and a girl. I named them Christian and Keona. They are nine now. I love them so much, Chris, I can't tell you how much these children mean to me. Jamal has been an excellent husband and father. My whole world revolves around them. Maybe if it were a different time, under different circumstances, it would have been you.

Chris, I received a letter from Sing Sing Correctional Facility stating that Michelle was being released from prison. I guess that because of her previous crimes, it's their policy to let the victims know that she will be out. I fear for you and Ashley, Chris. I know that she will be after you again. I know that she will be after Ashley. If you need me for any reason, I want you to know that I am here for you, Chris. Jamal and I will help you get through this. We will be there in any way that we can.

As a friend, I love you and I will always be there for you. I wanted so badly to be with you after the funeral to help you through that time, but you had distanced yourself from me. Take care, Chris. Here is my number if you need anything. I have also enclosed our latest pictures. You can tell Ashley that she has two cousins that would love to meet her.

Tears filled his eyes as he took in Keesha's beauty. She hadn't changed a bit since the last time he saw her. It had surprised him when she entered the church. If my mother only knew how much that woman loved her, he thought. Keesha wept horribly when she peered into the casket and saw her friend for the last time. It took two other people besides Jamal to pull her away.

He remembered the words Keesha spoke to the mourning spectators about her dear friend. Her eyes locked with those of Chris' and the look she gave him told of an eternal love and respect. If ever anyone cared for him, she did. Sometimes circumstances don't allow for two perfect people to come together, even if they are meant for each other. Those were the words his mother told him when he raced out of Keesha's house behind her. To think about it today, maybe that was his mistake. Maybe he should have stayed with Keesha instead of racing behind his mother. In the end, Chris believed that his mother understood how much Keesha meant to him, but it was too late. She had already pushed her into the arms of another man.

The birth of Ashley was the first time Chris felt peace since the death of his mother and losing Keesha to another man. His daughter brought so much sunshine to his life. If it wasn't for her being in his life, he would have never met Simone. Although it is said that everything happens for a reason and that your destiny is your destiny, he couldn't even imagine any other reason why he and Simone would have crossed paths.

Simone probably doesn't know it, but she saved his life. Not only because she won his daughter for him, but also because she came along when he needed someone. As vivacious as Chris understood himself to be, he had lived a life of celibacy for three years. When he and Simone started spending so much time together, things just seemed complete with her being around.

Being in the rut he was in, Chris never considered that Simone was interested in him until one day when Ashley was at school and Simone stopped by to do her routine house visit. Something magical happened that day; Simone unexpectedly locked lips with him and engaged him in a kiss that was full of so much passion. At first, and more out of reflex, Chris pulled away, but her persistence overwhelmed his emotions and he began kissing her in return. She had so much fire in her, so much desire. This was a road Chris had been down before and unlike before, he would be skeptical of her intentions and take things very slow - seven years slow. Of course, it wasn't his intentions to wait this long to ask her to marry him, but at the rate things were going, he didn't want to mess them up with a proposal of marriage. It didn't matter anyway; she still refused after seven years of waiting.

Relationships were all too confusing to Chris. He didn't understand women and he certainly didn't understand himself. Being a father to Ashley was the only thing that seemed natural and now with Michelle on the prowl, even that was uncertain.

His assistant's voice came in on his intercom breaking his thought. He pushed the pictures of Keesha and her adorable children back into the envelope and responded to her call.

"Mr. Walker, Mr. Thurman left some files on my desk he wants you to go over. Can I bring them in to you?"

"Sure, Patrice. Come on in."

Patrice entered his office with an arm full of large, expanding file pockets. Chris hurried around his desk to help her with the files before she dropped them.

"Thanks, Mr. Walker. That's very nice of you."

Patrice was about forty-five, but she looked much older. She too had gone through some hard times with relationships. She was just returning to work from an eight month-long term of disability. This was her third week back and, surprisingly so, she jumped back in the game better than anyone imagined. She has a son who was taken from her during the time she was sick, but she seems to be getting her life back together. Chris respected her so much because she was a strong woman. It took a lot for her to return to work and take charge of her life. In a few weeks she will be meeting with social workers to see if she's ready to get her five-year-old son back.

"It's no problem, Patrice. You should have told me that the files were heavy."

"I know, but I really thought I could handle them."

As Patrice finished putting the files on Chris' desk she noticed the pictures on it. She had seen them before, but Ashley's picture caught her eye.

"You know what's funny, Mr. Walker?" she asked while studying the recent picture of Ashley.

"What's that, Patrice?" Chris responded with amusement.

"You know the woman that left here earlier resembles your daughter. She could almost pass for her mother."

Chris dropped the files he was still holding. A ghastly look replaced his amused look.

"What is it? You don't think so?"

He pulled himself together.

"No. I hadn't noticed. You really think so?"

The look of fear left Patrice's face. "Yeah, I really do. They have the same eyes, the same smile and their complexions are just alike. It's funny, but they say everyone has a twin."

Chris forced a smile. Her statement had added salt to the already burning sore. Patrice didn't know the reality check she just gave him; a reality that Chris was not ready to face. Ashley looks like him until Michelle is around. The resemblance is striking.

"Thanks for bringing the files in, Patrice. I should get started on them," he said dismissing her from his office before another of her revelations pierced him.

Patrice turned on her heels and left the office unbothered. She was totally unaware of the damage she had just done.

It was a long day and Chris welcomed the opportunity to go home. He was surprised that he got anything done with all that he had on his mind. He tucked the letter Keesha sent to him in his briefcase. On his way out Patricia stopped him.

"See you tomorrow, Mr. Walker."

"Good night, Patricia. You get home safe and thanks for the files again. You're doing a great job."

"Thanks, Mr. Walker."

Her formal addressing of him seemed hardly appropriate, especially with him being so much younger than she is. Chris continued on his way.

Traffic was horrendous and it took extra long getting home. Chris couldn't believe the trip home took two hours, but accidents have been known to cause severe pileups. When he arrived home, the first thing he wanted to do was take a shower. Today was challenging and very stressful. He sat his briefcase on the floor by the steps. This would remind him to go through the papers he brought home and to reread Keesha's letter. He managed to climb the steps upstairs and he stood at Ashley's bedroom door. Her bed was unmade and the covers were rumpled by the pillow. It reminded him of their disagreement from yesterday. So much hurt for one little child. Chris wondered how his life had become so wrong. It was as though his life had become like dominos. Every good thing that has ever happened to him was falling in one swift move. Michelle was the antagonist that has upset his world and if he didn't do something about it, he would be consumed by it.

Chris went into the bathroom and set the water. He listened to the water spill onto the ceramic floor. He peeled off his clothes and stepped in. It kneaded into his blades soothingly. After fifteen minutes he felt so much better. He shut off the water and snatched the towel from the bar. He blotted himself dry then stepped from the stall. A reflection of his diminishing self stared back at him. His chaotic past was rapidly catching up with him. He leaned in toward the mirror and observed the prominent vessels etched across his eyeballs. They represented fatigue, hurt and stress. For a brief moment he closed them. The initial sting subsided to a teary cool. The stress lines that once decorated his corneas had vanished.

Chris burrowed his fingers through the mass of curls that adorned his head, forcing them out of place until his hands rested behind his neck. He twisted his neck from one side to the other to relieve the tension. The realigning of his vertebrae brought relief. While looking into the mirror he remembered the note Keesha had sent him and the pictures that were enclosed. As he stared not at his reflection, but through the dark passage of his mind, he remembered the day when his world began to crumble.

***

Chris sat in the front pew with his eyes fixed on the details of his mother's casket. It was late and everyone had already left the funeral home after giving their condolences and viewing the body. It had only been three days, but he missed her like hell. Normally, Chris would be full as a tick and on his way home from his mother's house by now, but that would never happen again. He missed her so much. So many of her friends came to see her and so many paid their respects, but because of bitter feelings and ill decisions, her best friend had to come to say her last goodbye.

"We're going to close up soon, son," the man said as he rested his hand on Chris' shoulder.

Sniffling, Chris nodded in acknowledgement. "Just give me five more minutes." The man gave him an assuring pat then walked away. Chris knelt in front of this mother's casket. "Mom, I am so sorry that I wasn't there for you. Everything that has happened was all because of me. You would be here right now if I had only listened. He paused, shaking his head at the memory. I know that you would have forgiven Keesha. You two had such a beautiful friendship and I had to mess that up. I wanted to tell her to stay, but I was afraid. Mom the two of you were more important to me than anything in the world and I have now lost both of you. I miss you so much and I want you to know that I am so sorry for leaving you. I'm sorry for being a bad son to you. You have always been my best friend and I wish you were still here. Well, I'm going to go now, but I want you to know that you can stop by to see me from time to time. I won't be afraid. He stood then leaned in and kissed his mother's head.

"I'm leaving now."

A hand rested on his shoulder.

He turned and suddenly found himself face to face with Keesha and all of her beauty.

"Hello, Chris," she managed, using her best effort to contain her emotions. "How are you holding up?"

Although his first instinct was to grab her and pull her into his arms, anger pushed rationale right out the door.

"Why are you here? Haven't you caused enough hurt?"

"Chris," she responded half believing what he was saying. A combination of hurt and dismay replaced her sorrowful eyes.

"My mom is gone, Keesha. She's gone forever and it's all because I chose you."

"Well, I'm sorry that you feel that way. I'm sorry that I have lost not only one friend, but two." For a moment Keesha forgot that she was holding a bouquet of orchids in her hands. She moved toward Christine and whispered a sorry and a plea for forgiveness to her friend then placed the flowers across her torso. "I love you, Christine," she said then turned away. Her steps were labored as she moved toward the door away from Chris.

"I'm sorry, Keesha!" Chris called out to her, but she continued down the aisle until she disappeared through the doors. That was the last time he saw her face to face.

A year later Chris received a letter from Keesha with pictures of her twins. When Ashley was born, Chris followed suit and sent pictures of his daughter and they continued communicating through mail. So desperately he wanted to ask her if she still had feelings for him or if Jamal was treating her the way he should, but his envelopes always contained the same things; pictures of Ashley and a take care of yourself card. That was all he could manage without opening a way for his hurt to resurface.

Chris returned to the foot of the steps and retrieved his brief-case. He went into the kitchen and fixed himself a drink because he needed one badly. Michelle coming to the office today was the last thing he needed. She was out to ruin him any way she could. It won't be long before she would be after his Ashley. This was something Chris knew would be unbearable. If I lost my daughter, it would kill me for sure, he told himself as he took his first swallow and moved to the table to sit down. He pulled the two latches apart and the clasps that held his briefcase closed popped open. He removed a few of its contents, focusing on Keesha's letter. He reread her letter uttering a quiet, I love you. He stared at the pictures and noticed that her two beautiful children looked so much like her. They had her eyes, her smile, and then something different...Jamal, the very one who stole his woman from him. Of course, if he had it his way, he wouldn't have let her go either. She was definitely worth fighting for. Now, Chris realized that he had something more valuable than Keesha to fight for...his Ashley. Michelle would die before he'd let her walk away with his daughter. He shuffled through his papers and lifted the file his boss apparently tucked within his other work for him to look at. He opened it and found that it pertained to Michelle Tanner's invest-ments. Her liquid funds exceeded three million dollars. Where the hell did she get all this money? he wondered. Sifting through the contents, he noticed a sizeable trust fund that was left to her by her grandmother as well as a substantial lump sum settlement from an automobile accident. There were several investment portfolios and vested assets that have been handled by Goldman, Thurman & Sacs' rival company - Morgan International Investments. Chris searched diligently for the name of her agent or broker, praying that it wasn't whom he thought it was. To his dismay, it was Justin Jones, known as JJ. Justin had worked for Goldman when Chris first arrived. He was there two years before he was offered a position at Morgan International Investments. Mr. Thurman was infuriated when he heard that Justin was working there, but it also opened a door for Chris to advance his career. This was a very bad situation because he knew that his boss would be anxious to take this account away from Justin and it was probably the only one that he had that was paying his bills.

Chris picked up the phone and methodically dialed Justin's number. He didn't expect Justin to be there, but if he left him a message he knew that first thing in the morning, Justin would call him back. Chris knew that he would have to open up to him if he were going to get Michelle out of his hair. The line rang twice before Justin picked up the phone.

"Justin Jones, may I help you?" he asked with his high pitched tone. Chris always teased him about his feminine sounding voice. He would always joke that the women liked it.

"What's up, man? I didn't expect you to be there. Burning the midnight oil?"

"Don't tell me this is Chris Walker, the prize accountant at our rival company."

"In the flesh. How are you, man? How's it going over there?"

"Things are going great. Don't tell me you want a job?"

Chris laughed. Justin told him that he should have come with him, that Mr. Thurman was never going to let him run his operation or join the board.

"You should be asking me that. You know if you want to be my secretary I've got nothing but love for you."

"I appreciate that, but I've got my own staff and my secretary is fine as hell. What can I do you for, man?"

Chris paused, mustering through his thoughts for the right words. He didn't want to be too forward.

"I've got a client that you might be interested in."

"Why would Chris Walker be giving me leads? Isn't that a conflict of interest? What, are you out of the financial business now?"

"Michelle Tanner."

The mention of her name sent an eerie chill up Justin's spine. He wondered what the hell was going on. He recognized that client off the bat. Michelle was a cunning, rich bitch with a whole lot of angry ambition. Justin met her a few years ago when some unexpected funds turned up. Michelle's grandmother had passed away and left a sizeable estate to her only granddaughter who happened to be in jail at the time. It took a whole lot of effort to find her, and working with her was difficult because she refused to meet with him in person. He handled her grandmother's estate before she passed and she entrusted her will and wishes to him to see to it that her granddaughter received her money. He wondered if she knew that Michelle was in prison would she have still left the money to her.

"Michelle Tanner was an inherited client. How did you come about working with her?"

"She just dropped her assets on the desk of Goldman Thurman & Sacs and she wants me to personally work on it for her."

"You don't want to mess with her, man. I had to deal with her from prison and she was an evil woman. I mean, I made a lot of money off of her, but you think she would be grateful for what I did for her? No," he answered before Chris could consider responding. "As soon as she was released, she made a point of visiting me and having the assets transferred from our accounts."

"Why did she do that? From the looks of things, you were doing an excellent job at making money for her."

"She just told me that she had a debt to score. I didn't ask her too many questions because she was too calculating for me and her expression told me that I had already asked too many. You seem to know more than you're letting on. How do you know her and why did she choose you?"

Chris thought about it. He had kept his previous relationship a secret too long and he knew that he needed someone to confide in. Justin was his partner before he left the company, and he still had respect for him. Clamoring out the words

"I used to date her."

"No freaking way, man. You have got to be kidding me. How did you land…"

"She was my first real experience."

"Holy crap! You mean to tell me that foxy woman turned you out? Dang, I got turned out by my biology teacher, but she looked nothing like this chick."

"I cut her off."

"You mean you let her go? It's usually the other way around. What happened?"

"I just grew up. When my dad died we moved away and I eventually forgot about her."

"Well, she apparently hadn't forgotten about you. But this makes no sense. Why would she want to do business with you if you dumped her."

"The truth is I never dumped her. I just stopped seeing her. When we moved I fell for someone else, an older woman that was beautiful, smart and sexy and I just stopped reaching out to Michelle."

"Why was she in jail? Don't tell me that she was stalking you and you pressed charges?"

"Worse."

"Don't keep me in suspense. What happened?"

"She tried to kill my new girlfriend or at least hurt her."

"I understand that. Why does she want you to handle her money?"

"She doesn't, she wants to ruin me. I don't know what her plans are, I just know that they can't be good."

"Why don't you just tell Mr. Thruman what's going on and let him assign the account to someone else? Don't let your personal crap get in the way of personal growth."

"We have a daughter together."

"Little Ashley is her daughter?"

"Yes. And I can't tell Mr. Thurman that Ashley is her daughter. I don't want him to know that I lied to him."

"Why did you lie about it? Why did you lie to me?"

"It was just better for me and for Ashley if no one knew that her mother was a convicted felon."

The line fell silent. This was more than Justin bargained for. There was definitely more to this than Chris was letting on. He wondered if he should pry or let it go. He decided to pry.

"What does Michelle want with you now?"

"Ashley."

"I figured as much. Why give you access to her accounts?"

"Leverage, I guess. She probably wants to use my job against me. This is her only way of communicating with me. Now that she's met with Mr. Thurman, she knows that I haven't told anyone about her."

"Well, now is the time to take her leverage away and come clean."

"You're right, man. I just don't know how to since I have already lied about it."

"You only said that her mother went away, but you didn't say where. You didn't owe him any other details and your reservations were totally understandable. But now is the time to come clean and stop Michelle in her tracks."

"Thanks, man. Mr. Thurman will be upset to lose an account this size."

"He's not losing an account. She never really intended to give you the account, but to only make it look like you fouled up. Look, if you need me, I'm always here, but think about what I said and do the right thing. Tell Mr. Thurman."

Although Chris didn't give a verbal response, Justin knew that his friend was listening and that he would make the right decision. After saying their goodbyes, the line was disconnected and Chris continued to sift through the work he had to do.

Chapter Seven

Keesha had turned over one time too many. Jamal knew that this whole Michelle thing was getting to her. Ever since she received the letter from the parole board about Michelle's release, she hasn't been able to sleep. None of this surprised him because it took her months to get over Chris blaming her for what happened to his mother. He had really hurt her that day at the funeral and she let so much time go by before she would even communicate with him. After a long while, she began sending him pictures of their children. At first he didn't respond, but soon he started sending pictures of his daughter. That was another blow for Keesha because the reality of Chris sleeping with Michelle became evident. Not only that he was sleeping with her, but because he wasn't totally honest with her about Michelle.

"Honey. You okay?" Jamal asked resting a gentle hand on her shoulder and lightly tapping her.

She turned to face him with her eyes glistening in the darkness. All night, the only thing she could think about was Chris and Ashley. Recounting the past events, she realized that Michelle was not only dangerous, but also cunning. Now that she had spent ten years away with God only knows what types of personalities and circumstances, she may be far worse now. The extent of any desired revenge may render far too many casualties.

Keesha snuggled into Jamal's awaiting arms. She buried her face into his chest and quietly wept. She knew that seeing Chris again was risky, not only to her, but also to her marriage. The last thing she needed was to make Jamal skeptical of their relationship. He had kept his promise to care for her and their children. He never forsakes to make her happy and their twins adore him. She couldn't dare let anyone come between her happy home. She wondered if Chris had totally buried his love and desire for her or would her trying to help him hamper her marriage.

"Jamal, I've got a really bad feeling about Michelle being released. I think Chris will need us. We should go to see him."

"He'll be fine, Keesha. Chris is a man. He'll be able to deal with anything that comes his way. He's a smart and talented young man. Believe me, he'll be just fine."

"I know, but his mother is gone and he has no one."

"Keesha, you are not his mother and he will not see you as his mother or his confidant. You were once his lover and this man had strong feelings for you. Why go there and open up his wounds?"

Keesha considered his reply. She always valued his wishes and opinion, but she knew that he was wrong about them. He was so wrong about her ex-lover. Chris is very smart and talented, but he is not emotionally strong. Keesha has seen first hand the defeat and hurt Chris harbors when something upsets his world. He was alone and vulnerable to anybody. Michelle would make him her footstool just because of his daughter and if she somehow managed to take Ashley away it would be like cutting his lifeline.

"I don't want to be his mother, Jamal. All I want to do is let him know that we are here for him if he needs us. Not me, us. I want you there with me in everything I do. I love you and I promise that I won't let anyone or anything come between us. You don't have to worry about me rekindling a physical relationship with Chris. I just want to be there for him when he needs me. I would feel really bad if I sat back and watched things happen to him and not help him."

Jamal listened intently, realizing that as much trust as Keesha has put in him, she deserved the same amount of trust, even in uncertain circumstances. Their relationship has been so perfect; he wouldn't dare risk anyone coming between them. He reached behind them and switched on the lamp. The three-way bulb cast a dull glow that provided just enough light so that Jamal could clearly read her emotions. What he wanted to ask or petition from Keesha was her understanding. It was never his practice to try to control her, but this issue was sensitive in nature and the potential for disaster and adversity was high.

Keesha knew from experience that when the lights came on it was serious and that Jamal was going to either lay something really heavy and profound on her or he was reading her again. Mentally bracing herself, she prepared for what Jamal was about to tell her.

"I'm going away on a retreat for two weeks in San Francisco and I'm hoping that you will wait until I return to be in contact with Chris. I'm sure that nothing tragic will happen during that short period of time. I know you don't like to attend these functions so I'm not going to ask you to go, but for me, can you promise that you will give me two weeks? I will make it my first agenda when I return."

Two weeks seemed like a long time when everything seemed so crucial. Deep down, Keesha still believed that all this was her fault and the least she could do was be there for him when he needed her. She didn't expect Jamal to understand how she felt, but she let Chris down before. He sacrificed so much to be with her and in the end he still ended up with nothing. No mother, no wife and no one to care about him. For the first time in their relationship, Keesha felt her back against the wall.

He waited for Keesha to respond. It was at that point that he realized how much this Chris character meant to her. He worried that he meant more to her than he imagined and her allegiance to him and to what they once shared may be greater than his own selfish insecurities. He feared letting her be alone with him. What sparks might be rekindled when he embraced her for the first time in ten years. Could a simple kiss on the cheek turn into enflamed passion? Jamal knew the dangers of being in a compromising setting. As loyal as he is, he was still a man and recognized that being faithful requires not only discipline, but also sense enough not to put oneself in bad positions. Keesha was blind to her genuine allegiance to Chris and may not realize the dangers of being alone with him. He also knew that if Chris had half the chance he would try to get her back at least that's what he would do.

Jamal cupped Keesha's face.

"Honey, promise me that you'll wait until I get back."

He was absolutely serious about his petition and determined to get her to agree to his request.

"Jamal, what if something happens? What if he calls and really needs me?"

"Chris hasn't called after all this time, I doubt that he will call before I get back. Just promise me. If anything happens, call me and I will get back as soon as possible. We will go together. How about that?"

"Okay. I've never seen you so adamant before. You don't have to worry about me. I'm not going to do anything that will jeopardize what we have. We have two beautiful children and I intend to be here for my family forever. I will never leave you."

Jamal held her close and was about to kiss when the door swung open.

"I can't sleep," Christian said as he entered the bedroom. He wore dinosaur print pajamas with matching bedroom shoes. Half-tired, he drug his slippers on the carpet making his way to the bed. He held on to the bed and hoisted himself up. Jamal held his arm down so that he could catch hold and pull himself the rest of the way up. He climbed over Jamal's hip and found a warm position between his parents. Keesha lifted the cover and welcomed her baby into their warmth. Almost instantly, Christian closed his eyes and fell asleep.

"This is why we haven't made anymore children," Jamal whispered.

Keesha giggled and kissed the back of Christian's head.

"Christian isn't ready for another sibling." She reached around Christian and felt Jamal's groan. "But it doesn't stop us from pretending."

"You know there's always tomorrow."

"I know, but not tonight," she teased. Although she closed her eyes, she still couldn't sleep. As much as she wanted to be by his side, she didn't want to give Jamal a reason to doubt the sincerity of their marriage. She also realized that Michelle was dangerous and would do anything to reach her goal.

It was three minutes to five and Keesha was just beginning to fall asleep. Jamal had hours ago drifted into a sound sleep. Christian had snuggled deep into the crevice of his father's chest and his dad rested his arm gently over him, creating a warm and safe haven. Keona was fast asleep in her bed clinging to a baby blue teddy her dad had given her.

***

Jamal was off to his convention. He assured Keesha that he would call her as soon as he arrived. Their earlier conversation was still on Keesha's mind. She knew that if Chris called upon her that she would hurry to his aid even though Jamal had asked her not to. She would not wait for his return before going to see Chris.

Ironically, before Jamal could reach his destination, Keesha received a phone call from Chris. His tone immediately gave Keesha the impression that something was wrong. He sounded desperate and out of his mind.

"Chris, calm down," she advised while trying to make sense of his report. "Tell me what happened."

"Ashley's missing!"

"What do you mean she's missing?"

"I took her to school and when I got there she wasn't there."

"How can that be? Did she wander off? Maybe she went to the bathroom and they weren't aware of it?"

"Keesha, I'm not a fool. My daughter is gone. They told me that someone had picked her up already."

"Did they say who took her?"

"Her teacher told me that Ashley told her that her ride was here. I called Simone and she said that she didn't pick her up."

"Her ride?" Keesha exclaimed, not believing what she was hearing. "Her teacher didn't ask her who was picking her up? Did you call the police?"

"Yes. They said that it was too early to report."

"That's preposterous. Do you think Michelle took her?"

"That was my first thought. I went by her house and no one was there."

The phone fell silent for a moment as they began contemplating their next move. Keesha didn't want to let Chris down again. She felt that if she had been there for him before, his mother would still be alive. Her battle with Christine left room for someone to come in and attack her.

"Chris, I can be there in about three or four hours if I can get a flight out."

"I don't want to inconvenience you, Keesha."

"It's no inconvenience. I can take the kids next door to my neighbor's house."

"Keesha, please don't rush over because of my dilemma. I just didn't know what to do. I'm afraid that if Michelle has taken my daughter I will kill her."

"Chris, don't talk like that. I'll be there shortly."

"Let me know what flight you're coming in on."

"Don't you dare come to the airport. I can take a cab to your house."

"Are you sure?"

"Listen, if Ashley tries to call, you should be there. Don't worry about me. I'll be there soon."

Keesha hung up the phone and called the airport to reserve the earliest flight out. There were plenty of open tickets and Keesha purchased a ticket for the six o'clock flight. That was the earliest that she could make it considering traffic. She took Christian and Keona to their neighbor's house and asked Mrs. Ambross to watch them for two days for her. Of course, Christian made a big fuss about it. He always gave trouble when Keesha had to leave him. Keona was free-willed and less clingy. She comforted her brother when her mother wasn't there. Keesha told Mrs. Ambross that if she needed her, she can always reach her on her cell phone and that Jamal would also have his cell phone on.

Keesha got in her car and drove for forty-five minutes to the airport. When she arrived, she swiped her credit card in the machine and her electronic ticket printed. She went to the appropriate gate and after checking in she went to the terminal going to New York. She knew that she should call Jamal and let him know what happened, but she knew that he wouldn't agree and would insist that she not go. She knew that he would be upset with her, but it was something she would deal with on her return.

After waiting for longer than she wanted, the attendant announced that the flight was ready to be boarded. When her seating was called, she boarded the plane with other passengers who would be sitting in her section. She placed her overnight bag into the overhead compartment then took her seat. A young gentleman took a seat next to her. He smiled as he sat down. He was a good-looking guy, probably no more than twenty-seven. He reminded her of Chris basically because of his age and demeanor than anything else.

Keesha leaned back in her seat and waited for the plane to take flight. Her cell phone rang. She looked at the display and saw that it was Jamal calling her. It rang again. The stewardess asked her to turn off her cell phone. Keesha did as instructed. She suspected that Jamal had reached his destination and was safely in his room. She also knew that if he called a second time he would be upset. She then reasoned that the only reason he would be calling is because he must have gotten the news from Mrs. Ambross that she was keeping the children for the weekend. Keesha tucked her phone away in her pocketbook after turning it off.

She was now on pins and needles because she wasn't able to answer Jamal's call. His being uneasy about her previous relationship with Chris didn't make matters any lighter. It was going to hurt him that she disobeyed his request to wait for him. Keesha reasoned that she was already in the air and she couldn't turn around now. An hour later she was landing at JFK airport. She secured a taxi to Chris' house. When she arrived she expected to see Chris distraught, but he was happy and in extremely good spirits. This all surprised Keesha and she wondered if this was his ploy to get her to come. Ashley came to the door safe and sound.

"Keesha, please come in," Chris instructed. "Ashley had come home with our neighbor and forgot to call me. I tried to call you to let you know that she was here, but you had already left. It's good to see you," he said while desiring to pull her into his arms.

"Come in, Auntie Keesha," Ashley told her as she caught hold of her hand. She pulled her into the house and led her to the living room.

Moving through the corridor, Keesha felt Christine's presence. She had missed her friend so much. Chris did little to change things from the way his mother had it. The limited modifications he made only enhanced the place but maintained the serenity it always possessed. Keesha took a seat next to Ashley. She realized that she was more beautiful than the pictures displayed. She looked so much like Chris.

"You love my daddy?" she asked out of the blue.

Keesha looked from Ashley to Chris then back to Ashley.

"Of course I love your daddy. He is my best friend." Keesha returned her attention to Chris again. In his eyes was a familiar pensive look that told her that he had not let go of what they had. Jamal was right, coming here without him was dangerous, she told herself.

"Will you marry my dad?" Ashley persisted.

"Ashley, sweetheart, let me and Aunt Keesha talk a little while. Okay?" Chris said hoping to keep her from asking anymore embarrassing questions. Ashley nodded in agreement and dismounted the seat. When she left the living room, Chris gave Keesha an embarrassed look.

"You two are quite close," Keesha told him, realizing that Chris must tell her everything.

"Yes, we are, but most of her zealousness is just her being perceptive. Ashley is especially smart for her age."

"Yes. Like her daddy."

He smiled sheepishly at the realization that Ashley was so much like him. He remembered how his father would go on about how smart his boy was.

"I guess we are really alike. So how have you been?"

"I've been good," she replied, now realizing how much she had missed him. Being alone with him felt awkward. The desire to fly into his arms crossed her mind, but she struggled to suppress that urge.

"I'm really sorry about what I told you at my mom's funeral. It was totally undeserved. I just want you to know that I don't regret a day I spent with you and I don't blame you for what happened. If anything, I should have been mad at myself because I should have been there for her."

"I don't regret it either. I just wish that things didn't turn out so badly. Christine didn't deserve that. She only wanted to protect her only son."

Changing the subject, Chris diverted from discussing his mother any further. It hurt so much talking about her. It reminded him of how he abandoned her. Michelle was right, he did abandon her.

"So, how's Jamal treating you? Is he keeping you happy?"

"He's wonderful. I love him so much. The twins just adore him. He is so patient and loving."

"That's good to hear," Chris managed. "I miss you, Keesha. I miss being with you." He couldn't believe the words that escaped his mouth.

"I know you do, Chris. I miss you too. But…"

Before she could say anything, he stopped her by placing his finger to her lips. He moved closer to her causing her to freeze. She knew he was going to kiss her and she wanted to stop him, but she couldn't.

"Don't say it. I know that I can't recapture the past and I don't want to do anything to jeopardize your marriage. I respect you that much, Keesha. As much as it hurts me to be near you like this, I couldn't live with myself if I defiled your marriage. I will always love you, Keesha. I will always want you and I will always be here when you need me in whatever way you need me. But I too have moved on and I can not jeopardize that relationship."

An unfamiliar feeling welled inside her. It was the feeling of rejection. Chris was no longer captive to her love-spell. She blinked in disbelief. For her own selfish reasons, she wanted him to be there for her forever and no matter how unfair her desire was, she knew that it had to end somewhere.

"I feel the same, Chris," she lied, trying to conceal her hurt. She now felt foolish running to his aid. It seemed as though she could hear the laughter inside him.

"What's wrong? Did I say something wrong?" Chris genuinely asked.

Keesha quickly snapped out of her trance.

"Nothing. I'm glad to hear that you are dating. What's she like?" Keesha asked trying to hide her hurt.

"Simone is great. She reminds me so much of what we had. Ashley adores her. I've asked her to marry me."

Keesha felt so jealous. She regretted jumping at his call. She expected him to still be swooning over her and denying him a passionate escapade, but he threw a monkey wrench in that idea. He seemed the least bit attracted to her. What was the close encounter with the lips about? Was he teasing me? she wondered. Did he plan to intentionally make me envious of his new relationship? How did he turn my ploy against me?

Keesha now remembered that she had turned off her cell phone. She reached into her pocketbook and retrieved it. She noticed that Jamal had called several times and that her neighbor had also called twice.

Chris noticed the concerned look on Keesha's face. He watched as she studied the numbers on her cell phone. He knew that Jamal must have called her several times knowing that she had come to New York to see him.

"Do you want to use my phone to call Jamal?" he asked genuinely concerned for her relationship. "You should let him know that you arrived safely and that everything is okay."

She turned to face him.

"I didn't tell Jamal that I was coming."

"Why not? You should have asked him how he felt about it."

"I couldn't tell him. He would have said no. There is no way Jamal would let me come here to see you."

"And that's all the more reason why you shouldn't have come."

Keesha couldn't believe he said that after all she put on the line to help him.

"I let you down before, I didn't want to let you down again. I -
"

"I am a man, Keesha. You don't have to come running whenever something happens. I just wanted someone to talk to. You've got to think about your marriage and your children. How could you drop everything to come here? Call Jamal right now and tell him that you are on the first plane back."

Keesha wanted to slap his face. How dare he tell me what to do? She was an excellent mother and wife. She was a good friend if he had bothered to notice instead of wallowing in his own self-pity. He shouldn't have called her if he didn't need her. Keesha refused to call Jamal. She would deal with that issue when she got home.

"Well, since I am no longer needed here I should get to the airport and see if I can get a flight out."

"Why not call first? I don't want you to get there and there is no flight available."

"I'll be fine. I'm sure there is a seat available. There is always a seat available."

"Are you upset with me?"

"No. Not at all."

"Good, then you won't mind if I take you to the airport."

"That won't be necessary. You should stay here with Ashley."

"You are angry."

Chris noticed the hurt in her eyes and the tears she struggled to hold back. He placed his hand on top of hers as it rested on her lap. His hand closed around hers and he gingerly looked into her eyes. His sincerity and sensitivity were evident. He was about to take the ultimate risk and kiss her. His hand slowly traveled from her hand up her arm and to her shoulder. So far so good, he told himself. Their eyes never abandoned the long gaze they shared. His hand reached behind her neck then cupped the lower part of her head and he gently pulled her toward him. She didn't resist. When her face was close enough he opened his mouth and placed it around hers. Slowly and cautiously, their tongues met and the passion they once shared returned. Ever so tenderly he continued to kiss her. In his mind he told her how much he loved and missed her. He told her that he would leave Simone in a second if he knew that Keesha would be his forever. He said that he would make love to her until she cried in his arms. None of these words he spoke, but his kiss said it all and he never wanted to break from it. He wanted so much to let her know that this was not just a moment of gratification, but an eternal endearment. His hands ached to touch and fondle her body, but he forbade that urge. He would not allow his emotions to get the best of him. He would kiss her as though their bodies were intertwined with each other. In his mind he said to her, I'm forever your slave.

When their lips parted they stared into each other's eyes, not an empty stare, but one that was full of unsaid emotion.

Chris had successfully pulled Keesha into his world and momentarily away from Jamal's. Without thinking, she said what she felt.

"I love you, Chris."

***

Jamal lightly shook Keesha to wake her from her sleep. She had been muttering and moaning for two minutes. When she confessed her love for Chris, he had heard enough.

"Keesha, honey, wake up. I'm about to leave."

Keesha groggily opened her eyes. Jamal was squatting beside her fully dressed. He watched her lovingly. When he was certain of her being awake, he told her that he was leaving and that he would call her everyday to check-up on her. If she needed anything, he would be back in a flash. Keesha nodded in acknowledgement. Remembering her dream, she felt guilty of cheating on him.

Jamal pressed a kiss on her lips and stood from his squatted position. He had taken Christian to his bed when he got up and looked in on Keona. She rested so peacefully. On his way out he left a note with his hotel information on it as well as the number to the convention center. He said that his cell would be on vibrate so whenever she called he would know.

He grabbed his suit bag and started out the door. In the car, Jamal looked back at the house. Keesha was at the window watching him leave. He waved and blew a kiss up to her. She had no idea that he knew of her passion with Chris last night or that she confessed her love for him. He prayed that history wasn't about to repeat itself.

Chapter Eight

Ashley was up bright and early. She felt so much better since the day before. Simone made a wonderful stepmother, but she was not her real mother and she could not portray her mother. Everyone seemed to be against Michelle except her and Simone. Simone understood what it was like to be without a mom because she too had lost her mother at a very young age.

She sat quietly on the side of her bed looking at herself in the mirror. Although she was a distance from her reflection, she could see that she looked a lot like her mother. Remembering her mother with her long braids, caramel brown complexion and slightly pug nose, she was more like her mom than she ever imagined. She reflected on what her mom told her. She said that she loved her so much that she allowed her father to take care of her so that she wouldn't have to live in a shelter with other bad or abandoned kids. She wanted her to have the best and she knew that Chris would take good care of her baby until she came out. She also told Ashley that her dad didn't want her when she first told him that she was pregnant and that she had to make the hospital force him to take care of her. Now that he realizes how beautiful and smart she is, he doesn't want to let go. She told her that she didn't want to take her away from her father but only to be able to spend time with her. They could share, but Chris doesn't want to share. He wants to punish Michelle for wanting to be with him and getting pregnant in the first place.

Ashley was disappointed in her father. She could not believe that her father could be so selfish. He always taught her to share and to love everybody and now he was doing just the opposite. Ashley didn't want to leave her father, but she didn't want to be away from her mother any longer. She didn't care what her mother did to be where she was. She was still the mother and deserved to have her daughter.

Ashley heard Simone go to the door and talk to someone very quietly. She could hear them move through the living room and into the kitchen. Ashley quietly left her bedroom and went to the top of the stairs. She looked through the banister and couldn't see neither Simone nor the visitor. She stayed where she was and just listened as best she could. Simone seemed to be arguing with the person, but she couldn't hear what they were saying. She did manage to hear them mention her dad's name followed by some more dialogue that didn't seem to make Simone happy. When she heard them moving around in the kitchen, Ashley hurried back into her bedroom and sat on her bed. Not long after, Simone was letting the visitor out and shuffling around in the living room.

After a while when Ashley didn't hear Simone moving around anymore, she called out to Simone before descending the stairs. Simone answered her telling her to come join her. Ashley reached the bottom step and realized that Simone had been crying. She tried to dry her eyes before Ashley reached the sofa.

"What's wrong, Simone?" Ashley inquired. She could tell that something was bothering Simone, but she didn't want her to know that she heard her talking to someone in the kitchen.

"I'm okay, baby," she told her while trying to cover up the quiver in her voice. She looked at Ashley and knew that she was not buying her response and that if she didn't want her to pry any further she had better tell her something.

"Baby, are you hungry? How about I fix you some waffles and sausage?"

"Okay," Ashley responded, but was hardly finished inquiring about her crying.

"Can I turn on the radio?"

"Of course you can," Simone responded turning toward the living room and directing Ashley to the stereo. "Not too loud, okay?"

"Okay," Ashley said making her way into the living room and finding the power button on the stereo. The station was turned to 98.7 Kiss FM and the R&B tune "Closer than Close" by Jean Carne blared through the speakers. Upon hearing it, Simone began singing with the radio. Ashley loved to hear Simone sing because she had a beautiful soprano voice. She shifted her hips seductively to the music as if she were dancing with someone. She wrapped her arms around herself as her eyes glazed over. She stared lovingly out the kitchen window while dancing.

"What are you thinking about, Simone?"

She smiled and her eyes never left that beautiful place she was lost in.

"Your dad," she told her. "I don't want to let him go."

"What do you mean?"

"Things are about to change for all of us, Ashley. I only hope that when that time comes we all make the right choice for all the right reasons."

"I don't understand." Her big, innocent eyes stared up at Simone. She had no idea of all the hell that was about to break loose. Her mother was going to upset their world drastically and there was nothing Simone could do to stop her. Even if she warned Chris of what was about to happen, she would also have to tell him the truth; that she was in on it too. She would have to tell him that she was Michelle's secret weapon and that she was about to hurt him, Ashley and now herself because it was never in the plan for her to fall in love with him.

Simone realized that Chris didn't deserve the hand that was dealt him even though he was playing it as best he could. If he was really smart he would have taken his daughter and moved far away. He would never have moved into the house his mother had died in. He would never have stayed in the same area that Michelle lived in. She knew exactly where to put her hand on him and her daughter. She wondered why he didn't just read the papers. If he had only read them, none of this would be possible. But she couldn't blame him. All this was thrown in his lap at the last minute and he did the noble thing and came for his daughter. Her eyes watered again and if not for a little will power, she would have broken out in a full bawl.

Ashley looked on in wonderment. She had absolutely no idea what Simone was talking about or why she was crying. When Simone turned the flame off from under the sausage, Ashley took her hand and held it.

"Who was here earlier?"

Her question took Simone by surprise. She didn't know that Ashley was awake because when she had passed by her door earlier she was sound asleep. Michelle had called her early in the morning to let her know that she was stopping by. Simone tried to discourage her from coming, but Michelle insisted. She didn't tell her that Ashley was right upstairs because she would have raced right up there and tried taking her.

Michelle wanted Simone to tell Chris who she really was and why she was really there, but Simone didn't feel that it was necessary to tell him everything. Simone felt that she had done her part by keeping tabs on him and keeping him around and feeling comfortable. She was not going to take any part in the circus act Michelle had planned for him. She wanted his soul to bleed. She wanted him to wish that he was dead just like she felt when he abandoned her. When Michelle first told her about all that Chris had done to her, she hated him. She despised men that took advantage of a woman's feelings and left them pregnant. She wanted to help her get the ultimate payback, but now that she has gotten to know Chris and Ashley, she realized that Michelle had lied to her.

Simone quickly fixed Ashley's plate and hurried upstairs to her bedroom. When she reached her room, she threw herself onto the bed and cried into her pillow. She was about to lose everything that meant anything to her.

Ashley entered the room. She didn't ask Simone anything; she only climbed onto the bed and lay next to her. She put her arm around her and kissed her arm.

***

"Who the hell does Simone think she is, asking me to leave Chris alone?" Michelle barked turning into her driveway. "Did she forget why she's there? Did she forget whose child Ashley is?"

Michelle was furious. She turned off her engine and opened her car door. When she entered the house she went into the kitchen and retrieved from the cabinet a box that she kept all the way at the back behind her canned goods. She carried the small cigar box to the table and opened it. Inside the box were some photos of her and Simone as little girls. There were two pictures of them as teenagers and one of them as adults. Michelle knew that she could always count on Simone, if nobody else, to have her back no matter what. But somehow, Chris had dick-whipped her and she's forgotten why she was with him in the first place. "I will have to remind her that Chris is mine and will always be mine. I will have to make her witness the passion."

Michelle gave off a hearty laugh. She would make Simone hand Chris right over to her. She wanted Chris to feel hurt and alone. Remembering something an inmate told her she smiled…It's not the bars that makes one a prisoner, but the state of his or her mind. If you are at peace, no prison can take away your serenity. Ashley and Simone made Chris serene, but all that was about to be taken away.

***

Justin couldn't believe how sinister Michelle was. He was not about to let her ruin his friend's life or that little girl's. Chris had done such a wonderful job raising her and she was so smart. It would be wrong for him to just turn his back and pretend that he didn't realize what was going on. He looked into his Rolodex and found Thurman Goldman and Sacs' phone number. He never thought he'd see the day when he would call that old man again, but there was more at stake here than his pride. He took in a deep breath and dialed the number.

"Goldman Thurman and Sacs," a woman's voice answered.

"Good morning, Patrice. Is Mr. Thurman in yet?"

"Yes, he is. I'll let him know you are on the line."

The line fell silent momentarily. Patrice returned to the line and told him that Mr. Thurman asked her to take a message and that he'd call back when he got off his current call.

"I'll hold for him, Patrice. This is really important and it can't wait."

"Okay. I will make sure that he calls you back."

"Patrice, Mr. Thurman isn't on the line. I know that he doesn't want to talk to me, but I need to talk to him and I am not going to let you hang up the phone until you put him on the line."

She exhaled revealing her exasperation for the situation.

"How about I give you Mr. Walker?"

"No. You can't let him know that I am on the line. You get Mr. Thurman on the phone right this minute, Patrice, otherwise someone might get hurt."

"Are you threatening me, Justin?"

"No, Patrice. That's not what I meant. All I'm saying is that it is a life and death situation so please tell Mr. Thurman to pick up the phone."

The line went quiet again and this time Mr. Thurman picked up the phone and answered in his deep, monotone voice. He meant to intimidate Justin, but with what was at stake, he ignored the gesture.

"Hello, Mr. Thurman. I have something important to tell you and I need you to listen carefully."

"You have some nerve calling me, Justin. You stole a lot of business from my company and now you want to ask favors?"

"I'm not calling for any favors. I'm trying to save someone from a whole lot of pain."

"Whose pain could you be telling me about that I would be interested in saving?"

Justin looked at the phone and made an ugly face. He mimicked the words you old cantankerous bastard.

"One of your prospects used to be a client of mine."

"Are you afraid that we will be getting some of your old business?"

"No. Actually, one of my old clients is about to seriously hurt one of your employees and if you don't listen and stop tooting your own horn, you are about to lose the best thing that ever happened to Goldman Thurman and Sacs."

"And who might that be?"

"Michelle Tanner. Does the name ring a bell?"

Mr. Thurman thought for a minute. "Yes, she was in here only yesterday. I knew that you were up to no good. You are not going to steal that one from us. Besides, she wants to especially work with Chris."

"That's Ashley's mother."

"Who is Ashley? And why would I care about that?"

"Chris Walker's daughter! Chris lied to you about Ashley's mother. Michelle Tanner has been locked up for some time and I used to handle her financial accounts. She wants to ruin Chris and make it look like he sabotaged the account. I don't know what else she has planned, but if someone doesn't help him, he may lose his daughter."

For the first time, Justin was able to get through to Mr. Thurman. Normally, he would dismiss him or any of his suggestions, but this time it involved someone he had grown to respect and care for. Chris impressed Mr. Thurman and he wouldn't be able to bear knowing that he sat back and let something bad happen to him when he could have helped.

"What do you suggest I or we do about it?"

"For one, you have to forget about getting that account. The next time you speak to Ms. Tanner you let her know that you are unable to handle her account. You can use your own discretion concerning telling her that her actions are intolerable and any further efforts she make to hurt Mr. Walker will be handled with strong consequences."

"I really appreciate you going out of your way to tell me this?"

"Well, I have always had the company's interests at heart, you just didn't think so. Although it's too late to make it right with me, you can consider giving Chris a shot at partnership. He will not only make you proud, but he will make you grow in ways you wouldn't believe."

"I'll take that into consideration. Thanks, Justin."

"It's all for a common interest. Take care, Mr. Thurman, and don't tell Chris about this."

He hung up the phone exhaling. The feeling of betrayal crossed his mind, but he couldn't help but think that his intentions were good. Although Chris had confided in him and probably didn't want him to tell anyone about it, he reasoned that it was for his own good.

Chris you owe me big time for this, he told himself. He pulled Michelle Tanner's file from his metal cabinet and started breezing through its contents.

***

Mr. Thurman pushed his leather chair back and got up from behind his desk. He went to the window and watched as the cars and people passed by thinking, You can never tell about people. He heard Patrice speaking to Chris and it sounded like he was about to walk out of the office. He hurried to the door and called Chris to his office.

"Good morning, Mr. Thurman. I didn't realize that you were in your office," he said as he entered the office and took a seat.

"You're off to a client? I guess that you've had a chance to go over the files I left for you yesterday?"

"Absolutely. I can brief you on it later, but I promised Mr. Zelda that I would come by first thing this morning."

"Chris, I just wanted to see if everything was okay with you. Is there anything you want to talk about?"

Chris looked at Mr. Thurman strangely. He wondered where he was going with this line of questioning. Did Michelle discuss any of their personal history with him? Was he talking about the files he left me? Was I acting strange and Mr. Thurman noticed?

"I'm sorry, Mr. Thurman, I don't understand what you mean?"

"I just thought that you might have some things on your mind that you wanted to discuss."

"No. I'm fine," Chris said, still baffled. "Everything is fine."

Mr. Thurman was not pleased with his response. He thought that Chris valued him as a mentor and father figure and that he would share anything with him. He worried that Chris had bought into his own lie and delved into it so deeply that he couldn't discern the truth. He wanted to tell Chris all that he knew about his previous relationship with Ms. Tanner and that he didn't have to worry about her sabotaging his job. He would fight with everything they had to protect him from her plight.

"How is the Tanner file coming along? Anything I should look into?"

Chris felt a chill slither up his spine. He could feel perspiration beginning to bead on his forehead. Mr. Thurman's fishing had become evident and his questions were deliberately steering him to confession, but he still fought to maintain his silence.

"I haven't had a chance to fully go through her file, but I intend to look into it when I return from Mr. Zelda's office."

"That's good. Maybe I should take a look at the file before you get started."

This was more difficult than Mr. Thurman had anticipated. He just knew that Chris would have opened up to him at this point. They continued to play cat and mouse, avoiding what was evident to the both of them that they both knew the truth.

"It's in my office, but I have it locked in my desk. How about we look at the file when I return. Really, I don't need any help. There wasn't anything complicated about it. She has acquired some substantial funds that are sitting in a dormant account that should be placed somewhere with growth. I'll call some brokerage firms we have relation with and have them put something together."

Chris got up from his seat and was turning toward the door when Mr. Thurman stopped him in his tracks with his next statement. He had played cat and mouse enough.

"Chris, I don't want you working on your ex-girlfriend's account. I know about her and what her plans are."

Chris turned around to face Mr. Thurman. At this point he was leaning forward over his desk and making direct eye contact with Chris.

"Come sit down, Chris," he instructed. "Why would you keep this from me? You should know by now that I have your best interest at heart. I want to help you, but you are making this very difficult. I want you to tell me what is going on."

Chris moved toward the seat and sat down. Shame was written

all over his face. He regretted not telling his boss about his relationship with Michelle, but he also felt that he had his reasons. Oddly, he felt really short sitting in front of his boss. It seemed as though he was no taller than the desk in front of him. He finally managed to meet his boss' stare.

"Michelle and I used to date and she had gotten pregnant with Ashley. Because she was sentenced to prison for a substantial number of years, she decided to turn Ashley over to me to care for her."

"That doesn't explain why she is so bitter. It would seem to me that she would be happy that you took care of her daughter."

"She isn't angry about me taking care of her daughter, she is angry because I left her."

"Okay. Why did she go to prison?"

"She got a charge of attempted murder and possession of an illegal drug."

A ghastly expression displayed on Mr. Thurman's face. He couldn't imagine the beautiful woman that walked into his office yesterday could be so vicious.

"She tried to kill you?"

"No. She tried to kill the woman I was with at the time."

"Is she all right?"

"Yes. Luckily, she received medical treatment before any damage could be done."

Chris fell silent. He didn't want to explain anymore to his boss. He already felt that he told him too much and now felt uncomfortable.

"What can I do to help you?"

"Nothing. Everything is under control."

"Is that what you believe? Or is it that you don't want my help?"

"The truth is she hasn't presented any problem yet. She just showed up yesterday and I was surprised to see her."

"Has Ashley seen her?"

"Ashley has never seen her. The only time Michelle has been near Ashley is when she was born."

"You don't think that she will try to regain custody of her

daughter?"

"I'm sure she will, but she signed her daughter over to me and I have custody of her."

"Okay, but you watch out because a woman's scorn is not to be taken lightly."

"Thanks, Mr. Thurman. I appreciate your concern. I should be getting to my client's office before I am late."

Mr. Thurman nodded in agreement. Chris got up from his seat and left the office. Although Mr. Thurman's forwardness had taken him by surprise, he felt a sense of peace knowing that he didn't have to continue carrying the horrible secret around.

Chapter Nine

Michelle was ready to put her plan into motion, but her attorney had advised her that she should wait at least six months before trying to implement any changes. This really went against the grain since the only thing she could think about was getting even with Chris and taking her daughter. She also realized that if she waited any longer, Simone would get too close with Chris and spoil her plans. She could tell that Simone had formed a real connection with him. Of course, this was of no surprise since Chris was a good catch, not to mention that he was fine as hell. Ashley seemed pretty close to her as well. They were like one big happy family and if she didn't do something quick, they would become a permanent one.

It was time to begin working on Ashley and building a motherly bond with her. Going to court wouldn't mean a thing if she didn't want to be with her mother. Michelle had to appeal to the soft side of Ashley and make herself the victim if she was going to win her daughter back from Chris. She picked up the phone and dialed Simone.

"Hello, Simone," Michelle offered as she heard the phone line open. She didn't even wait for Simone's voice to come on.

"This is Ashley. Who's calling?" the tiny voice replied.

"Ashley, sweetheart, is that you?"

"Yes. Who is this?" she said listening to see if she could make out the voice.

"This is Michelle…your mother."

"Mom!" she screamed. "Is it really you?"

"It is, baby. How are you? I've been trying to reach you all week."

"I've been here with Simone. Dad didn't tell you."

"Yes. He told me that you were there."

"Mom, when are you coming home? I really want to see you?"

Michelle wanted to cry. Her daughter had hit a spot that had been surrounded by anger for so long that she forgot how wonderful it could feel.

"Oh, baby, I am home. I will be right over to pick you up. We have so much to talk about. How does that sound?"

"I'll have to ask Simone if I can go. My dad said that I have to listen to her when he isn't around. Hold on a minute."

Before Michelle could say anything, Ashley dropped the phone and dashed upstairs to Simone's room. Simone was taking a bubble bath when Ashley came in out of breath.

"Hey, take it easy. Are you okay? What's the hurry?"

"My mom is on the phone and she wants to pick me up. Can I go?"

Simone was horrified. All week she had been trying to keep Ashley out so that Michelle wouldn't catch them at home. If she didn't keep her promise, this would be the ultimate betrayal. She thought for a moment and realized that blood was thicker than water. There would be many more men to come into her life. Why should Chris be any different?

Ashley was becoming impatient waiting for Simone to answer her.

"Simone, please. I really want to see my mom."

"Okay, but on one condition."

"Anything," she said excitedly.

"You remember that I love you. Now come give me a hug and find out when your mom is going to get here."

Ashley ran to Simone and gave her a big hug. Simone put bubbles on her nose and Ashley raced back out of the bathroom and downstairs to the phone again.

"I can go," she told her mother. Her jovial tone let Michelle know that she really did want to spend time with her. "What time are you stopping by?"

"I will be there in an hour."

After sounding a kiss, Michelle hung up the phone. It was twelve o'clock. She wondered why Ashley wasn't at school. She wondered if Chris was trying to hide her, but just as quickly shook that thought. He would never get in the way of Ashley's education.

She picked up the paper to see what was playing in the movies. X-Men, that's perfect! She checked the timetable to see when the movie was playing. Michelle found a few pictures of her and Chris when they were seeing each other and placed them on the coffee table. She also found some pictures of Chris and Keesha. Tonight she would bring Ashley over and introduce her to the real Chris.

Michelle went outside and stood in front of her door. She looked up and down the block at her neighbors' homes and noticed everyone was at work. Losers, she thought. She moved to her car and got in. For some reason, she got the nerve to drive past Christine's old house. She remembered the day she went to see Christine about her relationship with Chris. She remembered telling Christine that she was pregnant with Chris' baby and how much she wanted to save her relationship with her son. Christine ridiculed her and told her she was nothing. She told her that she had tricked her son and that she would take no part in reuniting them. In a rage, and determined to salvage the relationship, Michelle did what she thought would protect her relationship—she got rid of his mother.

As she drove past Christine's old house, she realized that some-one had moved in and updated the property. Things were a bit more modern and better maintained. She kept going and took notice of Keesha's old house. She didn't expect to find her there anyway. Keesha went off and got married. This reminded Michelle of how much of a fool Chris was to try to hold on to something that was never his. In the end, Keesha still went with the other man. Michelle wondered if Keesha moved to Virginia with her Jamal. He was a nice piece of work, Michelle remembered. Keesha had good taste, that was for sure.

Michelle sped up and started on her way to Simone's house. When she arrived, Simone was not thrilled to see her. She tried to hold her emotions at bay, but they were evident. Michelle told her that she wanted to see her upstairs in private. Ashley wondered what they wanted to talk about. She didn't realize that Michelle knew

Simone so well. They told Ashley to wait in the living room until they returned.

Upstairs, Michelle shoved Simone into her bedroom.

"What is your problem?" Michelle asked speaking a bit over a whisper. She didn't want Ashley to hear them arguing.

"Nothing. What are you talking about?"

"You seem a little too close to my daughter and you shiver when I mention anything about Chris. Did you forget why you are here?"

"I have not forgotten, but I think you are rushing things. This is too soon for you to be trying to take Ashley."

"Too soon!" Michelle barked. "I have been locked up for the past ten years. How dare you suggest that I am trying to rekindle things too soon?"

"Why don't you just work things out with Chris? This does not have to turn out to be some kind of war."

"You're not worried about me rushing things. You're worried about your relationship with Chris. Well, he's not yours and you can't have him."

This angered Simone. She was tired of fighting Michelle's war. What? Did she think that when she came out things were going to go back to normal? Me and Chris are in love with each other and now Michelle wanted to break that up with her fantasy war.

"This isn't about me having Chris. This is about what your war will do to Ashley when you hurt her father. She has been with him for all of her life. She doesn't know you. All she knows is that you are her mother. Now I care a whole lot about Ashley and I will not let you hurt that child with some personal vendetta."

"Oh, you won't, huh?"

"I'm not trying to get in your way, Michelle. All I'm trying to say is that you don't have to fight Chris to see Ashley. He had already decided to let you see her when you were still locked up. I don't know what you did or said when he went in to see you, but Ashley was waiting for his return so she could go in and see you."

Michelle couldn't believe her ears. Simone was a traitor. She had gone against family.

"Ashley is my daughter and I don't need Chris' permission to see her."

"Well, that's where you're wrong, Michelle. Chris has custody of Ashley and you are going to need his approval to see her."

Michelle laughed. This was the exact reason why she didn't let Simone in on her little scheme. She knew that she would get dick-whipped after being with Chris all this time. She was in love with him and she was not going to give him up without a fight.

"We'll deal with that issue when it arises, but for now, my concern is Ashley. When are you supposed to return her?"

Simone hesitated. She wondered if she should pull out of this fiasco now before it was too late or help Michelle with her devious plight. She realized now that Ashley was not Michelle's real concern. She wanted Chris. Maybe not to be with him, but she wanted to punish him once and for all.

"Chris is supposed to stop by tomorrow night. So you will need to get Ashley back to me either tonight or tomorrow morning. I don't know what time he is coming so please have her back first thing."

Simone has some nerve giving me orders about my daughter. When this is over, I will show her who runs the show! "Fine. She will be back here by 10:00 A.M. Bringing her any earlier would be unethical."

Simone nodded her head in agreement. She stood with her hands on her hips, more for support. She did not want to go to war with Michelle, especially not over her own daughter.

Michelle glared at Simone for another moment then turned on her heels. Another day, another battle, she thought.

Downstairs, Ashley was waiting patiently for her mom and Simone to return. When they came down, Michelle was first, and then Simone descended the steps behind her mother. She didn't look her normal happy self. Ashley tried to evaluate her expression, but she couldn't imagine what had made her become so uneasy. She didn't want to ask her now with her mother there, but she would ask her when she returned later.

"You ready to go?" Michelle said with a big, motherly smile.

"Yes," Ashley responded and she turned to face Simone. She could tell that she was forcing a smile back.

"Okay, sweetie. You enjoy yourself and remember, I love you."

Ashley went over to Simone and put her arms around her. She held her tight.

"I love you, Simone. I'll be back soon."

"You promise? You know if you don't, I'll miss you too much. You're my little heart and if you leave it won't beat again."

Oh yes, Simone is definitely going to be a problem, Michelle told herself. "Okay, Ashley. We should be going now. We're going to be late."

"Late for what? Where are we going?"

"Oh, it's a surprise. You're going to like it, I promise."

Simone kissed Ashley's cheek then released her to go with Michelle. Without hesitation, Ashley hurried out the door that Michelle was holding for her. She watched as Ashley got into Michelle's car. It took her only twenty seconds to drive off with both her and Chris' heart. Simone stood at the door for a while watching Ashley disappear up the street. If Chris knew about this he would never forgive her. No matter what she would explain to him, nothing would make her deception understandable. She went inside and closed the door.

***

Michelle was right. Ashley did enjoy the movie X-Men. By the time the movie ended, she was hyper and ready to do whatever Michelle wanted. She took her to Fun Time USA, which was an indoor amusement park for children and adults. She took Ashley to play Laser Tag. She had a lot of fun there. Michelle was surprised at how good Ashley was at shooting. She knew exactly how to hold the gun and how to aim it as well. Ashley had caught and shot six of the eight opponents.

"Where did you learn to shoot like that?" Michelle asked her after they left Laser Tag. They had played two competitions.

"My dad and I play a lot of video games and one of our favorite games is shooting the ducks. He taught me how to hold my gun and aim it at whatever I wanted to hit. I am really good at it now, but Dad is great at it. I could never beat him."

Running around with Ashley at Fun Time USA had just about worn out Michelle. She was ready to go home and call it a day, but all that excitement warranted dinner. She and Ashley decided to eat burgers. Ashley liked Wendy's so that's where they went.

Michelle was ready to drop at this point, but she wanted to show her daughter a wonderful time so that she would always want to be with her. Once they arrived at Michelle's house, she went to the bathroom and ran some water in the bathtub for her daughter. She filled it with lilac bubbles. Ashley came into the bathroom and Michelle told her that she would return shortly with some pajamas for her and a towel.

While Michelle was getting Ashley's things, Ashley got into the tub. She quickly washed up and was ready to get out when Michelle finally returned. She placed the items on the floral hamper then left the bathroom, giving her daughter some privacy. Once Ashley was out, she joined her in her bedroom. To Ashley's surprise, Michelle had bought her the cutest outfits. Her dad liked dressing her in jean outfits that Ashley liked, but these were big girl clothes. She had nice tops that showed off her belly button and nice pants and skirts to match it. Her mom had even bought her shoes with a little heel that exposed her toes. Michelle took notice of Ashley's surprise and went a little further. She loosened Ashley's ponytails and proceeded to comb her hair. She told Ashley to come and sit in front of her vanity. Michelle went to the bathroom and got her blow dryer and some styling mousse. She sprayed a large ball of foam into the palm of her hand and massaged it throughout Ashley's curly hair. She sectioned her hair and held it apart with clamps and proceeded to blow her curls straight. After that, she took a curling iron and curled the ends of Ashley's hair. Ashley wanted to turn to face the mirror to see what her mother had done to her hair, but Michelle insisted that she wait until she finished. She parted across from Ashley's ears, separating the front from the back and flat twisted the front portion of Ashley's hair then caught the rest of her hair up into one big ponytail. Ashley's hair was so long that when she pulled it up to the upper rear of her head, her hair still spilled around her shoulders. Once finished, Michelle spun the seat around so that Ashley could now see herself in the mirror. A look of pure gratitude showed on her face. Ashley had no idea that she had so much hair. Her curls were very tight so that her hair seemed medium length, but when her mother straightened out her curls, it was well past her shoulders and onto her back. Simone had done her hair in the past, but nothing like what her mother had performed. She was definitely her mother because she knew what looked good on her.

Michelle picked up one of the outfits and told Ashley to put it on. Ashley did as her mother told her. After fixing the clothes on Ashley and showing her the new look in the full-length mirror, she laughed at her daughter as she spun around and posed, admiring her own reflection. It was as though she had never seen herself before. Although Ashley didn't want to take off her clothes, she did, and was pleasantly surprised when her mother gave her some equally nice pajamas.

They did the mother and daughter thing as Michelle polished her fingernails and toenails and Ashley did the same for her mother. They went to the living room and talked most of the night.

Ashley noticed the pictures on the table of her mother and father. She realized that they looked so happy together. She blushed at the pictures of her dad kissing her mother. She looked up at Michelle.

"What happed to you and Dad? Why did he leave you?"

Michelle picked up the picture of Chris and Keesha then handed it to her daughter. Ashley studied the picture. She recognized the woman's face as her father's princess.

"This is Princess Keesha. My dad really loved her, but she left him to be with uncle Jamal," Ashley told her mother while still looking at the photo.

"Well, your dad left me for Keesha and God punished him so that he could see how I felt when he left me. I was so hurt when he turned his back on me. He didn't even care about you. I thought he would be happy to know that we were going to have a baby together."

"My dad didn't want me?" she asked her mother, not wanting to believe her. She knew how much her father cared about her. He would do anything to make her happy.

"No. He told me that you were my baby and he would not have anything to do with you."

"Why did he come and get me then?"

"Because he had to, the court forced him to take you. He was your father and it was his responsibility to take care of you even if he didn't want to."

Ashley felt bad. She didn't want to accept the fact that her father could be so mean. She wondered if that was why Simone told him no. Maybe she knew that he wasn't nice. Michelle could tell that Ashley was upset with her father.

"But you won't have to worry about that anymore because I am going to take you away soon and Chris won't have to pretend that he wants to keep you. How does that sound?"

"You promise?" she asked trying not to cry.

"I promise. Let's make some hot chocolate."

"Okay," she said and followed her mother into the kitchen.

Michelle placed a pot onto the stove with some water. When it came to a boil, she put three heaping spoons of cocoa into the water with a dash of salt and some sugar. Once it had blended well, she poured it into a cup with cold milk. She and Ashley sat at the table and talked while they enjoyed the cocoa. When they finished, Michelle took Ashley to her room. She didn't want to sleep by herself. She wanted to be close to her mother so Michelle allowed Ashley to sleep with her.

"Mom, if I tell you something, you promise not to get mad?"

"I won't get mad, sweetie. What is it?"

"My dad loves Simone and he asked her to marry him."

"He did?" Michelle said attempting to sound surprised and hurt.

"Yes. But Simone told him no."

"Why did she say no?"

"I don't know. I don't think she loves my dad. I'm glad she said no because my dad should be with you. Do you still love my daddy?"

Michelle forced a smile.

"I will always love your daddy."

Ashley turned over and closed her eyes.

Michelle stared up at the ceiling. She knew that she would have to work fast to get Simone out of the picture. Although Simone told Chris no, she would soon say yes. Simone was becoming all too attached to Michelle's old flame.

***

It was ten o'clock. Simone was still up worried about Ashley being with Michelle. She hated to let her go with her, but she didn't want Michelle to cause a scene or to ruin her relationship with Chris so she pretended to be nonchalant about the whole matter. Her biggest worry was whether or not Michelle would get Ashley back to her before Chris stopped by. Simone also knew that Michelle was not just trying to get custody of Ashley, but that she still wanted Chris. She would try to wear him down until he finally gave in to her.

The phone rang at eleven o'clock. It was Chris.

"Hey, sweetie. You don't sound sleepy," Chris teased.

"Hi, Chris. What are you still doing up?"

"I was just checking to see if we were still on for tomorrow?"

"You know I wouldn't cancel on you."

"How's Ashley?"

"Ashley is fine."

"Is she still angry with me?"

"No, baby, she was over that tantrum a long time ago."

"What do you have on?"

"Nothing," she teased. "Why?"

"Neither do I. What do you think we should do about that?"

Oh, Chris, this is the wrong time, she thought. I can't ask you to come over now. What will I tell you about Ashley? Please don't say you're coming over. "I don't know. Maybe put something on so we don't get cold?"

"How about I come over now and start our romance a night early?"

"Oh, baby, I would love for you to come over, but I want to wait. I will have something extra special for you tomorrow. Can you give me one night?"

"Only if you're going to plan something special," he teased.

"Anything on your mind you want to talk about?" she asked changing the subject.

"I'd like to talk about us."

This is going to get really complicated now. Michelle is getting ready to bring our happy little relationship to a serious halt, Simone thought as she mustered through her mind for something to say. "Chris, do you really want to be with me? I mean, I know that you have depended on me to help you with Ashley and that she has grown fond of me, but are you sure that I am the one you want?"

"How could you ask me that? Simone, I care a whole lot about you and I want nothing more than to make you my wife. We have spent so many years together. I couldn't even imagine not being with you. Don't you want us to be together?"

"Oh, Chris, I do, but I'm afraid that if you knew all the secrets of my past that you wouldn't love me anymore."

"Simone, I will always love you. You have never done anything to hurt either Ashley or me. You have been the best thing that could have happened to me, and God sent you at just the right time. How could I judge you when you didn't judge me? Everyone has a past and that's exactly where it should stay…in the past. I don't want to second-guess you or us. I want you to sincerely decide what you want. Don't worry about the past. What you do from this point forward will make all the difference in the world. If you have demons that you need to make peace with, then do that, but don't base your future on your past. I'm going to say goodnight for now, but when I come by tomorrow, I will be expecting my extra special surprise and the whole heart of the woman I love. Okay?"

Simone wanted to cry, but she knew he was right. She had to deal with her demons once and for all, but she was not sure that he would still be there if he knew that they share the same demon and that she was once a part of that demon.

"Okay. I love you, Chris, and I am going to make things perfect and right between us. I promise, even if I have to lose you to do it."

Chris wondered what she was talking about. Even if she has to lose me to do it, maybe I'm reading too much into this.

"Goodnight, Simone."

"Goodnight, Chris. I will see you tomorrow evening."

"No, I will be there early afternoon. I want to spend a whole lot of time with you."

"Okay, but give me until two o'clock. I want to have time to put my surprise together."

"Okay," Chris laughed.

They hung up the phone. Simone realized that things were about to become really dicey. Her battle with Michelle was about to begin. She expected that she would probably lose Chris in the interim. It's better to lose a good man on good terms than to ruin a good man so that he's no good to anyone else, she told herself.

Chapter Ten

Michelle arrived at Simone's house with Ashley at ten o'clock as promised. She needed to keep things cool with Simone long enough for her to win the affection of her daughter. She didn't expect Simone to flip when she came in. Simone let out a hideous shrill when she saw Ashley.

"What did you do?" she screamed at Michelle when she noticed how straight Ashley's hair was.

"What are you talking about?" Michelle genuinely inquired.

"You straightened out Ashley's hair. Look at these clothes. Her father will never approve of this. Ashley, go upstairs right now. I will be up in a second."

Ashley was confused. She didn't understand why Simone was making a big deal out of her hair. She thought it looked really nice.

"Michelle, are you crazy? Why would you make such a dramatic change to Ashley? What am I supposed to say to her father?"

"Her father!" Michelle barked. "I am her mother. I have every right to comb her hair."

"What are you trying to do? Get me in trouble? Chris will know right away that something is wrong. I'm trying to help you and this is what you do to repay me? Ashley, please go upstairs. I need to talk to your mother alone for a moment."

Ashley hurried upstairs. When she started mounting the steps, she turned to face her mother. Michelle blew her a kiss and told her that everything was okay. When Ashley was out of sight, Michelle let Simone have it.

"How dare you admonish me in front of my daughter?" she wailed, her voice slightly higher than Simone's initial shrill. "Ashley is my daughter and I couldn't give a damn about how Chris feels about her hair. If he or you had paid any attention, you would have realized that you've got Ashley looking like a tomboy."

"I understand, Michelle," Simone said lowering her voice. "But you've got to understand that he left her in my care and he won't be pleased if he knew that you have changed her look. Chris likes her the way she is. I mean, look at her clothes. Do you really think that her father would approve of his baby showing people her belly button? Keep this in mind, if he finds out that you are seeing Ashley and that I am the one making it possible, neither one of us is going to be able to see her. He will forbid me to see her or even talk to her. Then where will you be?"

"Fine, but I don't appreciate you yelling like that as if I had no right to do it, especially in front of my daughter."

"You have no right to jeopardize Ashley's life the way you are trying to. I understand the fact that you are angry with Chris, but think about what all this might do to the child."

"This has nothing to do with Ashley. You're concerned that you will lose Mr. Walker. Well he was never to be yours in the first place," Michelle spat.

"I want you to leave, Michelle. I am expecting Chris and I don't want him to find you here. We can discuss this later."

"I think we should discuss it now. Maybe it is time that Mr. Walker finds out just how loyal you are to him."

"Michelle, this is not the time. I promise you that I will see you next week. Chris will be here all weekend and I will call you so please, just give me time to get things ready for you. Chris is not an issue and you will have Ashley, but please, you have to go now. If Chris finds you here or realizes that you are involved in Ashley's life, he will beat you to the punch and you will lose her forever. You don't want Ashley to see you as the bad guy. Let her think that her mother is the victim."

Michelle shrugged her shoulders and turned toward the door. She called Ashley to say goodbye. Upon hearing her mother's call, Ashley hurried downstairs and gave her a big hug.

"I will see you next week, okay?"

"Okay, Mom. Are you alright?"

"Yes, baby. Remember that our visit is a secret for now. You must not tell your father that you've seen me. Okay?"

Ashley nodded and told her mother that she loved her. Simone turned her back. She hated what Michelle was doing, but what could she do? It was her daughter.

Michelle left and told Simone that she would see her next week. Simone nodded in agreement and opened the door. Michelle left the house and got in her car. Moments later, Ashley watched as her mother disappeared in the distance. Simone closed the door then turned to Ashley. She knew that Ashley was going to be hurt about her changing her hair and clothes, but she couldn't let Chris see his daughter dressed like that. She caught hold of Ashley's hand and led her to the living room. She sat on the sofa and pulled Ashley in front of her so that she could face her.

"Ashley, I need a favor from you and I need you to trust me. Do you trust me?"

Ashley nodded her head. She had no idea what Simone was talking about, but she knew that it had to do with her mother or father.

"Your dad will be very upset if he sees you dressed in those clothes."

"What's wrong with these clothes? My mom bought them for me. I like them."

"I know you do, honey, but they are not appropriate for a little girl your age. Your father wouldn't want to see his little girl dressed like an older woman."

"But I like them and my mom said they look nice on me."

"They do look nice on you, but you can only wear them when you are with your mom. We can't do things that will make your dad know that you've seen your mom. Do you want him to stop you from seeing her?"

"No."

"Then you will have to trust me on this. I need to wash your hair too."

"Why?"

"It looks a little mature for you."

"Please don't make me change my hair, Simone. I can take off the clothes, but please leave my hair like this."

Simone felt bad about asking Ashley to change everything her mother did for her.

"Okay, but if your dad asks, I did your hair, okay?"

"Okay," she responded and wrapped her arms around Simone's neck.

She took Ashley upstairs and found her another outfit to put on. Ashley put the outfit her mother had bought her in the closet. She would save it for the next time she was to see her mother.

Simone stood at the door watching Ashley put away the outfit her mother had bought her. Michelle was going to steal Chris' daughter right from under his nose. He had no idea how dangerous Michelle was or to what lengths she would go to get what she wants. Ashley had already grown fond of her mother and it wouldn't be long before her relationship with Chris diminished.

"So," Simone started, "what do you and your mom talk about?"

Ashley felt no threat in talking with Simone about her mother. It was Simone who had allowed her to see her in the first place. Even though they seemed to argue a lot, she didn't think that Simone would do anything to hurt her mother or keep her away from her.

"We went to Fun Time USA and played Laser Tag, then we had dinner, and then we went back to her house."

"You had a lot of fun with your mom?"

"She's really fun."

"Oh, yeah? More than with your dad and I?" Simone asked with her face twisted into a frown.

Ashley laughed at the face Simone was making.

"You are both fun to be with."

Simone wanted to jump right to the point, but she didn't want Ashley to clam up. She decided to give it a shot and if Ashley responded negatively she would make light of it and turn it into a joke.

"If you had to choose between living with your mom and living with your dad, who would you choose?"

She could see that Ashley was giving this a great deal of thought, which meant that it has been a consideration.

"I really love my dad, Simone. He makes me happy and I have a lot of fun with him."

Simone knew that Ashley was going to lay some heavy material on her. She was such a young prodigy.

"But," she hesitated, "my mom says that he didn't want me at first and that the court forced him to take me."

Simone wanted to cry. Michelle had broken Ashley's heart with that. That was a cruel thing for her to tell her daughter about the only person she's ever really cared for.

"That's what your mom told you?"

Ashley bobbed her head up and down in agreement.

"Well," Simone started while pulling Ashley to the bed to sit down, "I know your father very well and I was there when he came to get you. Your father didn't know that your mom was really pregnant. They broke up a long time ago and your mom was already pregnant when that happened. Your mom went to jail for doing something bad. I called your father to tell him that your mom was pregnant and that she said that he was the father. When it was time for you to be born, your father was given the choice to claim you as his child or let you go to an orphanage and he didn't want his child to grow up that way. He hurried over to the hospital and signed the papers to take you. He didn't ask for any proof and he didn't care if it were true or not, he just cared that much about an unborn child that was said to be his. So believe me when I tell you that your father cared about you then and he loves you to death now. It would kill him if you didn't love him or want to be with him."

Ashley began to cry. She wanted to believe Simone, but Michelle was her mother and she couldn't believe that her mother would lie to her about anything like that.

"You should love your mother just because she is your mother, but Chris has been an excellent father to you and done as best he could. He has been a father and that mother as well. He took you to the last place he would ever take you just to make you happy. He took you to see your mother in prison. He did that for you, Ashley. He didn't have to. I don't know what happened when he went in there, but whatever it was, he didn't feel that he should take you in there to see her then. Whatever you do, don't turn your back on your father. Okay?"

Ashley nodded her head, but deep inside she wanted to get to know her mother and spend as much time as she could with her.

"I took you to see your mother because it meant so much to you, but now I don't know if it was a good idea."

"Thank you for taking me, Simone. I'm glad that I met my mother and now I want to be with her. She is wonderful and -"

Simone cut her off. "This is too much for a little girl to bear. Come on. Let's get some food on. Your dad is coming over later and we want to make it special for him."

"Are you going to marry my dad?"

"I made a terrible mistake the last time, Ashley, but if he asked me again, I would say yes without thinking."

"Why don't you ask him?" Ashley asked.

"I don't know. Ladies don't ask men to marry them."

"Who said?"

"I don't know. It's just the rule."

"Well, it's a silly rule. You should ask him."

"What if he says no?"

"I don't know. I'm only ten-years-old."

"Smart aleck. You know, I'm going to do that. Come on, let's go shopping."

She and Ashley went shopping for something special for Chris.

***

Chris arrived as planned. It was two o'clock on the dot. Simone had made a delicious seafood spread. She prepared a seafood salad, fried scallops, shrimp, crab cakes and catfish. She made onion hush puppies, tossed garden salad and homemade punch. The three of them sat down at the table.

"This was Ashley's idea, wasn't it?"

"Yep. She thought we should have something fun today, not to mention seafood being your favorite dish.

They enjoyed dinner together, but this wasn't the end. They went into the living room and Ashley got a blindfold for her dad and told him to sit down on the sofa. He did as she told him and Ashley tied the blindfold over his eyes. Simone went upstairs real quick and returned with the surprise. She placed a large bowl on his lap that was filled almost to the top with clear marbles. She told Chris to stick his hand in and take out three envelopes. Whatever was in the envelopes would become his present.

Chris shoved his hand into the bowl, swished around, felt an envelope and pulled it out.

"Should I open it?"

"Nope. Not yet. You have to pull three. Whatever you leave behind, you don't get."

He smiled showing his deep-set dimples. He pulled another envelope out then went in again and found another. He realized that there were a few more, but he left them in the bowl.

"Are you satisfied with your picks or do you want to put one back and try your chances again."

"No. I think your first choice is always your best choice. I will stay with what I got."

"Okay," Simone teased.

"Are you going to take the blindfold off now?"

"Not yet. You have one more task. You have to pull one marble out."

Chris fumbled through the marbles. He could hear Ashley giggling behind him as she watched him go through the marbles. When he heard his daughter catch her breath, he grabbed the marble his hand was on. He knew that he found the special one because his daughter gave it away.

Simone removed the bowl from his lap and carried it to the mantle. She tilted her head sending Ashley quietly upstairs. Ashley fought to contain her laugh. She returned wearing a white leotard dress. Simone had gone behind Ashley and changed into the same dress. She turned on Phil Perry's song "If Only You Knew." Chris could not take the suspense any longer. He removed the blindfold and was delighted to see Simone and Ashley dancing. The two of them had attended ballet together on weekends. Chris had never seen them dance before now. It was a beautiful sight to see. They were angelic together. He sat back in the seat and watched. He realized at this moment how much Simone meant to him and to his daughter. Simone was indeed Ashley's mother in his eyes. Not her biological mother, but the one who has shared her ups and downs and her triumphs and weakness with. They have shared so many joys together. He wasn't concerned anymore about Simone turning his marriage proposal down. He now realized just how much she meant to him. The way she danced and her expression let him know that she felt deeply about him.

Ashley danced away and went upstairs leaving Simone to her private stage. The music changed to "Do Me Baby" by Melissa Morgan. Simone's dance changed from sweet to seductive. She moved toward Chris with her belly dancing and writhing tantalizing-ly. Simone called Chris with her finger telling him to bring out what's been in me for far too long. He came to her and placed his hands around her waist while she danced in his arms. He dipped her when she leaned back then lifted her into an embrace. Their lips met into a deep, meaningful kiss.

"I want to take you to bed," he whispered, "but it's too early to send Ashley to bed."

"I know," Simone mused. "But there is plenty of time for that later."

Marvin Gaye began to croon "Sexual Healing" and their embrace became a longing. Chris stiffened his tongue and pressed it deep into Simone's mouth and she tightened her lips around it as they motioned the act of lovemaking. She could feel her cave deepening to welcome him and moisture began to build between her thighs.

Ashley came downstairs again.

"Simone, can I go next door to play with Janine?"

Simone, released Chris.

"Let me see if they are back. I told Janine yesterday that you would be over this evening and she asked if you could spend the night." She turned to Chris and asked if it was okay. He nodded. Simone went to the phone and dialed her neighbor's house and briefly spoke. "Janine's mom said it was okay for Ashley to come over now."

Ashley already had her overnight bag together. She ran to her dad and gave him a big kiss and then gave Simone one. Simone took her to the door and waited until she saw Ashley welcomed in by Mrs. Roberts.

When Simone closed the door, Chris snatched her into his arms. Simone held him for a moment then told him to follow her to the sofa. When he sat next to her, she picked up the three envelopes he chose and handed them to him.

"Open them."

Chris shook the envelope, but nothing moved. They all felt the same so he couldn't determine what was inside. He opened the first one and retrieved cardboard with a key taped to it. He looked at her.

"That's my house key. I want you to be able to come in whenever you like."

He kissed her and couldn't believe that after all this time she was letting him all the way in. This was definitely a good sign. He opened the second envelope. He could see that Simone was nervous and she apparently had no idea what he had chosen. She seemed just as excited about his surprises. Again, he found a cardboard sleeve, but this one had a ring attached to it. Chris retrieved the ring and looked inside. It read "forever my love." Chris didn't grasp what this symbol meant. The ring was gorgeous. Simone took the ring from him and knelt in front of him. She caught hold of his hand and kissed it. Her eyes filled with tears as she mustered up the courage to break tradition.

"Chris Walker, I love you dearly and I want to spend the rest of my life with you. I have done so much wrong to you in the past, but I hope that you can forgive me and accept me as your lifelong friend and wife."

She lifted her face to meet his stare. Chris couldn't believe what she had done. She took the ring and placed it on his finger.

"Chris, I made a terrible mistake the last time when I refused your proposal. I love you so much and I know now that I don't want to go on without you. You and Ashley are my family and I want us to be together."

"I love you too, Simone, but I get the impression that you're not telling me everything. Before we can go any further, I need to know about the wrong you're talking about." Chris wouldn't let Simone look away. He loved her and would forgive her for anything, but he knew that she wasn't just referring to her not accepting his proposal. In order not to make the same mistakes he made before, he wanted to use more than his little head to make his decisions and he would not let his feelings be a doormat for anyone else.

"Tell me the truth, Simone."

"Chris, I have every intention to tell you everything, but first I want you to know that I love you and I love Ashley."

Chris nodded. Simone placed her hands on Chris' cheeks and pulled his lips to hers. He didn't resist, but he was determined to know what was going on. They kissed passionately until Chris pulled away from her.

"I can tell this is hard for you, Simone, but I promise you that no matter what you say to me, I will not overreact and I will still love you."

She nodded. "Open your last envelope."

Chris opened the last envelope and inside it was a letter addressed to Simone.

"I don't want to read this, Simone. I want you to tell me."

"Chris, read it. I want you to read it first then let me explain what happened."

Chris read the letter.

Dear Simone,

Things are about to get really bad for me. Since you and I are cousins and we're very close, I hope that I can depend on you to have my back. There is no one else that I can depend on to do this. I am in

Sing Sing correctional facility and I am about to birth my baby. The father's name is Chris Walker. I don't know if he will come, but I want you to find him and convince him to take custody of his child. I don't want my baby to grow up in some orphanage. When you find him, let him know that if he doesn't claim his daughter that the State is going to take her. He will come in spite of me. I will then need you to stay involved with them until I get out. Please take care of this for me. My attorney will take care of the rest.

Michelle Tanner

Chris folded the letter neatly and returned it to the envelope. His heart was racing. He couldn't believe that everything about him and Simone was a farce. Didn't she have any consideration for Ashley? He could understand her wanting to hurt him, but not a child. As much as he wanted to, he couldn't look at her. How can I trust her now? How can I love her after all that she did? It was definitely clear to Chris now why she turned him down the last time. It was never her intention to stay with him. She was Michelle's pawn.

"Chris. I know you're hurt. But now I want to explain."

"Is there anything more damaging than this?"

"Yes," she managed. "But if I don't warn you, you will fall victim and so will Ashley. Now that I know, I can't allow that to happen."

"You've done enough damage already."

"No, Chris, this is nothing compared to what will happen if you don't listen."

"I love you, Simone, and all this time you were playing with my feelings. You deceived my daughter and me. We both thought you cared about us and, all this time, you were only carrying out Michelle's devious acts."

Simone caught Chris by the face. "I love you, Chris, and believe me, there was no reason to tell you this except that I love you. Now please, don't condemn me without hearing me out. Michelle and I were very close growing up. She was always there for me whenever I got into anything. Then she came to me with this little task, but I had no idea that I would fall in love with you. I had no idea that you were so attractive. You are a wonderful man, Chris, and even though my initial intent was to help my cousin punish you, I can't do that now. Ashley is like my own daughter and I have to do everything in my power to protect her."

"Protect her from what?"

"From being turned against you."

"How could she do that, Simone? Have you been taking Ashley to see her?"

"Yes, I have and Ashley is very fond of Michelle."

Chris pushed Simone from in front of him. He had heard enough.

"I can't believe you did that. I can't believe that you have taught my daughter to lie to me. That's why she's been so hostile toward me lately. You have been helping Michelle turn her against me. That's why she calls for you when we disagree. Simone, this is totally unforgivable. What gave you the right to make a decision like that? You don't know the damage you've done." Chris pulled the ring from his finger and slammed it onto the table. "I don't want to see you again, ever."

"Chris, wait." Simone ran to him and grabbed his arm and he snatched it from her. "Chris, if you don't listen to me, Michelle is going to take Ashley from you."

"She can't take Ashley because you've just lost your visiting privileges."

She grabbed him again.

"Chris, I know that you're angry, but you've got to listen to me. You said that no matter what I told you that you would forgive me. Well, are you going to go back on your word?"

"I had no idea that you had done something so evil and so conniving."

"Stop it, Chris. I know that you are upset, but this pill came to me without my knowing what I was taking. Now I do love you and I am not about to let you walk out on me."

"Oh, you're not, huh?"

He reached for the door and Simone stepped in front of him.

"Chris, I didn't have to tell you anything. We would be in bed making love right now if I didn't think it was important to have a clean relationship. I know this hurt you, but believe me, it's hurting me too. But I made a choice between you and my cousin. I chose you. Am I going to lose you both?"

"How many times, Simone?"

Simone looked at him confused.

"How many times did I lie to you?" she asked.

"No. How many times did you take my daughter to see her mother?"

"She's seen her three times."

Chris threw his hands up in disbelief. He shook his head from side to side watching Simone as she stood with her body spread out in front of the door in a poor attempt to block him from leaving.

"Simone, this is too much for me. I have been through too much in the past and I can't handle anymore heartache and pain. You've just hurt me."

"I know I did, but we can get through this. If you just give me a chance, I will show you that I love you and I will make you a very happy and proud husband."

"Right now, I need to be a happy father. I need to know what you and Michelle were planning."

Simone looked away. She was about to put a big rift in her family tree. Michelle was her first cousin and the only one who she depended on when anything went wrong.

"The papers you signed gives Michelle custody rights to Ashley six months after her release. She is about to execute this plan and she is already working on Ashley so that she would not want to be with you anymore."

"God, Simone. Couldn't you see that this was wrong? How could you do that, not just to me, but to anyone? Did you even think for a moment that you could be hurting the child?"

"Chris, I know, but the only thing I was thinking about was my cousin being hurt and that she should not have to lose her daughter."

"It's been seven years that we've been together. You told me that you loved me. You told me that you loved Ashley and still you would sneak around and take her to see her mother. No wonder I can't seem to talk to her. She has been so distant toward me. We don't even talk anymore. I can't remember the last time she wanted me to tell her a story."

"That's going to change. I made a dreadful mistake and I am going to fix it. You will not lose Ashley and you are not going to lose me."

"What assurance do I have that I will not lose Ashley? I will not let her go. Even if I have to kill Michelle, she is not going to take my daughter."

"Don't say that. You won't have to kill anybody. If you did, Ashley wouldn't have anybody so stop it. Let's work on a counter plan for now. A friend of mine drew up the papers and he's acting as Michelle's attorney. I will call him tomorrow and ask him what avenues we can take to have this amended or revised. If nothing can be done, I will ask him to discourage her plight or delay her until we can figure something else out. You will not lose her, Chris, I promise."

Chris dropped his head. As much as he wanted to walk out the door and never see Simone again, he knew that he needed her. He needed her to be the woman she made him believe she was. He looked at Simone spread out in front of her door trying to keep him in. She could have let him walk out, but she was going above and beyond to keep him and he didn't believe that it was to help Michelle. She was his ally and soul mate. She deserved another chance because she gave him another one.

Simone realized that Chris had softened his anger. She wanted him badly, not only for her own gratification, but to douse out the tension between them. She caught hold of his hand and pulled him toward the steps.

"I can't, Simone. Maybe some other time under better circumstances. I've got far too many worries now." It felt strange for Chris to turn down some good sex. He didn't feel that he could perform anyway feeling as he did at the moment. He wasn't even sure that he wanted to.

Simone wanted this tension to end. She had played this night out in her mind and she wasn't about to let him walk out on her lustful intentions tonight. Angry or not, he was going to get what he came for.

"Shhh…just come with me."

Chris followed her upstairs and she led him to her bedroom.

Why am I letting her do this? Chris asked himself while being led by the wiles of the woman he loved. Her betrayal became distant as he became absorbed by the light music in the background. Simone had put a lot into this evening and he was not going to let this drama ruin this special moment. The song "Just For Your Love" by K-Ci and JoJo started playing. Simone placed her arms around Chris' neck and started grinding against him. Chris placed his hands on her waist then slid his arms around her.

"For your love I will do anything, baby, anything," she sang.

"For your love I will climb any mountain no matter how high," Chris returned the song.

They kissed lightly while they caressed each other's back. Simone slid her hand down the firmness of Chris' arm then down under his shirt until she could feel his warm flesh. He removed his shirt for her. She kissed his neck and his lips then she moved down to his nipples. As she nibbled them, Chris began to feel his organ harden. It's on now, he thought. He put his cares aside and dug deep for the lover he wanted to be. With all the tension they had gone through, the last thing he wanted was quiet romance. He desperately wanted to see the smiles and giggles she gave him when they had fun together.

He slid his hands between the crisscrossed top of Simone's dress, pulling free her breast. He opened his mouth wide taking all of her areola in. He reached beneath her dress and felt beneath her panty. She was moist. He lifted her and carried her over to the bed and gently placed her there. He peeled her dress completely over her shoulders down to her waist and over her hips. Observing the fullness of her body excited him more. He loosened his belt, unfastened his pants and quickly pulled them down over his hips. After stepping out of them, he went to her stereo and pulled a Socalypso CD from her collection. A wide grin spilled across his face as he looked back at Simone on the bed watching him. When the music started and Simone heard the knocking then the man saying, "It's the plumber," she broke out into a laugh.

Chris started his seductive dance. Simone sat up and watched as Chris fondled himself and gyrated in front of her. As he pumped the air, Simone imagined his elephant trunk slapping against her mound. Chris then began crooning, "She wants to pull it out and turn it around, pull it out and turn it around, turn it around and push it back in, turn it around and push it back in. Oh baby the water is running."

As the song "Who Let The Dogs Out" started playing, he moved toward her pumping his hips to the music. Simone laughed heartily at the comical sight. Now realizing that the situation was no longer tense, Chris slid a condom onto his swollen member then climbed atop her and immediately worked his way into her never losing stride. Simone clawed at him.

"God," she cried out as he released his passion on her. His fury was well accepted. Sweat trickled from his body onto hers. Simone was coming. She pulled him so close that he almost couldn't move. She wrapped her legs tightly around him and something from the pit of his stomach pulled down to his balls and his member swelled so tight that Chris thought it was going to rip as his fluid shot from his body. He gripped the mattress for leverage and made strong plunges into the firm cushion. The bed danced wildly with his motions and finally it came to a complete stop.

They continued to hold each other while panting.

"I forgive you, Simone," Chris managed between gasps. "But you've got to promise me that this is what you want; that you will not do anything to hurt me or Ashley and you will make this right."

"Chris, I promise. You don't know how sorry I am about the way we started, but I hope that you do really forgive me and that we can start over. This is now our battle and not just yours."

"I love you for the better and never again the worse." He held her face up to his and made certain that she understood what he said. This would be the last and only time he would forgive her on this note. But if he lost Ashley over this, he would never forgive her.

"I love you too," Simone retorted.

They made love again after talking for an hour. Chris fell asleep in Simone's arms. For the first time in a long time, he felt that things were going to be alright.

Chapter Eleven

It was time to put her plan into effect. Michelle went to see her attorney. She knew that Simone was going to stab her in the back the first chance she got because she could tell that Simone was in love with her Chris and was not going to let him go without a fight. Okay, you little backstabbing bitch, it's time to teach you the dance of the devil. I'm going to show you how the big girls play.

Michelle didn't bother knocking; she entered her attorney's office and took a seat on the leather sofa. Her unannounced entry startled her attorney, as he was finishing up a phone call from one of his friends.

"Hello, Ms. Tanner. I wasn't expecting you."

The tremor in his voice let her know right away that he was up to no good. She wondered if Simone went as far as to call him.

"Hello, Simon. Sorry to drop in like this, but I want to get the wheels turning," she told him anxiously and waiting for the anticipated negative response.

He shifted in his seat looking at Michelle as though she was a ghost. He shuffled the papers on his desk together and shoved them into a folder. He hoped that she didn't notice her name on the file or the papers concerning her daughter. Things are about to get really hairy, he thought.

"I thought we agreed that we should give it six months before we started anything."

"Well, I don't have six months to wait. We need to get this started immediately."

"What's the rush? I'm sure nothing has occurred since your getting out. I think you should lay low for a while and let me put this together effectively. This is too soon to make a court petition. It may work against you."

Michelle got up from the sofa and moved closer to the desk

and took a seat right in front of Mr. Walsh.

"When I signed the papers you gave me, you said that this would be an open and shut deal. You said that we wouldn't have to take this to court."

"There are some complications. I mean you have been incarcerated for a terrible crime and her father has raised your child for ten years since birth. The court is not going to allow you to just take her away. For Christ's sake, Ms. Tanner, you've got to understand that this is more than just revenge."

"This is not about revenge!" she screamed. "This is about my daughter and I have a right to be with her! Now don't feed me this bullshit. I want you to do your fucking job. That's what I paid you for. It's time for you to earn your pay."

His pale skin turned crimson and his hands shook nervously and felt clammy. Considering Michelle's crime, he knew that she was potentially dangerous. He wouldn't tell her that the judge did not sign the document and that the notary will not hold up in court.

"I'm not saying that you won't get your daughter. All I'm asking you to do is give me some time to properly prepare for it. I want to be able to tell the judge that you have honored your parole and have exhibited responsible behavior. Have you tried talking to the father?"

"No," Michelle lied. "He told me when she was born that I would never see her again."

"That was ten years ago. He was angry then. Maybe he has changed his mind and wants to do the right thing for his daughter. Make contact with him. See what he says and maybe we won't have to exercise this request. Right now the judge will probably not give you full custody, but joint custody or visitation rights will undoubtedly be granted."

This was not what Michelle wanted. Her attorney was against her too. He had his own agenda and could care less what she wanted. He wanted the easy way out, the one without a fight. But this was Michelle's fight and she was not about to throw in her towel. He was going to do what she paid him to do and he was going to do it now.

"I don't want to wait and I want that petition filed today. Am I making myself clear?"

He shook his head in disagreement, but his response was clear. He had to do what she wanted otherwise she could file suit against him. Nevertheless, she would soon find out that she has no leverage in this case and her best option is visitation.

"I understand. I will begin working on it right now, but I must warn that you are jeopardizing this case and your chances at getting your daughter back."

Just as she entered, Michelle got up from the seat and left the office. She had not taken heed to her attorney's warning. Her determination to get Ashley outweighed any consequences of losing her for good. In her mind, she was the mother and has first right to her daughter no matter what she had done; even former drug addicts are entitled to their children; even pedophiles gain custody of their children. Michelle turned to her attorney's voice.

"Ms. Tanner, I should have the papers ready in two weeks."

Having heard his response, she waved at him and continued toward the elevator. Chris is not going to take everything from me, she thought to herself. He will learn what it feels like to be hurt to his soul.

***

Simone had been ducking Michelle all week. By Thursday, Michelle had started calling and leaving messages for her to call. A few times, Chris had heard the message and opted to call Michelle, but Simone petitioned him not to. He honored her request, but knowing Michelle, she was not going to stop there. Things were about to get a whole lot worse.

Someone was knocking at the door and Simone knew that it couldn't be Chris because he had his own keys. She hurried downstairs to answer it because the knocks became persistent.

"I'm coming," Simone called, feeling a bit annoyed that the person was banging on her door so urgently. "Some people have no consideration." While making her way to the door, she noted that the clock read nine thirty. Who would be knocking at my door this late? she wondered. As she reached the door, she opened it without looking, probably because of her annoyance she didn't take the time to see who it was. She was expecting it to be Michelle and this was the perfect time for her to bring an end to this whole mess.

When the door opened, someone sprung into the door placing a cloth over her face. Simone immediately felt dizzy and fell into the attacker's arms. She was carried into the house and the door was closed. Simone struggled to steady her vision, but she could not focus on her attacker. The thin, blue nightgown that she wore was pulled open exposing her full breasts. She fought to stop what was happening, but her arms grew numb. The matching panty she wore under her gown was pulled down over her hips.

"Please," she managed to say. Her voice sounded throaty and labored. Everything went into a full spin.

Something wet was smoothed around her opening and into her. Then something large and hard was pressed into her over and over again. Simone wanted to scream, but it was as though her mouth didn't belong to her. Her buttocks and shoulders burned against the carpet as her body shifted with her attacker's thrusts. The size of this man's penis was so thick and long, that it burned as he moved into her, stretching her opening wider than anyone else had. He pressed and hammered against the unrelenting wall of her cervix. A mordant twinge surged through her belly. The pain grew so great that Simone finally passed completely out, accepting the fullness of the chlorophyll that was administered to her two minutes ago when she opened the door.

When the man finished raping Simone, Michelle knelt down over her cousin and placed a kiss on her cheek.

"You wanted him that bad, huh? Well, give him this little package for me. Now you can be his dirty little bitch."

She stood up and told the man to carry her to her bedroom.

***

Ashley was sound asleep in her bed when Chris walked in. He sat on the side of her bed watching her. The moonlight had cast a beautiful glow on her skin. She was angelic. Ashley instinctively felt the warmth of her father and nestled her head on his lap and wrapped her arm around him. He lightly brushed her hair with his hand. Running all weekend must have worn her out because she went straight to bed after dinner and Chris had planned to tell her another story. This one was special. Although Ashley was asleep, he told his story.

***

"A young prince was in search of someone special, someone who would be true and dear to him. He stumbled upon a lady. She was just a little older than himself, but she was unbelievably beautiful. She would invite the prince to her castle and do things to him that felt too good to be true and they were. As the prince began to mature, he realized the lady he was with wasn't the one he wanted to make a princess so he stopped seeing her. He soon moved far away, but the lady found him. He would foolishly accept her when she came to him because she always made him feel greater than anyone else. That wasn't enough for the prince so he made it clear to the lady that he no longer wanted to see her, but it was too late. She had pulled from him something so great that he could never walk away from it.

"With her magic, she stole from him something so precious and so divine that only a princess should have. He was doomed to be joined with her forever because she held within her the greatest part of him. But that wasn't the worst of it, she was a really mean woman and she vowed to punish anyone who came near her prince. She did, but with God's mercy and compassion for the prince, He made it possible for him to claim his bride. He waited as a beautiful princess came into the world and, from that moment, loved her greater than himself. He vowed that moment that he would never let anyone or anything come between them. She was his heart and soul forever.

And when that day comes when a prince comes for her, only then will he reluctantly release his princess, but the prince better be good to his princess because he will feel the wrath of the King and the King always protects his princess. The end."

Being so involved in telling his story, he didn't realize that Ashley was awake and listening to him. She now understood what happened between her parents, not fully, but enough to know that although he doesn't love her mom that he still loved her. When her dad's voice fell silent, Ashley closed her eyes and returned to the silky place in her dreams. Chris slipped from under his daughter's head and went to his bed. It was now twelve thirty and his body was just realizing that it needed sleep.

Chapter Twelve

Simone went to visit her gynecologist because of the reoccurring burn that she had been experiencing lately. She suspected that it was probably an imbalance in her chemistry and she may be experiencing the beginning of a yeast infection. She waited for two other patients that were ahead of her. One of the women was a pregnant patient and the other was a teenager.

"Simone Grey," the nurse called and Simone got up and followed the young nurse into the next room. She told Simone to remove her clothes from below the waist and she would be back momentarily to take her vitals.

Feeling a bit awkward, Simone sat on the fresh chuck the nurse prepared for her. She returned and asked Simone to stand on the scale while she took her weight, then she took her temperature and blood pressure. After giving the favorable results, she told Simone that Dr. Pilman would be with her momentarily.

Simone scanned the colorful diagrams and charts that were posted on the walls with various vaginal and reproductive conditions. Since her first encounter with the light discharge, the odor had heightened to just under what she considered foul. She hated to expose her inappropriate odor to her doctor, but she understood that he needed to see and examine the discharge in order to cure it.

After ten minutes of sitting in the office, Dr. Pilman entered the room. He seemed happy as ever and never displayed signs of fatigue or concern.

Hello, Ms. Grey. You're a little early for your regular check-up," he said viewing her chart and nodding approvingly at her vitals. "What can I do for you today?"

Simone fought to control her discomfort and shame and explained her experience. She didn't tell the doctor that she thought someone had attacked her. She discarded the memory as a dream that left a scar. He told her to lay down and draw her rear end to the end of the table and place her feet in the adjoining stirrups. He shuffled through the cabinet and found the necessary jars and tools and gathered them on a table that he pulled next to him while he sat on a short stool that left his head level with Simone's opening. He tied a mask in front of his face and began collecting samples from her vaginal walls. He took the cultures and smeared them on the glass slide. Once finished, he told Simone that he wanted to draw blood as well. He took two tubes of blood and handed it to the assistant who now entered the room. By this time, Simone was again in a seated position. She had expressed to her doctor that she felt uncomfortable having the assistant looking on and that it made her feel like a piece of meat. Being compassionate of her concerns, the doctor remembered to keep the assistant out of the examining room during the physical examination.

He told Simone that he should have the results in a couple of days and that she should increase her yogurt intake in the meantime. He would call her in a few days with the results.

"Should I start taking some form of antibiotic too?"

"I'm not going to prescribe any antibiotics until I know what we're dealing with. If it's just a matter of yeast, giving you an antibiotic will only make your infection worse."

Simone nodded in agreement. Dr. Pilman moved the tool tray away and left Simone in the room with the assistant. She labeled the tubes and slides.

"Okay, Ms. Grey. You can get dressed now," she told Simone as she left the room.

Simone got dressed once the assistant closed the door. She had a feeling that something was very wrong.

***

Chris and Ashley went to the principal's office and joined Mr. Connor and his daughter Tiffany. The fury that the two girls shared a week ago had diminished. Principal Carmine had pacified the situation through Tiffany's parent. He explained to Mr. Connor that none of Ashley's teachers had any complaints with Ashley and that they validated that his daughter had indeed been provoking her. Chris was pleasantly surprised when the Principal told Ashley to go to her class and that this incident had already been resolved and no further action was necessary. From Mr. Connor's expression, Chris knew right away that Tiffany carried the greater punishment and that Ashley had been pardoned from the incident. Chris went with Ashley to her class.

"Simone will pick you up later. I will see you when I get home." He then got close to her ear and whispered. "Try not to beat up anyone today. Okay?"

She laughed and kissed her dad.

"See you later."

Ashley went to her seat. Some of her fellow classmates waved to her when she turned to them. Tiffany, of course, was still angry, but wouldn't dare confront Ashley again.

***

Simone woke up at eight o'clock. She pushed her feet into her slippers then shuffled to the bathroom. Her body ached all over as if she had been in a fight the day before. She looked at herself in the mirror stretching. God, my body hurts. She moved to the toilet and emptied her bladder. The urine stung as she slowly released it. Jesus, what the hell is that all about? I hope this isn't another episode of yeast. She wiped herself and examined the tissue. A clear emission clung to the tissue with a light, cloudy substance. It smelled funny; nothing like yeast and its texture was not like yeast either. It was slimy like semen. She shrugged, flushed the toilet then went to the shower to set the water.

After taking her shower, Simone dressed and gathered her papers together. She had two homes to visit today. One of her patients was a sexually abused little boy named Everett. His stepfather had been abusing him and because of it, he had episodes of self-abuse. Simone felt bad for him because his mother's disbelief allowed this abuse to go on for so long.

When she arrived at the Sherman's house, which was Everett's foster parents' house, she could already hear him upstairs arguing with his foster mother Debra Sherman. She rang the bell and heard quick footsteps hurrying to the door. The door opened and Simone was greeted by Mrs. Sherman.

"Hello, Mrs. Sherman? How's everything?"

"Oh, Simone, things could be better. I don't know what got into Everett this morning. I caught him masturbating in the bathroom."

Simone nodded without any expression. It wasn't his fault that he was experiencing these urges. He was ten just like Ashley, but his exposure to sex made his body more mature than it should be.

"Where is Everett now?"

She shook her head as though she was fed up with him.

"He's upstairs in his room now. I don't know if I am going to be able to handle him much longer."

Simone made a mental note of her comment.

"What were you two arguing about? I could hear you from outside."

"When I told him to stop what he was doing, he turned to face me so that I could watch him."

Simone noted her response again.

"Can you call Everett downstairs for me and leave us alone so that I can talk to him?"

"Sure."

She yelled out Everett's name. A few seconds later, Everett emerged from his bedroom and saw Simone standing by the door. He slowly descended the steps with the look of shame and exasperation on his face.

"Hello, Everett," she greeted him when he was fully in her sight.

His foster mother looked at him with disgrace, shook her head and ascended the steps to her room.

"You want to sit in the living room or the kitchen?" she asked him with a compassionate smile.

He shrugged his shoulders. He knew that his foster mother had told Simone what he had done. He couldn't control the sweet tingle he felt when he touched his penis. When he squeezed it, the sensation got stronger and before he knew it, he was massaging it. When his foster mother walked in, the fever was so intense that he couldn't stop. She slapped him so hard that he fell off the toilet.

Simone walked to the kitchen and sat in one of the seats at the table. Everett followed and sat directly next to her. He didn't want to sit across from her today because he didn't want to see her eyes when she made him explain himself or talk about what was going on inside him. He was grateful that she didn't ask him to change his seat.

Simone pulled her pad from her bag and sat it on the table in front of her. Today she didn't have to ask what happened, Everett was more than ready to talk.

"My stepdad used to hold my penis and pull up and down on it before he would hurt me," he said without looking up at her. He stared at the table as though it were a window that he could look into and see the past. "Sometimes, I feel a tickle inside that won't stop unless I massage it," he continued. "I try not to let my…mother," he stammered unsure of what to call her, "see it, but she's always sneaking around and watching everything I do."

"Have you tried explaining to her what you're feeling?"

"No, because she won't understand how I feel. She doesn't even care about me. Sometimes she twists my arm when she gets mad and today she slapped me."

Simone hadn't noticed the red finger marks on his face until he turned his face to the opposite side showing her where she'd slapped him.

Simone wrote that down.

"Do you mind if I take a picture of that?"

He shook his head. She took two pictures of the slap marks.

She moved toward him and lifted his shirt. While examining his chest and back, she realized that he was still being abused. There were four, long, fresh scratches across his back moving toward his side.

"How did that happen?"

"She did it while grabbing for me when I didn't take out the trash. I knew that she was going to hit me so I ran and while trying to catch me she scratched me."

Simone went to her bag and pulled out her cell phone.

"Everett, I am going to have to move you to another home. I don't think this is a good place for you."

She dialed Social Services and explained that she needed someone right away. She had Everett to sit again.

"Everett, I know that you are experiencing some strange sensations right now. I also understand that you don't know how to handle them, but I need you to try a little harder to fight those urges. I am going to schedule you for a special therapist who is trained to deal with your kind of situation. There is nothing wrong with you. Your stepfather just forced your body into a maturity that you are not ready for. That is why he is in jail, but it is my job to help you maintain a normal development both socially and physically."

She made a few notes on her pad and she marked "sex education" on it and then put it away.

When Social Services arrived, Simone had Everett to call his foster mother downstairs. Simone explained her findings and that Everett was being removed from her care and that she was going to see to it that she never got another child into her home. When social services had taken possession of Everett and his things, Simone went to her next case.

Like Everett, Wayne Green had gone through an abusive past. He was now sixteen and started on a bad trend of fondling little boys. Simone had been responsible for Wayne for four years. When she was assigned to his case, he had already gone through five other social workers and more foster homes than she wanted to count.

Simone had placed Wayne in a boy mentoring program as well as finding a home for him. Duane was a good friend of hers and she knew that if anyone would be able to get through to Wayne, he could. For four years, he has improved dramatically. Duane had taken Wayne to sporting events and got him involved with the big brother mentoring program. Teamed with Simone having him listen to the stories of other young boys that had been abused, Wayne understood the wrongness of what he was doing and actually felt remorse enough to want to help other young boys who went through what he had.

Wayne's foster parent had nothing but good things to say about him. Next year he would be graduating high school and continuing his education in forensics.

Simone looked at her watch. She remembered promising Chris that she would pick up Ashley from school. She had fifteen minutes to get there. This would be impossible if traffic was bad.

Simone arrived about ten minutes late. She didn't see Ashley in the yard with the other children who were waiting to be picked up. She went into the office and they told her that Ashley was picked up already. Not wanting to sound foolish, Simone didn't ask the principal who had picked her up because she didn't think anyone would be allowed to do so besides herself and Chris?

When Simone reached her car, she pulled out her cell phone and dialed Chris. Her heart was racing. She knew that if he didn't answer his phone at the office that he had indeed picked up Ashley and probably tried calling her, but she had turned off her phone.

"Chris Walker," he answered.

"Oh, hi, Chris. I just wanted to see how things were going at work today."

"Simone, how are you, sweetie? Today is wonderful. Did you get Ashley?"

"Yeah, she just went into the house. We're going to the mall so we'll see you a little later."

"That's fine. You girls enjoy yourselves."

Simone disconnected the phone and held it to her chest. She exhaled bringing her anxiety down two notches. She was glad he didn't ask to speak with Ashley. If he knew that she didn't have her, he would have come bolting home and all hell would break loose. She knew only one other person who could have picked up Ashley. She speeded to Michelle's house. Immediately, she noticed her car outside. Simone jumped from her Caravan and strutted to the door and began ringing the bell as if she thought no one could hear her. Michelle opened the door with a wide grin on her face. Simone looked past Michelle and she could see Ashley standing in the living room. Without saying a word, Simone reached back and hit Michelle as hard as she could and proceeded to beat on her.

"You bitch. How dare you pull a stunt like that?"

Michelle fought to get Simone off of her. She had surprise attacked her so she had an immediate advantage which soon faltered. The two women kicked and punched at each other, pulling hair and screaming. Ashley, realizing what was going on, screamed for them to stop. She was afraid. By this time, Michelle was holding Simone by the neck and dragging her toward the floor.

"Mom, stop," Ashley pleaded. "Please don't hurt Simone."

Simone dug her thumb into Michelle's armpit forcing her to let go. She charged at Michelle, but Michelle was too quick and kicked her in the stomach. Simone doubled over, but not allowing Michelle to gain advantage of her, she kicked Michelle's knee and forced her cap out of place.

Michelle howled holding her knee.

"Ashley, get your bag, we're going."

Ashley didn't move. She was afraid to move.

"Now, Ashley!" Ashley shot into the living room and started gathering her books and papers and putting them into her backpack. Tears forced their way out streaking Ashley's cheeks and falling onto her blouse. She was afraid for both of them and what they might do to each other. Ashley loved Simone just as much as she desired her mother. Under the circumstances, Ashley recognized Simone as her stepmother and the only mother that she really knew. Without thought, she obeyed Simone's requests although her real mother howled on the ground.

Simone stood over Michelle while she continued to howl and hold her leg. When Ashley had gotten her things together and waited for Simone at the door, Simone knelt down next to Michelle and caught hold of her leg while placing her hand on Michelle's knee.

"I don't want to have to repeat this incident again so you had better stop what you're trying to do here. I will not let you ruin this child and I am not going to let you hurt her father. I am not going to stop you from seeing Ashley, but you will not take her from her father and me."

With one quick effort, she shifted Michelle's knee back into place.

"Ashley, say goodbye to your mother. And from now on, you are not to leave school without me or your father unless we tell you that someone else is going to pick you up. Do you hear me?"

Ashley nodded her head. She felt bad for her mother.

"See you later, Mom."

Michelle nodded yes.

"You need help getting up?"

Michelle nodded again. She wanted to kick Simone's ass, but she would deal with her later. From her perspective, no harm had been done since Chris was going to legally lose Ashley to her and there was nothing Simone could do about it. She may have Chris, but she could not keep her daughter.

Simone caught hold of Michelle's arm and pulled her up. She then helped her over to the sofa. When Michelle was seated, she loomed over her for a moment.

"You know, I really thought Chris had done you wrong and I wanted to help you punish him, but now I know that you were the evil one. He didn't do anything to you. What? Did you think that you were going to have him forever? He's gone and you're going to have to deal with that. Your trying to hurt him by using Ashley is not going to work because I am not going to let you."

Ashley heard everything and looked at her mother wondering what Simone was talking about. Michelle didn't deny what Simone was saying or even try to justify her actions. Simone turned from Michelle and joined Ashley at the door. While Simone was ushering her out, Ashley looked back at her mother one last time before Simone closed the door.

Simone opened the Caravan's door for Ashley without saying a word. Ashley climbed in and she closed the door. She immediately noticed the hostility setting in. Ashley seemed cold and resentful.

"Don't hold it in, honey. Tell me what's going on in your head."

"Why did you fight with my mother? I thought you wanted me to be with her?"

"I don't want to keep you from your mother, Ashley, but what she did was wrong."

"She picked me up from school that's all."

"Without permission."

"She's my mother. She doesn't need permission."

"Your father has custody of you which means that your mother can not take you when she feels like it. She has to get permission from your dad and if he knew what she did today he would never let her see you."

"Are you going to tell him?"

Simone considered her question and the consequences of her telling Chris. First, she would have to let him know that she lied to him and everything else she would explain wouldn't even matter.

"No. I'm not going to tell him, but I want you to do something for me too."

Ashley waited for Simone to tell her what she had to do.

"I want you to tell your father everything your mom has said to you and I want you to give him a chance to tell his side of the story. He is going to tell you the truth, Ashley."

"No, he won't. I already know what he is going to say."

"What's that?"

"That she killed my grandmother, but she didn't. He just hates her."

"Just promise me that you will do that for me."

Ashley shrugged.

"Okay. But, I'm not going to believe him. Do I have to tell him tonight?"

"I think you should, but you can decide for yourself what you want to do."

Simone patted her on the lap then parked the car at the end of the driveway.

Chris was standing at the door when they got out of the car. He heard them when they pulled up and came to the door to wait for them. When Ashley rounded the van he could tell that something was going on. His daughter had not learned to hold her feelings inside. Simone displayed her normal happy to see you look, but his daughter had something heavy going on inside.

He approached his daughter and gave her a big hug. Then he held her away from him to get a good look at her.

"How was school today? Do I have to go to school tomorrow and beat up anyone?"

She chuckled. "No, Dad. Everything was fine."

"Well, what's wrong? Why the long face?"

She didn't answer him. He looked to Simone for answers. She locked eyes with Ashley then Chris. Simone moved toward Chris and gave him a quick kiss then moved toward the house.

"I'll see you inside. Did you start dinner?"

"I just got in, I was about to," he called to her as she went inside.

Chris turned his attention to his daughter. He grabbed her backpack, caught hold of her hand and walked with her to the steps. He sat down on the top step and patted next to him for her to sit down and she did so. They sat quietly for five minutes watching occasional cars pass by. A neighbor waved to them as he went into his house. Chris turned to face his daughter.

"Baby, I am so sorry that you have all this to deal with. I am not going to pretend that I know exactly what is going on in your head, but I have an idea."

Ashley listened, but didn't say anything.

"Simone told me that you have been to see your mother and I found the pictures under your mattress. I was very disappointed when I found them since I thought we had a close relationship. I really didn't think you would hide things from me, but I can understand why you did it. I'm not mad about it, Ashley, but I want you to be able to talk to me about anything. Hiding things from me only makes me believe that your mom is trying to turn you against me. She wants you to hate me. Do you hate me, Ashley?"

She turned her head away from him. Her eyes began to bulge as she fought to hold back her tears.

"No, Dad," she managed in a croaky voice.

"Look at me, baby." He turned her to face him and he put his arm around her and pulled her close to him. "I will never do anything to hurt you. No matter what your mom has told you, if it's true, I will tell you, but I don't think it's fair for you to hold something against me if you haven't given me a chance to explain. What do you think?" he reasoned.

Ashley muttered, "No."

"Well, don't you think I have a right to know what she said I did or didn't do?"

She nodded, but still said nothing. How can I tell him that my mother told me that he didn't want me and that the only reason he took me was because he was forced to by the court? "Did the court force you to take care of me?" she managed to ask him after a long silence.

"Oh, darling, no. That's far from the truth. I came to get you because you are a part of me. How can I not love you when you are from me? Part of me made you and to leave you would be to leave a part of myself. I love you, Ashley, more than myself. You are the best part of me. When I found out that you were coming into the world, nothing could keep me away from you just like nothing is going to keep you from me now. Your mother is evil to tell you a thing like that. To make you feel bad just so that you could hate me."

"She and Simone had a fight today."

"What?"

"Mom picked me up from school and Simone came to mommy's house and beat her up."

"Really?"

"She told her that she better not do that again and that she better not hurt you."

Chris knew for sure now that Simone indeed loved him and that she had his best interest at heart. He didn't let Ashley see his joy, but inside he was leaping.

"Ashley, don't let anyone tell you that I don't love you. Do you feel like I don't love you?"

"No. You are the best dad in the whole world."

"I am your father, Ashley, and that will never change. Your mom is going to try to take you from me. Is that what you want?"

Ashley didn't respond. She thought about her mom and all the fun they had together last week and how she wanted to be able to do that again. She also thought about all the wonderful times she shared with her father and how he always went out of his way to make her happy.

Simone came to the door.

"Hey, are you two going to come in tonight? Dinner is ready."

Chris didn't pressure Ashley anymore. He knew that she had a lot on her mind and he couldn't dare ask her not to want to be with her mother.

"Come on, let's go inside. I love you no matter what you choose. Forever," he emphasized.

Ashley kissed her dad's lips and held his neck tight.

"I love you too, Daddy. Are you going to stop me from seeing my mom?"

Chris sighed.

"No. If she learns to play by my rules I won't stop her from seeing you, but she has to stop trying to turn you against me. Come on before Simone comes out here again."

The three of them sat down for dinner. Simone could see that Ashley felt a lot better. She didn't know what they discussed, but whatever he said to her brought her to ease.

Ashley finished dinner and went to her room to finish her homework. She was surprised to see the pictures she took with her mother on top of her bed. She looked at them for a long while and then put them in her mirror.

Chris helped Simone clear the dishes. He stood pressed behind her while she washed them. He kissed the back of her neck and massaged her belly.

"I can't wait to put someone in here."

She smiled.

"Neither can I. I'm sure Ashley can't wait either," Simone remarked.

"Turn around," Chris whispered while nibbling her ear.

Simone turned to face him and was met with a deep kiss. He caressed and massaged her butt in his hands while pressing her against him.

"Want to take this upstairs?" he asked her between kisses.

Simone wanted him badly, but she felt really tender between her legs and every time she went to the bathroom it burned. She reasoned that Chris always wore a condom anyway so if it's yeast, he wouldn't get it.

"Honey, let me clean up first. Besides, Ashley is still up."

Chris pulled his swollen member from his Dockers and squeezed his muscles making it bob up and down.

"I'm almost fully erect. You want to waste it?" he teased. He looked delicious enough to eat.

"You go upstairs and wait for me. I will be there in a minute."

Chris tucked his gorged implement into his pants and walked stiff legged out of the kitchen. Simone laughed at this comedy then turned to the sink to finish the dishes.

Upstairs, Chris peeped in on Ashley. She was fast asleep in her book. He went in and took it from her and looked over her homework that was finished. He then put her books into her backpack and then pulled a blanket over her. He turned and realized that she hung her mother's picture up on her mirror. Chris moved toward the mirror and took a closer look at Michelle. She was a beautiful woman, but evil. Simone came in behind him and saw that Ashley had fallen asleep and Chris had covered her up. She lifted the covers and realized that she was still wearing her clothes. She removed her skirt and top and Chris handed her a gown and she pulled it over her head and put her arms in. Although Ashley was asleep, she groggily helped Simone put her clothes on then lay comfortably under her cover. Simone kissed her forehead and whispered, "I love you," into her ear. Chris then knelt down and kissed her. "I love you, Ashley, and I'll see you in the morning. Have sweet dreams." He kissed her again then followed Simone out of her room, cutting off the light behind him.

Simone went directly to the shower and cleaned to complete freshness. When she entered the room, Chris had already taken his clothes completely off and went into the shower. He returned to the bedroom where Simone began her seduction. She pushed Chris down onto the bed and took her trouser socks and bound Chris' hands onto the headboard. She then put his tie around his eyes. She kissed him passionately first then went downstairs to get the whipped cream she noticed in the refrigerator when she put the food away.

Chris was rock hard anticipating Simone's return. When Simone started back to the bedroom she felt something eerie behind her. She spun around and was again knocked out with chlorophyll. Michelle entered the room and became excited at Chris naked body. She moved over to him and placed her mouth over his erection and began sliding her lips over his hardness. Chris moaned. Simone was better than ever.

"Please, baby, I'm going to explode."

Michelle kissed him on the lips and touched his tongue with hers, but didn't allow him to lock lips with her. She straddled over him and began working him into her. Chris pushed up and met every movement she made. Michelle wanted to come. He was still good. His body was just made for hers. Chris began to tremble at how tight Simone felt. He knew she was going to come. Her walls became hot and she trembled trying to control what was about to happen.

Chris couldn't hold it in any longer and allowed his fluid to release. Michelle continued to move above him until her throbbing walls ceased to clamor at his ceasing hardness. She pulled off of him allowing his flaccid dick to plop onto his thigh. Once off, she kissed him one more time then went into Ashley's room to return the key she took from Ashley's bag. She slipped it back onto Ashley's key ring and put it back into Ashley's bag then left the house.

"Simone," Chris called after being there tied up for so long.

She didn't answer his first call. He called her again this time a little louder. She must have forgotten that she left him tied up there. Finally, Simone made her way into the bedroom. She turned on the light and was mortified when she saw the semen on Chris. His erection was gone and she now realized what had happened. She went over to Chris and removed his blindfold and untied his hands.

"That was good," he crooned rubbing her arms. He pulled her down to give her a kiss, but she wouldn't. She lay on his chest and started crying.

"Honey, what's wrong?"

She didn't want to tell him. She couldn't tell him because it was also her fault for making this possible.

"What is it? Are you afraid that you will get pregnant?"

"Chris, I'm sorry. I've got to go."

She turned to leave, but he grabbed her hand.

"Simone, I don't understand. Make me understand why you're doing this and what you're sorry for."

She turned to face him. Her face looked horrified. Right then, Chris knew that something was terribly wrong.

"I'll tell you later."

"Simone, you will tell me now. I don't want to know later. I need to know why you look like that. Tell me, Simone. I have to be able to trust you."

She knew that Chris was not going to believe her. He was not going to believe that she didn't have anything to do with it. She put her arms around him and rested her head on his chest and sobbed.

"Chris, something terrible has happened and I don't know how to tell you. This can be really bad, Chris."

He gently pushed her away from him and turned her face toward him so that he could see her face.

"I've got to know, Simone."

She took a deep breath, shifted herself away from him then looked him straight in the eyes.

"You just slept with Michelle."

"What?" Chris asked jumping up from the bed. "What do you mean I just slept with Michelle? What kind of game is this, Simone?

I don't think this is funny at all. How could you do something like this?"

"I didn't. I went to get whipped cream and she somehow knocked me out."

"That's bullshit, Simone. I don't believe you."

He moved toward her and felt between her legs. It was dry.

"Get out, Simone. I don't want to see you again."

"Chris, wait. I swear to you that I had nothing to do with this. I am just as upset about it."

"How could she have gotten in here, Simone? You must really think I'm stupid."

"Me? How the hell do you let someone else come in here and ride you and you don't know that something's wrong. You mean to tell me that you can't feel the difference?"

"Don't you dare try to turn this thing around. I should have never trusted you. Simone, I'm only going to ask you to leave one more time. The next time I say it, it won't be pleasant. You have no idea the trouble you've caused here. If she turns up pregnant…just get out."

Simone hesitated. Chris had hurt her, but she couldn't blame him, she wouldn't believe this nonsense either. It wasn't even something that could be reported to the police. This would definitely sound preposterous.

"When you want to talk, I will be home."

Simone wanted to scream. Chris was standing there angry with semen clinging to him like the stale aftermath of sex. Under normal circumstances, she would be angry about something like this. This is usually considered cheating. She left Chris' house after dressing. She drove by Michelle's house and she wasn't at home. She remained parked in front of her house until daybreak, but Michelle never showed up.

Chapter Thirteen

Chris went into his shower and washed away what had just happened. He was going to kill Michelle for this. This was an all time low. Chris felt bad about throwing Simone out, but he needed time to sort this whole thing out. If he didn't think a step ahead of Michelle, she was going to ruin him. He went into his room and changed the sheets on his bed. He woke up Ashley and told her to take a shower and get dressed. In the meantime, Chris fixed breakfast. Something came to mind. He remembered Ashley telling him that Michelle had picked her up from school. He ran up the stairs and looked in Ashley's bag for her keys. He noticed that the key was on the wrong ring. Okay, Michelle, you want to play this game? Let's play then, Chris laughed to himself.

He went back downstairs and fixed two plates, one for Ashley and one for himself. Ashley came downstairs in her school uniform. She sat down at the table and Chris gave her a kiss and placed a tall glass of orange juice in front of her along with a cod liver oil capsule and a multivitamin. He then sat across from her.

"How do you feel this morning?"

"I'm okay. How about you?"

"I'm good. Did you take your key off the chain for any reason?"

"No. Why?"

"I noticed that it wasn't on the blue ring but the red one."

"I don't know why that would be. I have never taken it off. Maybe Simone did it and forgot which one it was on. You should ask her."

Ashley didn't pay Chris' meaningless chatter any mind. She simply continued to enjoy her breakfast. When she finished, she took her vitamins and drank her orange juice.

"Where is Simone? Is she still sleeping?"

"No. Simone went home last night."

"Why? I thought she was staying over."

"She had something to do. She'll be away for a while."

"What do you mean? Simone isn't picking me up today?"

"No. I'm going to pick you up later."

"Did you guys fight last night?"

"No, but we have to sort some adult things out so until then, she won't be by."

"Is it because of Mom?"

"Yes, but that's enough questions for now. Let me work that out, okay?"

"Okay. I'm going to get my things."

Ashley went upstairs and got her backpack and rain jacket. Chris grabbed his briefcase and umbrella. He took Ashley to school then went to the office. When he arrived, he noticed that there were police cars outside the building and he wondered what was going on. He entered the building and took the elevator up to his office. As he walked in, he saw the police talking with Mr. Thurman. Not wanting to interrupt them, he bypassed them and went into his office. He would ask Patrice what was going on later.

Just as Chris was about to sit down at his desk, Mr. Thurman entered his office. He slid in and asked Chris about last night.

"I just went home, had dinner and went to bed. I didn't work on any files last night."

"Chris, the police are outside looking for you. I didn't tell them that you just walked in, but they are here to arrest you."

"Arrest me?" Chris repeated in surprise. "What for?"

"Rape. Your ex-girlfriend had told the police that you raped her when she came by to see her daughter."

"That's preposterous! It's a lie," Chris stated raising his voice a little over his normal tone.

"They want to take you in for semen testing."

"Oh my God," Chris said as he dropped down into his seat. This was really about to get ugly. He wasn't about to tell his boss that Michelle took advantage of him last night. Just as outlandish as it sounded when Simone tried to explain it, it was going to sound the same way to the police.

One police officer came into the office.

"Chris Walker?" he queried.

Chris looked from the officer to Mr. Thurman. He nodded.

"I am Chris Walker."

"I need you to accompany me to the precinct. Please come with me."

Chris rounded his desk at the officer's request.

"It's procedure to cuff you. Can you please turn around and place your hands above your head?"

Chris did as he was told. The officer approached Chris and placed the handcuffs around his wrists. He felt Chris' pockets and legs for any weapons. After finding none, he escorted Chris to his squad car. He was then taken to the precinct for a statement. This was becoming all too familiar. Chris denied the rape allegation. They told him that semen was collected from the victim and they would have to get a sample from him.

"I know how crazy this is going to sound, but Michelle Tanner…" he rethought his response; "she and I had sex last night. I had an issue of pre-ejaculation and she became furious and stormed out of the house. I don't know why she is saying that I raped her. Maybe she's just angry with me."

The officer nodded his head. He spread some photos onto the table. They were pictures of Michelle all beaten up and bruised.

"I didn't do that. I never hit Michelle. Never!" Chris explained while becoming excited. "I don't know how that happened, but it wasn't me. I swear I had nothing to do with that."

"Well, she reported you as raping her and if the semen matches…."

"Of course the semen will match. I just told you that we had sex. Listen, take this number and call Simone Grey. She will explain what happened. Instead of me trying to give you this absurd sounding story, I would prefer that you get it from someone who knows better what is going on."

Chris told him Simone's number and the officer wrote it down on his pad. He went to the phone and dialed her number.

Simone answered.

"Hello."

"Simone Grey?" the officer queried.

"Yes, it is. May I help you?"

"I hope so. Chris Walker has been brought in for questioning concerning a rape allegation."

The mention of rape made Simone's heart race. Michelle was a cruel and conniving bitch.

"That's ridiculous. Chris would never rape anyone."

"What is your relationship to Chris Walker?"

"We are engaged."

"Ms. Grey, it is alleged that the woman had traces of the attacker's semen in her and she was beaten pretty badly."

"Michelle Tanner and I had a fight yesterday around four o'clock and she probably sustained some bruises from that. I also hurt her knee. She wanted to punish me by sleeping with my fiancé. She snuck into his home last night and…" she hesitated, "took advantage of a situation."

Officer Mills had never heard anything so ridiculous in his life. But she did provide an alibi for him. This seems to be a love triangle situation and there was not going to be much to hold him on.

"Thank you, Ms. Grey."

"Excuse me, where is Chris Walker being held?"

"He's being released. We may have to call him in for questioning again if Michelle Tanner decides to fully press charges and maintain her story. I doubt that she will because the examiner just called and informed us that there was no evidence of rape."

"Where is Michelle Tanner now?"

"She's possibly at home, but your visiting her will only make things worse. I don't recommend that you go there threatening her."

Simone sighed. He gave her the address where Chris was and told her that he will be released momentarily and that she could pick him up if she wanted to.

Simone hurried over to the precinct. When she arrived, Chris was signing some papers at the desk. He looked tired and despondent. She waited by the door for a moment and took in her surroundings. She approached him and placed her hand on his shoulder. He turned to face her and pulled her into his embrace.

"Simone, I am so sorry about last night."

"It's okay. I can hardly blame you. I picked the wrong time to play reindeer games."

He smiled. "Is there a chance I can make it up to you?"

"There is no need. I already forgive you, but I need to tell you something when we get out of here."

After Chris finished signing the papers, he was released and he left the precinct with Simone. He climbed into her Caravan and they went straight to Ashley's school to pick her up. Once they acquired her, they went to Simone's house. Chris got out and helped Ashley down from the van. Ashley looked from her father to Simone wondering what was going on. Neither of them said anything to the other. Their silence was strange considering the amount of dialogue they normally have. Simone unlocked the door and they entered the house.

"Ashley, give your dad and I a second."

Chris held his daughter's shoulders, keeping her from moving.

"I think Ashley should hear this. I have spent too many years sheltering her from the truth and she should know what's going on."

Ashley looked at her dad puzzled. He ushered her to the sofa and they both sat down. Simone followed them and sat in the armchair across from them next to the fireplace. For a moment, no one said anything. The room was quiet and Ashley looked from one to the other. She imagined that it had to do with her mother again. She caught her breath as Chris turned to her to speak.

"Your mother did a terrible thing today, Ashley. She told the police that I did something that I didn't do."

Ashley's eyes spread wide and she drew in a deep breath with a gasp.

"You were in jail?" she managed once she released the air.

Chris' eyebrows furrowed into a frown and he drew his eyes

from his daughter and looked to Simone.

"Simone had come to pick me up, but I may have to go to court if your mom doesn't tell the truth."

Ashley leaned onto her father's arm.

"What did she say you did?"

Simone looked at Chris as if to say, You're not going to tell her are you? Her eyes bared an intense gaze and she muttered a weak, "No."

Chris noticed Simone's reaction, but he strongly felt that his daughter deserved to know the horrible things her mother was capable of. He hoped by telling her the truth and all that's transpired that it would lessen her desire to be with her.

"Your mom said that I beat her and raped her."

Ashley lifted her head and pulled away from her father.

"You wouldn't do a thing like that, would you, Dad?"

He turned to her and placed his hand gently on her shoulder.

"I would never do a thing like that. Not to anyone," he emphasized.

"Why did she do that?"

"Because she wants to hurt me and take you away. If I go to jail then there will be no one to keep her from taking you."

"I don't want you to go to jail."

"I know you don't, honey, but unless I can prove that I didn't do this then I may have to go. Right now, it seems impossible because it's her word against mine and there is nothing I can do."

"I don't like her anymore," Ashley pouted.

"Shhhhh. Don't say that. This is not your worry, baby. All this will be taken care of. Remember what I told you."

"I know. I must love everyone," Ashley recited. "Well, can I stay with Simone if you go away?"

Her words touched something deep within Simone.

"I'm not going anywhere, honey. Don't you worry."

The three of them sat quietly. The telephone rang and startled them and Simone went to answer it.

"Hello," Simone answered the phone. It was Dr. Pilman with

the results from her tests.

"Ms. Grey, how are you?"

"I'm well, Dr. Pilman. And you?" she asked politely wanting to get to the point.

"Same here. The results from your culture and blood test returned with positive results."

"What do you mean?" she asked. When a doctor says positive, the results are normally negative.

"I have room in my calendar to see you today. Are you able to come by within the next hour?"

"Sure, I can make it. Does it really have to be done today?"

"Yes."

"Then I will be there."

Chris, upon hearing the conversation, wondered what Simone was talking about. She looked very concerned about what her doctor had told her. She returned to the living room and sat stiffly in her seat.

"What is it?"

"I don't know, but I'm going to have to run. You can wait here for me if you like."

"I want to go with you."

Under the circumstances, Simone did not want Chris to go with her to receive the results from her doctor. Because he made it clear that he wanted her to come in immediately, she knew that it had to be bad. Considering the increase in odor and amount of her discharge, she knew that it had to be more than yeast.

"I want to do this alone, Chris. I promise that when I return I will talk to you about it. Let me have this moment to absorb what the doctor has to say and see how bad it is. I don't want you there with me when he tells me."

Chris stood up and faced Simone. This was more serious than he had thought. He wondered if she was badly sick and didn't want anyone to know about it. Not knowing what kind of doctor she was seeing, he really couldn't speculate.

"I'm going to go home. If you need me, I will be there," Chris assured her.

"Simone, can I go with you?"

"No, baby, you go home with your dad. I will see you when I get back."

"Promise."

"I promise."

Chris and Ashley followed Simone outside and then he realized that he didn't have his car.

"Looks like we will be seeing you here because I don't have a ride," Chris teased, but was serious at the same time. He was trying to make light of a seemingly tense situation.

"I didn't tell you that you are my prisoner?" she joked back, hiding her trepidation.

"No, but I know now. I'll be here."

Simone went to her Caravan and got in. She waited until Chris and Ashley were back inside before she let the tears flow. She knew that something had to be terribly wrong.

Thirty minutes later she pulled into the parking lot of her medical facility and she hurried to the GYN office. When she arrived, no other patients were waiting. The nurse led her into the empty examination room. Simone noticed that two of the doors were closed which meant that there were other patients waiting on him.

Shortly after, the doctor entered the room. Simone had undressed and waited for him to enter. He opened her chart and scanned the results.

Simone waited as patiently as she could, reasoning to herself that her doctor already knew what was wrong with her and this anticipation thing was bogus.

"Ms. Grey, your blood results show a significant increase in its hormone levels. This kind of change suggests pregnancy. When was your last menstrual cycle?"

Simone blinked and became distant for a moment until her doctor called her name.

"I'm sorry, what did you say?"

"You may be pregnant. Of course, this would be the very early stage. You may not even be a month yet. When was your last menstrual?" he repeated now that he realized that he had her attention and she had absorbed his revelation.

"What's today?" she muttered in her thoughts. "It was actually due yesterday."

"Has it ever been late in the past?"

"No. It's normally right on schedule, give or take a day, but even that is rare."

"Well, if you don't get your cycle in another day or two, I would like to get a beta."

Simone thought she was going to die. She knew that she and Chris practiced safe sex and there was no way he had done this. The horrible reality began to sink in that she was indeed raped.

"Ms. Grey," Dr. Pilman started as he sifted over the culture results, "I am going to write you a prescription for your infection. I am providing for double the dosage. You must be certain to give your partner the other dose."

"What do you mean? Wasn't it yeast?"

"No. According to the test, the infection is Gonorrhea."

A shrieking gasp startled the doctor as he was looking at her file.

"That can't be. Maybe there's been a mistake."

"I can repeat the test, but I'm almost certain that it's correct. Has the discharge lightened any since your visit?"

"No. Actually, it's gotten worse. The color has changed to a weird yellow-greenish color and I have been having painful urination."

"Uh hmm," he responded nodding his head adding up the description she gave him, which was exactly the same as what he saw the last time? "There is no need for you to get worked up about this. It is treatable and the good thing is that we caught it during the early stages of your pregnancy. Abstain from sex until you have completed the medication and you are no longer symptomatic. I want you to come back to me next week so that I can do a follow-up Pap and get new blood work."

Simone responded by nodding her head. She had never felt so

ashamed in her entire life. She was grateful that Chris was responsible when it came to protection and she was certain that it was not his child. Getting an abortion would not be difficult under these circumstances.

Her examination was over and her doctor left her in the room wallowing in her embarrassment. Simone knew that she would have to tell Chris what happened. She only hoped that he believed her. What she feared more than that is whether her cousin had anything to do with it or not.

Simone went to the pharmacy and secured the prescription. The pharmacist wanted to tell her about the medication, but Simone was too embarrassed to have them do that. She explained that her doctor already told her what needed to be done. After paying for her medication, she returned home.

Inside, she could smell cooked food and judging from the heat, it was prepared not too long ago. Chris and Ashley were sprawled across the couch sleeping. The television was going and neither of them budged when she entered. Instead of waking them up, Simone quietly went upstairs to her bedroom. She kicked off her shoes, flung herself across her bed, buried her face into the mattress and began crying quietly to herself. The bag with her prescription lay next to her on the bed. Chris would probably not even want her after knowing that she had something so nasty.

***

Chris could feel his stomach churning. He had fixed dinner, but he wanted to wait until Simone returned. He wondered if everything was okay with her at the doctor's office. Ashley was still asleep on the sofa. He quietly moved from the sofa and went to the window. He hated feeling stranded. When he noticed Simone's car right out front, he went upstairs to see if she was there. He knew that she would not have awakened him when she came in. When he reached her room, he noticed her sprawled across her bed with a CVS prescription bag next to her. Something was really wrong. He wondered why she didn't tell him that she was sick or had a problem. Chris rounded the bed and squatted next to her with his face close to hers. He kissed her forehead waking her. He could tell that she had cried herself to sleep.

Without saying a word, he stroked her hair, gently pushing it away from her face. He watched her stare at the wall as if she could see into the other room.

"Are you okay?" he finally asked breaking the silence.

She didn't respond. The tears that sleep had bridged were now broken and they began to flow again. Chris sat on the bed then pulled her close to him. She rested her head into the crook of his neck and cried.

"Whatever it is, we can deal with it together. I see the prescription bag, what did the doctor tell you?"

She pulled away and picked up the bag. She opened it and pulled two pill bottles from inside. There was one containing ceftriaxone and another with doxycycline. For cautionary reasons, her doctor gave her treatment for both Chlamydia and Gonorrhea. He explained that these two STD's usually go hand in hand. She clasped the two bottles in her hands, hiding them as though she held something ugly and vile.

She broke her silence.

"The other day something ugly happened. I thought I had dreamt it because I woke up in my bed. I felt strange that morning when I got up, but I passed it off as nothing. I just kept ignoring the signs, but something inside told me to go see my doctor and I did…" she paused looking at the bottles in her hand.

Chris listened intently. He didn't know what to make of her vague recap. She said a whole lot, but told nothing.

"Simone, tell me what happened."

"I didn't want to believe it. But after all that's happened, I knew that it was true."

"Simone, please. I can't take the suspense."

"Chris, someone raped me," she blurted out, no longer yielding her secret. "I don't know what to do."

This was hardly what Chris imagined. He stiffened for a brief second absorbing what Simone had just revealed to him. He knew that he had to pull himself together for both of their sakes. She was carrying that horrible secret around with her, but it was something they both had to deal with. He recounted her words and his attention drew to the bottles she was holding.

"I'm sorry that happened to you. Do you have any idea who did it?"

She sighed and straightened herself.

"No, but…" she hesitated.

Chris started to inquire, but she continued on her own.

"I think Michelle had something to do with it. I think she used something to knock me out the same as she did at your house and had someone rape me."

"Why would she do something like that? What would she benefit in having someone traumatize and abuse you? It makes no sense."

"Yes, it does," she told him holding the bottles toward him. Simone had to be strong to reveal her ugly secret. "The person who raped me had Gonorrhea. It was for you. She wanted me to carry it to you."

"Oh, God, Simone. I am so sorry." He moved closer and held her and she cried in his arms.

"Chris, I'm pregnant."

Before he could catch himself, his mouth flew open. It was obvious that it wasn't his because he always used protection. He also knew that he wasn't infected for that same reason. He was not going to suggest any solutions. This was something she had to decide and live with. Whatever her decision, he was going to be there for her.

"Chris, I'm afraid… afraid to do the wrong thing. There's a life inside me and -"

She looked at him and noticed the ghastly look on his face. This was more than Chris wanted to deal with and Simone realized that she was going to have to make a choice.

"What would you have me to do, Chris?"

His voice was chalky and low.

"I don't know. This is a big decision for you. I have no right making or aiding in a decision like that."

"You have every right to help me decide. We are in this together."

"But only you will carry it."

She knew what he meant by saying that. She would have to carry that burden alone. He was not going to take part in it. He and Ashley were leaving and she would have to look into the eyes of her rapist's child and find love for it, alone. This was harder than she imagined. Before the eyes of God, would he disfavor her if she killed one of His? Would this child be one of His? Or is he doubly cursed at birth? So many thoughts came to her mind, thoughts that would not be answered today, but had to be decided upon soon.

"Chris, if I keep the child will I lose you? Will you take Ashley from me?"

As much as he wanted to say no, the truth was, he would not be able to handle Simone carrying that child. It was bad enough that bastard gave her an STD, but to bury his seed in her womb was too far. How could she even consider keeping it? How could she even want to bring this man's child into the world? Just then, his heart softened. He thought about Ashley and Michelle. He thought about Michelle being pregnant again by him and he knew that he was wrong to feel that way. If he found out that Michelle was carrying another child for him, he would feel the same for that one as he does for Ashley. No matter how he feels about Michelle, it will never make him love his child any less.

"I will be right here, Simone. I'm not going anywhere. You do whatever you feel is best and I will support you one hundred percent."

She jumped into his arms.

"I love you so much. I am glad that all this happened because now I realize just how special you are and no matter what, I am with you forever."

"You need some water to take your medicine?"

"Yes. Thank you."

Chris got up from the bed and placed a kiss on her forehead.

"You know, I have a prescription here for you as well. Just for precautionary reasons. You should have yourself checked out as well."

He smiled at her.

"I'll make arrangements tomorrow."

Chris knew that he was alright, but he knew that he was better safe than sorry. He left the room and went downstairs to the kitchen and fixed a tall glass of water for Simone. He returned with the water and handed it to her.

"Are you in any pain?"

"Only when I go to the bathroom. It burns like hell."

He frowned thinking that it must feel pretty awful. He fought not to feel squeamish around her. He had heard enough about it to know that it was extremely contagious. He explained to Simone that he and Ashley would check up on her, but it was better that they didn't stay over while she was still systematic. He told her to use only white sheets and use bleach to clean them. He also told her to use bleach and disinfectants to clean her tub and toilet as well. He helped her clean and disinfect the house. This was more for his daughter than himself; he wouldn't live with himself if he knew that he allowed something like this to get on his daughter.

Simone understood and did not take offense to his help. In fact, she appreciated it. He handled the news better than she expected.

Chris heated up dinner and woke up Ashley. They sat together at the table.

"Was everything okay, Simone?" Ashley asked.

"Everything is fine now. You are such a wonderful girl, Ashley, and you are a perfect daughter."

Chris smiled at Simone. He knew exactly what she was saying to his daughter. Although her compliment pleased Ashley, she did not grasp the depths of what Simone wanted to say to her.

When dinner was finished, Simone and Ashley went into the living room while Chris cleared the table and washed the dishes.

In the living room, Simone whispered to Ashley that she was

going to marry her father. Ashley grinned brightly at her revelation.

"You are?" she asked thrilled at the news.

"Yes."

"You're ready now?"

"Yep. I am going to be Mrs. Simone Grey Walker."

"Wow! You're going to be my new mom?"

"If you want me to be."

"I do!" she said jumping from the sofa and hurrying into the kitchen to tell her father what Simone had told her. She totally bypassed the concept of whispering. Simone laughed at Ashley's enthusiasm and zeal. She heard her as she excitedly told her father about their discussion. He too thought well of his daughter's acceptance.

After drying the dishes, he went into the living room and sat with Ashley and Simone. He stayed longer than he had planned so they spent the night there.

Chapter Fourteen

Chris stopped by his house before going to work. He went to his answering machine and saw that there were eight calls since yesterday. He checked the ID box and realized that someone from his office called five times. *Probably Mr. Thurman checking up on me.* He saw that Justin had called him as well as Simone earlier that morning. There was another number he didn't recognize. He jotted the number down on a pad he kept next to the phone and placed it into his pocket. After gathering some necessary papers, he left the house and went to work.

Patrice was at her desk and when Chris entered, she stared at him as if she had seen a ghost.

"Good morning, Patrice. Do I have any messages?" Chris asked her hoping to remove that ghastly look from her face."

"Oh, good morning, Mr. Walker. It's so good to see you this morning. How is everything?" she managed after getting herself together.

"Just fine, Patrice. Is Mr. Thurman in?" he asked almost certain that he was.

"He stepped out for a moment. He should be back shortly. Would you like me to notify you when he does?"

"Yes. Thank you."

She handed him his messages and a file. Chris took them from her and went into his office. He was annoyed when he noticed that Michelle had called him. He felt that she had the nerve of calling him after what she put him through yesterday. He had never felt so embarrassed in his entire life. He crumpled up the paper and tossed it into the waste basket beneath his desk.

Mr. Thurman walked in while Chris was sifting through the file. He closed the door then sat down.

"How are you, son?" he asked pulling Chris' attention from his work.

Chris hardly wanted to discuss all that was going on in his life and definitely didn't want a reminder of yesterday's events.

"I'm good," Chris offered trying not to sound dismissive although he really wanted him to leave. "Thanks. How about yourself?"

"Chris, what's going on? I've got the distinct feeling that your life is about to take a disastrous turn if you don't address what is going on here."

"I know, but I don't know what to do. I can't give her my daughter. That's what she wants."

"Did you file the papers necessary to get full custody of her?"

Chris paused while taking a deep breath then forcing it out.

"No. It wasn't necessary when Ashley was born. Michelle had already taken care of that. She had me contacted when the child was about to be born and I signed a paper acknowledging I was the father of the child. Nothing else was necessary concerning paternity. Blood was drawn, which proved that I was indeed the father and that's all she wrote. I didn't think about anything else. I accepted responsibility of my child and I didn't think about Michelle ever trying to take my daughter away. Besides, Ashley would have been an adult when Michelle was scheduled to be released."

"So right now, neither of you have custody?"

"I have assumed custody, but this will probably become an issue of the court."

He nodded, taking in the assessment of his employee and possible partner. Mr. Thurman realized that Chris was a very smart and savvy young man, but he lacked the insight of someone with experience. Chris would have to learn to cover up his emotions and not wear them on his sleeves. Michelle should not have become a thorn in his side nor have him hopping from one foot to the other. She seems to be ten steps ahead of him and if he didn't learn to play the game, she would ruin him.

"Son, you can bet your last dollar that she is going to take you to court and I assure you that she is. You need to start preparation for what is to come. I have a friend who is an excellent family attorney." He handed Chris a card. "Go see him and tell him everything about your situation. He can help you."

Chris took the card and scanned over the text. The name sounded familiar. He was certain that he had heard it before. He went into his briefcase and pulled from it the papers he signed from Michelle's attorney. He handed the papers to Mr. Thurman.

"He's the one I'm up against."

Mr. Thurman located the name and quickly placed the paper on the desk faced down.

"This is going to be tough. He would have been your best bet. Let me talk to him and see if he will tell me anything about this case."

Chris took the papers and placed them in a drawer.

"How is Ashley dealing with all this? Does she know?"

"Yes. She knows some of what's going on, but…" he paused with a sigh, "Ashley likes her mother and she now wants to be with her."

"You're going to have to give her joint custody."

"Then I may totally lose her. Michelle is dangerous. I don't know what she may do to or with my daughter."

"She is still the mother. The court is not going to stop her mother from seeing her. Plus she has a whole lot of money to fight you with. That money is going to be her angle. If it were the case that she had nowhere to live or had to get a job, things might have been different, but none of this is true. She has the money and she's shown a very disciplined love for her unborn child by handing her over to you. In the eyes of the court that is commendable, especially under the circumstances that you two had her."

This was not the kind of battle that Mr. Thurman liked to fight. All odds were against him and as much as he wanted to help Chris, he couldn't.

Patrice interrupted them.

"Mr. Walker, someone is here to drop off a package. He said he can only hand it to you."

Chris got up from his desk and went out to the reception area. He didn't recognize the young man. He looked like a regular messenger. His shirt read Quality Transportation.

"Hi. May I help you?"

"Are you Chris Walker?"

"Yes I am. What can I do for you?" Chris asked while accepting the envelope the young man handed to him.

"You have just been served."

The young man turned on his heels and left the office leaving Chris standing there with the envelope. Chris was infuriated. He returned to his office and slammed the envelope on his desk. Mr. Thurman only watched him. There was nothing he could do to help him in this situation.

"I've just been served," he told his boss.

"I heard. Nothing you can do now more than get an attorney and adhere to the decision. Believe me, this isn't as bad as you think. I'm sure it will bring closure to this chapter. Worse case scenario, you will have to share Ashley. Nothing wrong with that." He didn't wait for Chris to respond. He left him alone in his office and returned to his own.

Chris opened the envelope and retrieved the summons. He had two weeks before the shit hit the fan. He returned the summons to the envelope and tucked it away in his briefcase. In an attempt to distract himself, he began working on some client files.

***

Judge Rachel was having her usual lunch alone at Oikawa Japanese Restaurant. She tilted the small cup of tea to her lips and was suddenly joined by a man she was unfamiliar with.

"Mind if I join you?" he politely asked, taking a seat before she could answer.

She looked up at his attractive features and smiled.

"I guess it's too late to say no."

He waved to the waiter for a menu and quickly browsed its contents. He closed the menu and returned it to the waiter.

"Give me what she's having," he indicated with a tilt of his chin.

The waiter nodded and walked away with the menu.

"So, what can I do for you?"

He absorbed the bitter lines that traced her face. Although her expression was a kind one, he knew that she was not easy. The man reached into his inside jacket pocket and retrieved a manila envelope and placed it on the table in front of the Judge.

She looked down at the envelope.

"What's this? You're dressed too nice to be a mailman or a delivery boy."

He smiled.

"Open it. It won't bite."

"What's in it?"

"A gift."

"What for?"

"For the little deed you are about to do."

"And what is that?"

"Open it."

She gave him a scrutinizing look then reached for the envelope. What harm can looking do anyway? she asked herself. She opened it and there was a single sheet of paper that read $100,000 in cash. This could compromise my entire career and for what? A lousy hundred-thousand dollars? Then again, it would pull me out of the red, she thought. Judge Rachel had accumulated a lot of debt and this was just the break she needed to make her righteous again. She looked up at him.

He now realized that he had her attention.

"You will be presiding over a case in two weeks - Tanner vs. Walker. It's a custody issue. The only thing you have to do is order in the favor of Tanner. She wants full custody."

Judge Rachel mustered through her memory for the details of that case and vividly recalled it. In theory, it wouldn't be difficult to rule in her favor because he did agree to turn the child over to the mother upon her release. She has demonstrated her financial capabilities and a stable environment.

"Done," she answered.

The waiter returned with his tea and Makki. He ate his meal, thanked the judge and got up from the table leaving fifty dollars for the check. After straightening his trousers, he shook her hand.

"I know you have a habit of neglecting your mailbox, but today you should check it. I'm sure you will find something worthwhile in there.

He left the table and returned to his car. Using his car phone, he dialed Michelle's cell phone number. She answered.

"Everything is arranged."

"Thank you. When this is over, there'll be a bonus waiting for you."

"Greatly appreciated," he said and hung up.

***

Principal Carmine called Ashley to the office. She had never been called to his office before and the only time she visited there was when she got into the fight with Tiffany. Her teacher gave her a pass. She took it and hurried downstairs to the office. When she arrived, she was surprised to see her mother standing there. She ran into her arms forgetting that her mother almost sent her father to jail.

"Hey, sweetie. I've missed you so much," she crooned in a velvety tone.

"Me too," Ashley responded. "I can't leave with you," she coyly told her mother remembering Simone's words.

"I know, but that's only for a little while. Soon you will be able to see me whenever you want. How about that?" Michelle told her daughter excitedly. A wide, proud grin spilled across her face as she absorbed Ashley's expression, which actually displayed confused joy.

"Come with me," she told her leading her into the auditorium where they could talk alone.

Ashley sat nervously fidgeting with her skirt.

"There is no need for you to be afraid of me, Ashley. I could never hurt you and would never hurt you."

"But you're hurting my dad. Why did you make the police

come and get him?"

"Is that what he told you?"

She nodded.

"Your dad blames everything on me. Every mistake he makes is my fault. His falling in love with me and making you is my fault. His changing his mind about the relationship is my fault and even his dating my cousin is wrong. Now he wants to take my daughter away."

While Michelle rambled on, she forgot for a moment that she was talking to Ashley. Her tone turned bitter and that saucy, sweet voice she always used when talking to her daughter evaporated.

"Mom, you're scaring me," Ashley pleaded.

Michelle snapped out of her trance.

"Oh, baby, I'm sorry. I didn't mean to make you feel that way. I just get so angry when I think about it."

She took Ashley into her arms.

"Do you love me?"

Ashley nodded yes while in her mother's arms.

"Do you want to live with me?"

Ashley shrugged her shoulders. She had been so preoccupied with meeting her mother and being with her, it never occurred to her that she might not see her dad again.

"Will I still see my dad?"

"Of course, sweetie. I don't want to take you away from him, I want to share him with you."

Buried in her mother's arms, Ashley couldn't see her mother's sinister grin.

"Well, time flies when you're having fun," she told her daughter, noticing her principal standing at the door looking at his watch and indicating to her that her time was up. She nodded and released her daughter. "I'm going to let you return to class. I promised your principal that I wouldn't keep you long."

"You should get back to class. Don't tell your father you saw me, okay?"

Ashley nodded with a look of uncertainty. She knew that she shouldn't be keeping secrets from her dad, but this was her mother.

Besides, he wouldn't be pleased if he knew that she came by the school again. Ashley kissed her mother once again before hurrying off to her class.

Michelle pushed off the tiny seat and met with Principal Carmine at the door. She extended her hand out to him.

"That was very nice of you to let me speak to Ashley."

He curled her hand up to his lips and pressed a kiss on the back of her hand.

"It was my pleasure. Anything I can do to help a student such as your daughter will always be a pleasure. So you and her father are no longer involved?" he asked with his motive clinging to his face like a mask.

"No. We've parted long ago. My mother was sick during the time Ashley was born and I left town to take care of her. Chris took on the responsibility of caring for our daughter until my mother recovered. She died a few months ago."

"That's terrible. I'd love to take you to dinner some time," he told her, changing the subject.

"That sounds wonderful, but I'm currently seeing someone."

"Oh. Well, it was a pleasure meeting Ashley's beautiful mother. I can see where she gets her looks from. I won't hold you up any longer. If you change your mind, my offer is still open."

"Thank you, again."

He stepped aside so that she could pass. He walked with her to the door discussing briefly Ashley's outstanding academics and the settled dispute she had with one of the students.

Michelle exited the building with Principal Carmine waving at the door. She could feel his eyes tracing every detail of her well-formed body. She opened her Mercedes door and got in. Within seconds, she sped down the street leaving the school distant in her mirror.

***

Simone arrived to pick up Ashley from school. After waiting

for fifteen minutes, she went to the office to see why it was taking Ashley so long to come out. She ran into Ashley's teacher at the door as she was entering.

"Where's Ashley?"

"You didn't take her?" The teacher said casually. "She left a little while ago."

"Who picked her up?" Simone became emphatic. The teacher's nonchalance was annoying, especially since she recognized the panic she was displaying.

"Oh, yes, that's right, her dad came by to pick her up."

Simone immediately changed mood and offered her apologies. She totally forgot that Chris had told her that he would be picking Ashley up this week. She returned to her car and went to see Chris.

Chapter Fifteen

Two weeks flew by quickly. Chris had gotten Ashley up early and combed her hair. Although Simone was there, he wanted to do it himself. He pulled her hair into one ponytail and let her curls fall freely onto her shoulders. He stared at her reflection in the vanity and noticed that there was a strange anticipation in her eyes. It was as if she knew of some turn of events that would change everything she knew and she was the least bit worried about it. There was no question in his mind that Michelle had gotten to his daughter and she was anticipating a reunion with her mother. After watching her reflection in the mirror and seeing how mature she looked with her hair spilling on her shoulders, he then twisted her curls together and wrapped them around the ball barrette that held her hair together. Just as he expected, the innocence he cherished about her returned.

"What's wrong, Dad?" Ashley asked seeing the trepidation in his eyes. He looked as though he didn't expect to see her again.

"Honey, I know that this is too much for you to understand right now, but I want you to know that no matter what happens today, I will always love you and you will always be my daughter."

"I know, Dad."

"Your mom may have told you some ugly things about me, but I have always loved you and always will. There was never a moment since you were born that I regretted you being here. You are the one thing that I am thankful for that has come from your mother."

He gently kissed her.

"Wait here. I have something that I want you to have."

"He went into his room and found his mother's charm necklace that held his picture. He placed it around her neck."

She lifted it gingerly and pulled it into view. She opened the heart and peered at the tiny picture of her dad. He looked so much like her when he was young.

"Thank you, Dad. I will never take it off."

"I know you won't. Come on, it's time to go. I don't want to be late."

Simone entered Ashley's room.

"Chris, it's time to go. It'll be alright. Stop worrying. There is no way the judge is going to take Ashley away from you. Come on, I'll drive."

Simone was nervous about this whole ordeal herself. She knew how sinister her cousin was and she also knew that she would do anything it took to get whatever she was after. They took Simone's Caravan and Ashley got in the back and Chris got in next to her so that he could comfort her. Simone didn't mind, she knew that Chris was very worried about his daughter. She dropped Chris off at the court doors and went to park the Caravan. Chris held Ashley's hand as they mounted the court steps. They went through metal detectors and were given a calendar. Chris scanned over the list for his name. When he found it, he went to the appropriate courtroom. He and Ashley sat in the rear of the courtroom.

***

Simone found a parking spot two blocks from the court. After parking, she stepped out of the Caravan and a silver Mercedes pulled into the spot two cars ahead of hers. As she neared the car, the door swung open and Michelle stepped out. She had loosened her braids and had her hair wrapped. Her long hair fell softly over her shoulders and down her back. She had apparently cut it a little so that it wouldn't fall past her butt. She wore tall, mint green sling backs, and sheer stockings that were perfectly sheer with a very faint shimmer when she stepped. Her long, curvy legs moved smoothly under her mint green, tapered suit. She twisted her hips as she walked. She stopped in front of Simone with a very confident look in her eyes as they twinkled.

"Hello, Simone. I'm so glad you could make it."

"You know all this that you're doing is only going to hurt

Ashley."

"No. It's going to hurt Chris. Ashley is going to be with her mother," Michelle retorted. "You would understand that if you had stayed off his dick. I don't blame you, that shit is magical. I kind of miss it myself. Of course I did appreciate that little piece you gave me. For that, I'm going to let you live."

"If I can help it, you are not going to get Ashley."

Michelle smiled and shook her head.

"And what are you going to do, Simone? You're damaged goods. You can't go around fucking your clients. I don't suggest you speak on that at all. I'll bury your career if you do. Besides, I've got all that worked out. You know I'm always on top of my game. I don't want to be late so I'll see you inside."

She stepped off leaving Simone at her heels. She turned to face Simone again.

"You know, I let you beat me the other day at your house. I just needed to get that off my chest. You could never really beat me."

"You don't think so, huh? How about we find out right now?" Simone said stepping up close to Michelle.

"Calm down, little bitch. There will be enough time for that. I don't want to mess up my suit and I don't want my daughter to think I've been roughhousing when there is something as important as a court date needing to be settled."

"Michelle, I can smell the fear all over you and you could never beat me. I don't care how many years you spent in jail lifting weights. Don't forget who used to protect your coward ass."

Michelle laughed and turned away from her. When she rounded the corner, she saw her attorney waiting for her by the steps. When she got close to him, he kissed her politely on the cheek.

"You look wonderful, Ms. Tanner. Are you ready?"

"Absolutely."

They climbed the steps together with Simone at their heels. When Simone entered the courtroom, she saw Chris talking with his attorney. She joined them, sitting next to Ashley.

"How are you, kid?" she whispered. "I know all this is frightening for you, but everything is going to be alright. Your dad is a good man and a great father. No one is going to take you away from him." She squeezed her hand then put her arm around her.

Michelle walked in and the pleasant floral fragrance she wore caused everyone in the room to turn around and take notice of her. Chris also noticed her as she entered. She smiled and winked at him as she passed. When she got eyeshot of Ashley beside him, she stopped and blew a kiss to her daughter and motioned her lips to say, "I love you."

Chris turned to face his daughter and noticed that her entire demeanor had changed. She watched as her mother took a seat toward the front in the row to the right. Her expression showed longing for her mother. It was then that he felt he was going to lose his daughter to Michelle even if the court ruled against it.

The judge entered the courtroom. Five cases were heard before theirs, which took up most of the morning. After a fifteen-minute break, the judge returned and the case of Tanner vs. Walker was called. Chris and his attorney moved to the table across from Michelle and her attorney. Ashley sat next to Simone behind Chris.

The judge scanned over the documents.

"Ms. Tanner, you are seeking full custody of your daughter Ashley."

"Yes, Your Honor."

"Is she here today?"

"Yes, she is," she responded, indicating with a point of her finger at her daughter, which prompted Simone to tighten her arm around Ashley.

"Chris Walker, you are countering with a request of no visitation."

"Yes, Your Honor." He sat down and noticed Michelle watching him and he turned away from her.

"Ms. Tanner, you are aware that you are still under the boundaries of the parole board?"

"Yes. I am."

"You also know that you will have to provide proof of adequate means of support for this child and a stable home as well."

"We have all of that information here, Your Honor," The attorney spoke up extending the papers for the bailiff to take and give to the judge.

The bailiff took the papers to the judge and she scanned over the bank statements and personal assets records.

"The documents provided prove that you are financially capable of taking care of your daughter. However, I need to question your reasons for wanting to take your daughter away from her father. According to the papers they submitted from her school and her medical records, she has been well cared for. She appears to be in a very stable environment."

"Your Honor, if I may," Michelle's attorney began, "Ms. Tanner did the responsible thing in account of her daughter by providing information about her daughter's father. She contacted someone from Social Services to get in contact with him so that her child would not have to be moved from home to home through the system. She wanted the best possible home for her child and she placed her in the temporary care of her biological father. He agreed to the terms offered him in regard to their daughter. I have here a copy of the signed agreement." He held it up for the bailiff to take to the judge. She looked over the documents and noted the highlighted areas of the agreement where Chris Walker agreed to care for the daughter until Michelle Tanner was released or paroled.

"Ms. Tanner, your daughter is ten-years-old now and she is accustomed to the rules and care of her father. A positive relationship would need to be developed between you and your daughter with counseling before this arrangement can be made."

The attorney again responded.

"Ms. Tanner has met with her daughter on numerous occasions and has had positive connection. Ashley has expressed enthusiasm about being with her mother. In fact, it can be a remedy for the feelings of incompleteness she has expressed to her school counselor. More than that, Your Honor, she has been in a fight with another student about her not having a mother. All Ms. Tanner is asking for is a chance to be the mother Ashley needs."

She nodded.

"Thank you. I would like to hear from Mr. Walker now." She turned to Chris. "Mr. Walker, you are requesting that Ashley's mother be denied the right to see her child. Why?"

"Your Honor," Chris' attorney began, "Michelle Tanner has been convicted of a horrible crime against another human being. Her tactics can be lethal in instances where she does not get her way. She has also been suspected by Chris Walker of killing his mother, her daughter's grandmother."

"I have a copy of the transcript and that issue was found inconclusive. I sympathize with Mr. Walker's grievance, but that has no bearings on this issue," the Judge retorted.

"Your Honor, Ms. Tanner has used poor and unethical tactics in seeing her daughter. She has exposed her to lying and deceiving her father. She took Ashley from school without permission, leaving her father in a panic and her unannounced presence has caused a great deal of mayhem in the Walker household. If these are the type of tactics and examples Ms. Tanner is going to instill in her child, her best interests are in the custody of her father. This kind of drastic change can be detrimental to the child's normal development."

"I want to hear from Mr. Walker. Mr. Walker, you agreed to the terms stated by Ms. Tanner in respect to her child. At the time, you didn't have any concerns about her mother caring for the child. Why do you have these concerns now?"

"Your Honor, at the time, Ms. Tanner was at the last stages of her pregnancy and labor was expected very soon. I was given the honor of caring for my child and that was the only thing I thought about at the time, not whether or not her mother would be trying to take her away from me later or even that she was a terrible person. My concern was that I had a child coming into the world and it was a horrible thought to see her grow up in the system when she has a loving, able father to care for her. I love my daughter more than my own life and if I thought that her mother was a missing part of her life or could even do a better job at caring for her, I would unselfishly give her my Ashley. But I know Michelle, her only objective here is to punish me. She doesn't care about Ashley's well being; otherwise she would realize that taking her away from me is the worst thing she could do. She would consider Ashley's accomplishments. She is a wonderful child and she makes me so very proud everyday, not just with her grades, but her entire personality. Ever since her mother has been out of prison, she has done nothing shy of corrupting our daughter. She lies to me, she hides things from me and all of this had been hard on her. She cries at night, she sometimes goes through emotional changes because she doesn't know if she should love her father or her mother. I have never, in the past ten years, tried to turn Ashley away from her mother. I have protected her from her mother's ugly past. It is only since Michelle's pending release that I have found it necessary to tell my daughter about her mother. All I want is what's best for my daughter. She is a loving child. I only want my daughter to have a chance to be a smart, healthy young lady and eventually a woman. I don't want her to feel that she has to lie to get what she wants or hurt other people because she's afraid they won't understand how she feels."

Chris fought to control his emotions. His response was heartfelt by everyone in the courtroom including Michelle. For a moment, she felt herself shrinking in her seat. Tears flowed from her eyes and she dabbed at the tears that revealed the hurt she felt. She always knew that Chris would make a wonderful father. He really did love their daughter and care for her, but she had to punish him for the hurt he put her through. Ashley was her daughter and if it wasn't for her unyielding love for him, none of this would be happening; there would have been no wasted ten years, no Ashley and definitely no courtroom. She looked over at her daughter safe within the arms of her traitor cousin. That sight reminded Michelle of her goal.

Judge Rachel acknowledged both statements and went to her chambers to evaluate the documents. She knew that the right thing in this case would be to leave the daughter in the custody of her father, but denying visitation would be unsound. Her inclination was to favor Chris Walker's petition. However, stuck to the back of

Michelle's papers was a yellow sticker that read, Remember our agreement, and that reminded her of her deal.

***

Chris was shaking all over. He could not make any sense of this whole situation. The judge didn't seem to favor either of their requests. He turned back to look at his daughter. There was a well of fear in her eyes. Her trapped tears revealed her trepidation. Simone also had an uncertain look of fear. Even Chris' Attorney seemed undecided of the events. Chris cut his eyes over to the other table and noted that Michelle was calm, too calm under the circumstances. She seemed to have a sure card. The judge reentered the courtroom. After sitting, she started her deliberation.

"Mr. Walker, I totally appreciate your heartfelt expression for your daughter. I also commend you for stepping up to the plate to take responsibility for your child. Everything that you have presented to the court today reflects your effective parenthood."

She turned to Michelle with a very controlled, brooding look on her face.

"In lieu of the documents provided, I have ruled in favor of the prescribed signed documents. Ashley Walker will be turned over to Michelle Tanner with full custody effective today."

A rue of cries broke out in the court. Chris screamed out his objection with his horrid cry. Ashley jumped from her seat and ran to her father. She had never in all her days heard him cry out like that. She feared for him. Simone also let her regret manifest with tears. She cried silently. There was murmuring within the listeners in the courtroom. They too muttered amongst themselves their distaste.

"Chris Walker will be allowed weekend visits commencing after a two-month-period. This will allow the mother to bond with her child and for the child to become adjusted to her new environment."

The bailiff took the endorsed papers from the judge and took them over to Michelle.

"This hearing is adjourned," the judge finalized.

Chris didn't hear anything else after her decision. He held firmly to his daughter while she was pulled away from him by Michelle. Ashley fought to go to her father, but Michelle pulled and hurried her out of the courtroom. She screamed for her father, but his attorney held him. Things got out of control quickly. Chris struck his attorney and leaped from his seat and hurried after his daughter. Simone ran behind him trying to stop him. Three court officers ran behind both of them blocking them from the doors. One officer caught hold of Chris and forced him to the floor. He used his two hundred and ninety pounds toward his advantage over Chris. He pressed his forearm behind his head while another officer controlled his arms.

"Calm down, buddy. Calm down. Don't get yourself arrested. Take it easy." He held him to the floor with his arm still pinned behind him. "These things can be appealed."

Simone approached the struggle.

"He's okay now, get off of him!"

The officer finally released Chris and Simone knelt in front of him.

"Chris, I am so sorry."

"Get away from me, Simone. This is entirely your fault. You are the one who brought me the papers to sign. You are the one who took my daughter to see her mother. You are the one who gave her the advantage over me. You helped her steal my daughter away from me. Be sorry for Ashley."

He pushed her away from him and got up from the floor.

"But, Chris!" Simone cried.

"What am I supposed to do now? What do I have now? You? How can I love you now?"

He walked away from her.

She got up quickly and hurried over to him.

"Chris, we'll get her back. Michelle isn't going to hurt Ashley. She does love her."

"Simone, I don't want to talk to you. My life is worthless now. You have stolen my life from me with your ignorance."

"You're angry right now. Let me take you home."

"Why? So you can try to seduce me and make me forget that I've just lost my daughter? Well that's not happening, Simone. You have rolled with me for the last time. Get lost. Go find your cousin and share in her celebration. Tell her that she won. Tell her that she's finally paid me back for not loving her. Tell her that she's taken the only thing that mattered to me. You two celebrate that because it was the both of you that pulled this scandalous thing off. I hate you and wouldn't dare let you set foot in my house ever again. Stay away from me!"

He left the court and walked until his legs hurt, that was two and a half miles later. He wanted to die. His mother was gone, Keesha was gone and now his daughter. Everyone that meant anything to him was gone. His dad was even gone. He had nobody.

A cab pulled up to where he was standing at the corner.

"Sir, you need a cab."

Chris snapped out of his stupor. He walked over to the cab, opened the door and got in.

"Where are you going, sir?" the driver asked. She could see that her passenger had a lot on his mind.

Chris gave the driver his address then sat back into the cushions of the town car. The young woman became inquisitive of his worries.

"Mister, if you don't mind, I was wondering what could have an attractive man like yourself this upset."

He looked into the rearview mirror into the woman's eyes.

"Why, should attractive men not have any worries?"

"No, they shouldn't. Women would do anything to protect them and keep them happy."

"Women are usually the problem," he retorted. "Listen, I really don't mean to be rude or disrespectful to you, but I'm not in much of a dialogue mood. I'd like to just ride in silence."

"Okay. Sorry about that."

She pulled up to Chris' house. Chris handed her three tens and got out of the car.

"Thanks for stopping for me."

"Don't worry about it. Your friend asked me to offer you a ride."

"What friend?"

"The young lady driving the purple Caravan."

"Thank you," he said again then turned to walk up his driveway. He found his keys and opened the door and went into his home. All of his bottled up emotions surged forward. He started knocking things down and banging on the walls as he moved through the house. He went to the basement and retrieved his shotgun. He wanted to kill Michelle. She is a sneaky, conniving bitch and she now has my daughter in her clutches, he thought. She pulled my Ashley away from me screaming and I have to protect her no matter what the court says. She's my daughter. I took care of her, raised her and taught her everything she knows. I'm so sorry, baby. Chris slid down in the corner and wept. He held the shotgun upright between his legs with the barrel's opening pointing toward the ceiling. He would kill Michelle, but he had no idea where to find her.

***

Ashley's cry had finally calmed down to a quiet sniffle. She sat curled up on the sofa with her face hidden behind her palms and knees. She was so angry at her mother for hurting her father. She had never seen him cry like that. She occasionally peeked out from between her fingers at her mother who left her to cry alone. Michelle moved through the house casually as if she didn't notice her daughter shudder when she passed by.

Michelle hated to see her daughter crying like that. Today's event was far too traumatic for such a young girl. She sat on the sofa next to her and tried to pull Ashley into her arms, but she stiffened her body so that her mother had difficulty moving her.

"Ashley, don't fight me. I didn't do this to hurt you. I know how you feel, but how about how this makes me feel?"

Ashley didn't release her restraint. She continued to pull away from her mother and prevented her from holding her. Michelle moved closer to her so that she no longer needed to pull her daughter to her. She started to speak, but Ashley pulled from her arms and quickly sprinted up the stairs into the room she slept in before and fell onto the bed and started crying into the pillow. Michelle followed behind Ashley and stood in front of her room. She watched hurtfully at her daughter's display of anguish. Michelle respected her daughter's loyalty to her father. She surmised that trait as one of her own, and for that reason she would not be mad at her. She entered the room and sat on the side of the bed. She rested her hand on her daughter's back and began her act of consoling.

"I thought you wanted this. I thought you wanted to live with me and to be my precious little girl. You know all I've ever wanted in this world was to have a beautiful little girl that I could dress up, hang out with and become best friends with. Your dad was the selfish one. At least I left opportunity for you to see him; he wanted to prevent me from ever seeing you again. I couldn't let that happen. I carried you in my belly for nine full months and I made the biggest sacrifice to let you stay with him. You know, I could have kept you with me for two full years, but I thought about you. I didn't want you to spend even a day in that horrible place. You are a princess and you deserve the best. I know your dad loves you, but so do I. He couldn't possibly love you as much as I do. I took every pain in stride as I brought you into this world. There is nothing more precious to me than you. I know that you're hurting right now so I'm going to leave you alone. You cry all you need to and when you're ready, I will be right here waiting for my baby."

Michelle got up from the bed. She leaned down and kissed the back of Ashley's head then left her to cry herself to sleep. Tomorrow she would feel a whole lot better, and with all that I have planned for her, she will forget about the tragic events of today.

Chapter Sixteen

Keesha became really concerned when Patrice told her that Chris had taken two weeks off after losing his daughter in a custody battle. She explained that Ashley's mother was given full custody and had a two-month delay before visitation could commence. Keesha phoned Jamal at the office.

"Honey, something terrible has happened," Keesha began when Jamal came on the line.

"What do you mean? Are you or the kids hurt?"

"No. It's Chris," she stammered.

"Sweetheart, Chris is okay, he can handle -"

"He lost Ashley to Michelle!"

"He what? How could that happen?"

"I don't know, but he just took two weeks off from work and he's not answering his phone. Jamal, I'm afraid that he is going to do something terrible."

"Okay. I'm on my way. You don't do anything until I get there, promise?"

"I promise. Jamal, please hurry."

***

Jamal looked over his calendar. There was nothing pressing that Dr. Rich couldn't handle. He cleared his calendar and had Linda to coordinate his calendar with the rest of the staff. He told her that he would be away for a week. He then went to his car and hurried home. When he arrived, Keesha had already packed their bags.

"You took the kids next door?"

"Yes. Mrs. Ambrose said that she could keep them for us this week"

Jamal drove the Escalade to New York. He had no idea what to expect. He had only met Chris once and that was on uncertain terms. Barging in on his personal life was probably going to be a big mistake, but if he didn't, Keesha would never let him live it down. They arrived at Chris' house around eight o'clock. Keesha wouldn't hear of them going to a hotel before stopping by.

When Jamal parked, Keesha immediately hopped from the Escalade. Jamal caught hold of her waist and they both mounted the steps. Jamal rang the bell then waited. No one answered the door. Chris' car was in the yard so he knew that someone was home. He rang the bell again. The chime was loud enough for anyone to hear.

"Jamal, I think something is wrong. We've got to get in there."

"Keesha, we can't just break into his house. What if he shoots us?"

"Jamal, please."

He shrugged his shoulders.

"Okay, hand me your ring," he told her. Keesha pulled off her engagement ring and handed it to Jamal. She wondered what he wanted it for. He turned the ring sideways and, using the edge of the diamond, ran it across the glass in a wide circle. He then held his elbow up and forced it into the cut glass. It crashed in and fell onto the carpet on the inside. Jamal looked into the house for any movement. When he was comfortable that no one was there, he reached in and unlocked the door. He cautiously pushed the door open and Keesha moved around him and called out Chris' name. He didn't respond.

"Stay behind me," Jamal told Keesha holding her arm. They moved into the kitchen and noticed there were dishes in the sink that had not been washed. The trashcan was full of empty beer cans and vodka bottles. The stale scent of liquor was in the air. All of the windows were closed preventing the circulation of fresh air. Jamal went to the kitchen window and opened it and he did the same in the living room. Suddenly he noticed the loaded shotgun on the table. He turned the light switch on and observed the surroundings. There was no indication of struggle. Keesha started up the stairs and Jamal moved up the stairs behind her.

They looked into the first bedroom, which was apparently

Chris' room. There was no sign of him. They went to the next room, which was Ashley's. Chris was sitting down on the floor with pictures shredded all around him. He looked terrible and uncared for.

Keesha entered the room and knelt in front of him. She held him tight and he let all of his hurt rush forward.

"Chris, it's going to be okay. I'm here."

"She was screaming for me and I couldn't help her. She didn't want to go."

"I know, sweetie. I've lost everyone, you, my mom, Ashley, Simone. I have no one."

"It's okay."

"It's not okay, Keesha. I feel like I'm about to lose my mind. I'm trying to do what's right, but I can't. I'm not going to let Michelle keep my daughter."

Jamal entered the room and stood behind Keesha.

"Honey, wait for me downstairs."

Keesha turned around and looked up at Jamal. His face was serious and she saw something she had never seen in him before.

"Jamal, I was…"

"Please, Keesha. Everything is going to be fine."

She stood up and slowly walked out of the room. Jamal waited until he heard Keesha's footsteps on the carpet below. He reached down and quickly caught hold of Chris' shirt and snatched him up from the ground. Before Chris could react, he flung him onto the bed and leaned down close to his face.

"You are going to pull yourself together right now. How the hell do you expect to get your daughter back acting like this?"

Chris brought up his knee into Jamal's stomach forcing him to let go. He then pounced onto him with his fist and knocked him down on the bed.

"How dare you come in here demanding I do something? You stole her from me."

Jamal blocked the punch that was aimed right for his eye. He kicked Chris backward causing him to stumble into Ashley's vanity. Jamal quickly sprung up from the bed and hurried over to Chris. The two men struggled back and forth trying to gain control of the other. They kicked, flipped, yoked and punched at each other until they stumbled out of the room and into the hallway.

"Your concern is Ashley," he said punching Chris in the stomach, which knocked the wind out of him. "And if you don't pull yourself together you are going to lose her permanently. Is that what you want, man?" Jamal said collapsing next to Chris on the floor. They both were out of breath. "Man, I'm sorry that you keep being dealt a bad hand, but I know that if I lost my two babies that I would die. I know that's how you feel right now, but this is not the way to fix things. We'll get Ashley back and you won't have to go to jail in the process."

Chris laughed. He couldn't believe Jamal was ripping this bull off on him.

"How did you expect to help me? By beating the crap out of me while I'm drunk?"

"Beating the crap out of you? Man, have you had any pussy lately? You've got a whole lot of built-up power in you. Where's your girl, man? You should be married by now."

Chris smiled weakly.

"When I lost Ashley, I told my lady that I never wanted to see her again."

"Why did you do that?"

"Because it was her fault that I lost Ashley in the first place. She's Michelle's cousin."

Jamal shook his head.

"Man, you always got drama. Why the devil would you get involved with Michelle's cousin? That's plain crazy."

"I know. She was the social worker that told me about Michelle's delivery date and petitioned me to come and get my daughter. I had no idea that she was Michelle's cousin until she confessed it a week or so ago, but the damage was already done. I signed papers agreeing to return Ashley back to her mother when she was released."

"Why did you do that?"

"I didn't think about it. Michelle was supposed to be in prison for twenty years. By then, Ashley would have been old enough to make her own decisions. It was a fruitless threat that backfired."

"Well, Michelle is about to lose her mind."

"What do you mean?" Chris asked Jamal.

"You want your daughter back, right? Well, I'm going to help you get her back using the same system she used against you."

"How are you going to do that?"

"I'm a doctor, remember?"

Jamal held his closed fist foward and Chris did the same.

"Now, I'm not as young as you. Can you help an old man up?"

Chris pulled himself up although his stomach ached. He held his hand out for Jamal to take hold of, then pulled him to his feet.

"Thanks, man," Jamal told him.

"Thank you for coming. I guess this was Keesha's idea."

"Yeah, she was afraid you were going to do something crazy. I guess she was right."

"Well, thanks for kicking my ass."

"Anytime. I'm going to kick it again if you don't stop whining about my wife."

Chris laughed.

"I will always love her, man…but I know that she's your wife."

"What about that social worker? Are you going to call her?"

"I don't know."

"Everyone makes mistakes and the important thing is that she told you. She didn't have to do that. In my book, she betrayed family for love."

Chris' eyes became distant as he thought about Simone. He thought that maybe he had been just a little harsh. The two men stayed in Ashley's bedroom and picked up the things they had knocked down. Chris then straightened his daughter's bedding. Jamal picked up the torn pictures. He noticed the familiar face.

"Michelle hasn't changed a bit, has she?"

"Yeah, she's gotten worse."

He looked at a recent picture of Ashley.

"She is a gorgeous little girl. She looks a lot like you."

"I know, but she looks a whole lot more like her mother if you see them together."

Chris left Jamal upstairs and found Keesha in the living room looking over some pictures of his mother. He sat next to her on the sofa.

"Thanks for coming."

She patted his hand which rested on his lap.

"There is no need to thank me. You will always be my family. Our family," she said smiling up at Jamal who now descended the last step."

"Jamal's been treating you good. It shows."

"She deserves to be treated with the best," Jamal added, joining the conversation. "I owe you a glass," he stated pointing to the door.

"You broke the glass?" Chris responded half believing him.

"I had no choice. You didn't answer the doorbell. I couldn't have Keesha outside all night. We'll stop at Home Depot and get whatever it takes to fix it."

"You guys want anything from the kitchen?" Chris asked while changing the subject.

"Yes," Keesha answered. "I'll go with you." She looked at Jamal and he knew that she wanted to talk with Chris alone. She followed him into the kitchen and took a seat at the table. Chris went into the cabinet and pulled out a few teabags and placed them into the boiling water. He then took out three mugs for the tea.

"So much time has gone by. I can't believe it's been ten years since I've seen you."

He turned to face her and his heart melted.

"I know. Unnecessary time. I'm sorry about the way I acted at my mother's funeral. I shouldn't have blamed you for what happened to my mother. That was wrong. I guess the truth is I couldn't handle losing everything at the same time. But it was never your fault. I don't regret a moment we spent together. In fact, they were some of the most memorable times of my life and for them I am eternally grateful."

"I don't regret any of it either, and if not for the circumstances, I would have proudly married you. You were a wonderful man then and you are an even more wonderful man now because you are also a loving and kind father."

They shared an awkward moment thinking about the past.

"How did you find out that Michelle got Ashley?"

"Patrice told me. I called to see how you were doing and she told me that Ashley's mother got custody and that you took time off. I was afraid that…" she paused not wanting to tell him the horrible thing she imagined him doing. "So, tell me about this woman you've been seeing. Do you want to marry her?"

"I do. I love her a lot and she's just perfect with Ashley. She's really something. I want you to meet her before you go."

"I would love that. I mean, I can't have just any woman taking your hand."

He laughed. His mother would have said the same thing.

"Keesha, all my life I've been taught to be responsible, to do the right thing, and to do unto others as I would want them to do to me, but right now I can't."

His mind drifted to the look on Michelle's face when she pulled his daughter away from him screaming. The torment in Ashley's eyes and the look of vulnerability he saw clearly.

"Keesha, I want to kill Michelle."

"You won't have to," Jamal interrupted. They had been in the kitchen whispering long enough. At least it sounded like whispering to Jamal. "We'll take away her mind."

"How do you propose we do that?"

"Drugs."

"Michelle doesn't take drugs," Chris defended.

"Maybe not knowingly."

"She isn't going to let me near her or Ashley and I can't take Ashley right now anyway according to court mandate. She's allowed two months to bond with Ashley and by then it may be too late. I know my daughter very well. Because of the way Michelle took her, she is going to be rebellious. The problem is I don't know what Michelle would do if she pushed her too far."

"Ashley is still in school, isn't she?"

"Yes."

"Then you've got access to her."

"Michelle will cover that base. She will probably wave her court order to the principal and request that I don't see her."

"She can't do that. Just talk to Ashley and see what's been going on. Find out how her mother's treating her."

"Tell me more about the drugs. What did you have in mind?"

"Something untraceable, something that is so natural that it would have to be an accident."

"I'm listening," Chris retorted.

By then, the water began to boil. Chris poured tea into the three mugs and placed them in front of Keesha and Jamal with one additional cup in his place setting.

"Jamal, stop it. If you did that, you would be no different than Michelle is. That's not the way to get Ashley back by destroying her mother. What if she dies? Can either of you live with that?"

Jamal and Chris looked from one to the other then at Keesha who was standing now with her hand rested on her hip.

"Yes!" they synchronized.

She hit them both on the shoulder and sat down.

"Well, I'm not having it. You two are going to have to come up with something better."

Keesha finished her tea.

"I'm tired. I'm going to lay down."

She headed upstairs and to the left, which was the guest bedroom. Keesha went in and fell across the bed. Chris and Jamal talked for another hour then they too turned in for the night.

***

It was ten o'clock the next morning and Ashley had not emerged from her room. Michelle had fixed breakfast early and it had gone cold. She felt a little annoyed that Ashley was acting selfishly, but she tried to understand how Ashley felt. She climbed the stairs and went to Ashley's room. Ashley was in the same tight position she was in the night before. It was as if she was afraid to move. Upon seeing her, Michelle knew that she was awake. She squatted in front of her and called her name.

Ashley didn't respond. She lay stiff, loathing what her mother had done. She forgot all about the excitement she felt when her mother visited her school the other day. The desire she held to be with her mother diminished in the courtroom when she was pulled away from her crying father. Deep inside she felt awful, now remembering something her father had told her before, When you keep secrets, you only hurt yourself because no one can save you from what they don't understand. Ashley stared at her pillow ignoring her mother's words. She could hear the annoyance in her voice as she continued to talk to her. Her words were muttered behind Ashley's silent scream. Her eyes burned from crying and they felt as though they had closed up and she couldn't see. She badly wanted to tell her mother to let her call her father, but she knew that her mother wasn't going to let that happen. Her mother's hate for Chris was in her eyes as she walked away from him in court. Ashley pleaded with Simone with her eyes to save her, but Simone only sat in her seat crying and covering her face. Nothing could be done; she was going to her mother's house forever and would never see her father again.

Michelle fought to control her fury. She was not going to let her ten-year-old daughter manipulate her and she was not going to drive her crazy either. Ashley was going to learn that she had to follow her rules now. She pulled Ashley up from her pillow and turned her to face her. She could see the hatred in her daughter's eyes, but this did not deter her from making her point.

"Ashley, I want you to stop this nonsense right now. I am your mother and I will not have you disrespecting me. You will act like my little girl and not some snotty nose brat that cries when she can't have her way. You had all night to cry, but now you will stop it. I am going to fix your bath water for you. After your bath, you will come downstairs and eat the breakfast I fixed for you this morning. Do you understand me?" she demanded an answer from her daughter. Michelle's face was mean and agitated. She knew that if Ashley didn't comply that things were going to get ugly very fast. This was not the relationship she wanted to have with her daughter, but she left her no choice. She was not going to spend an entire day fighting with her for every little thing.

Ashley nodded, now afraid of her mother. She has never seen such anger before. Even when her dad was upset with her, he didn't scrunch up his face like that or make his eyes narrow the way her mother did just now. She fought to keep from screaming, only the new flow of tears showed the hurt she felt.

Once satisfied, Michelle released her grasp of Ashley's arm. She didn't say another word while leaving the room. She went to the bathroom and filled the tub with warm water and bubbles. She returned to Ashley's room and retrieved an outfit. Ashley cut her eye at the outfit her mother pulled from the closet. It had a short, cropped top that would fall above her belly, and the pants didn't have a waist ban. She didn't want to put on that outfit because Simone told her that her father didn't want her to dress like that. She lowered her head and cried even more.

Michelle placed the outfit in the bathroom.

"Ashley, your bath is ready. I want you to go right now and get into the tub and clean up."

Ashley didn't respond. She slid off the bed and moved past her mother toward the bathroom. She was so scared that she was shaking inside. Michelle turned away from her and went downstairs to the kitchen. She didn't want to slap her daughter, but she felt that she was trying her very last nerve.

Ashley went into the bathroom and closed and locked the door. As she pulled her clothes off, she noticed that Michelle had left the cordless phone in the basket by the tub. She leaned against the door and listened for Michelle. When she was certain that Michelle was nowhere around, she quickly dialed her father's number. The phone rang three times before Chris answered the phone.

"Hello," Chris responded groggily. "Who is this?"

"Daddy," Ashley sobbed.

Chris sprung up at attention and grasped the phone close to his ear. All sleep disappeared at the sound of his daughter's voice.

"Honey, what's wrong?"

"Daddy, I'm scared. Please come and get me." Ashley began sobbing uncontrollably. She covered her mouth with her hand and fought to stay quiet. "Daddy, I'm sorry I lied to you. I'm sorry I didn't tell you that mommy came to the school. I love you, Daddy, and I want to come home."

Chris felt sick. He hurried over to his closet and pulled on a pair of jeans and a t-shirt.

"Honey," he coaxed, "where are you? What street are you on? Do you know the address?"

Ashley cried. "No."

"Where is Michelle?"

"She's downstairs. She's angry with me and she squeezed my arm and it hurts."

Chris was enraged. He would kill Michelle for hurting his baby. He understood her being angry with him, but hurting an innocent child was beyond forgiveness.

"I'm coming, honey. I'll find you. Stop crying. I'm coming."

Suddenly, Chris heard the door bust open and Michelle begin yelling at Ashley. He then heard Michelle slap the phone away from his daughter. Ashley shrieked in pain and everything fell silent.

"Hello! Hello!" Chris called into the receiver. There was no noise. He yelled into the phone again. He slammed the phone down onto the nightstand and put on his sneakers. Jamal heard the noise and hurried to Chris' room, with Keesha at his heels, to see what was going on.

"What's up, man? What happened?"

"Ashley just called me. She's terrified of Michelle. She said Michelle squeezed her arm and wanted to come home. I just heard Michelle strike her."

Jamal became angered too. He couldn't believe that Michelle

would do something as horrible as that to her own daughter. Keesha was trembling all over. She feared for what Chris might do if he got to Michelle at this moment and worse, what Jamal would do for the sake of a child.

Jamal had already gone back to the other bedroom and dressed himself to go outside. He returned moments later ready for whatever came next.

Keesha ran to the phone and dialed 911. When the emergency service answered the phone, she explained the situation that just happened. They informed her that she would have to contact the local precinct for help. They gave her the number and hung up the phone.

"Keesha, where does Michelle live?" Chris asked turning to face her.

Keesha explained to Chris that he should let the authorities handle this and that he shouldn't jeopardize losing Ashley completely.

"Keesha, tell us now," Jamal told her. "What if she hurts Ashley? We don't have time to explain that to the police. Ashley needs her father right now, not an hour or two later when Michelle has had time to hurt her."

"Jamal, please, promise me that you won't do anything to jeopardize our marriage. We need you."

"She's right, Jamal. You stay here. I'll deal with this myself."

"Chris, I'm going. I know that you can handle Michelle, but I don't want you getting into any trouble. She has a court order that says that she has custody of Ashley. Let's do this thing the right way."

Keesha gave them Michelle's address reluctantly. She didn't know what to do. She hated what Michelle had done, but she knew that with the law on her side, Chris would still have to leave his daughter there. She also knew that if anything happened to Michelle, Chris would be punished for it.

Chris darted down the stairs with Jamal right behind him. They rushed to Jamal's Escalade and quickly left. Shortly after, they pulled up to Michelle's door, parking the truck in her lawn and uprooting her manicured bush. Chris and Jamal forced in the door and hurried into the house and up the stairs looking for Ashley. No one was there. He went into the bathroom and saw the phone floating in the water. There were speckles of blood on the floor and sink. Chris kicked the door when he saw it because he knew that Michelle had struck Ashley very hard and probably busted her nose or mouth.

He turned and saw a trail of blood on the floor leading out of the bathroom and through the hallway. He didn't notice it when he entered the house, but it was evident now. Jamal had already checked the kitchen and backyard. Chris looked into the rooms for them. When he didn't find them, he feared for what could have happened.

Jamal came into the bathroom.

"Let's check the hospitals first," Jamal told Chris. "Maybe she took her there to get medical attention."

Chris nodded and followed Jamal back to the car.

"I am going to kill Michelle!" Chris yelled. "I can't believe that she hurt Ashley. My baby better be okay."

He sat back while Jamal drove to the nearest hospital. When they arrived, Jamal parked the car in front of the hospital doors. His medical license plate would prevent him from getting a ticket. They hurried into the emergency room and scanned the patients, but there was no sign of Michelle or Ashley. Jamal went over to the triage window and asked where pediatrics was. She indicated the room across from them and they hurried there, but there was no sign of Ashley there either. He asked the nurse if there was an Ashley Tanner there. She shook her head no after scanning the patients' names.

Chris and Jamal returned to the car and went to three other surrounding hospitals and found that Ashley hadn't been to any of them.

"Listen, man, this is crazy. Let's go back to the house and wait. Michelle probably took her to the doctor, but not a hospital. She will be back later. There's only so far she can go. She's still on parole."

Chris agreed to Jamal's assessment. They returned to Michelle's house, but this time Jamal parked his Escalade down the block. They then walked to Michelle's driveway.

"I guess we made a real mess here, huh?" Jamal asked Chris referring to the torn shrubs and tire tracks in her grass.

"She'll definitely know that we've been here."

They entered the house closing the door behind them. Chris went into the living room and took a seat on the sofa. His hands shook nervously. Never had he wanted to kill anyone so badly. In a way, he was glad that Michelle wasn't at home because if she were, he would have beaten her to death with his bare hands. Jamal returned with two cold beers.

"Here, this will help calm you down. She's not going to hurt Ashley. She may have slapped her in anger, but she's not crazy. It's her daughter too." Jamal then thought about what Michelle had done to Keesha. It was a horrible thing to do to anyone and it almost cost Keesha her life. Had he not gotten there in time, she would have been dead. Of course, this was not the time to second guess their one and only hope that Michelle was sane.

Jamal sat in the armchair swallowing his beer. He realized that Chris was in deep thought.

"What's the story with you and Michelle? Why is she so bitter toward you?"

Chris shrugged.

"She was my first real woman; she was older, sexier, and prettier than any of the girls I had dated if you want to call it that. I guess I was supposed to be her pet, but I grew up and moved on."

Jamal nodded while taking another gulp. He could relate to Chris' story. Women could be crazy when their pride is hurt. The extent of what they would do in revenge was limitless. She may not hurt Ashley or kill her, but she would make damn sure that Chris never see or hear from his daughter again. Ashley's defiance toward her mother only heightened her anger and the yearning to punish Chris all the greater.

***

Keesha waited at Chris' house worried that things had gone drastically wrong. Four hours had passed and she didn't hear a peep out of them. Jamal, hurrying out with Chris, had left his cell phone on the nightstand. Remembering Michelle's number, she took a chance and dialed it. After the phone rang for several times, a recording came on stating that the number had been disconnected and no further information was available.

Chapter Seventeen

Night came quickly. Chris and Jamal had spent the entire day waiting for Michelle to return. Chris pressed the button on his watch, lighting the screen so that he could read the time. It was one fifty-four in the morning. He stretched his arms then got up and stretched his legs. Jamal was still asleep with his head thrown back into the cushions. When Chris turned on the light, Jamal sprung up at attention. He immediately looked at his watch.

"Oh, God, Keesha must be worried sick."

"I'll call her," Chris comforted. "When he reached for the phone, he thought about the redial button. He pressed it and a line started to ring. He waited. An answering machine picked up from a Poconos real estate company. He waved to Jamal for a pen. Jamal looked around quickly and noticed a pen on the counter. He hurried over to Chris with it. Chris jotted the name of the place down. He then dialed information for the address, but strangely enough, the phone message now told him that the line was disconnected and that he should contact his local telephone company for service. He hung up the phone.

"What is it?" Jamal asked.

"The last number Michelle dialed was a real estate company in the Poconos. She must have taken Ashley there."

"You got an address?"

"Not yet. Besides, the only way to find her address is to talk to the real estate company."

Jamal noticed the answering machine next to the phone. He pressed the play button to listen to the messages:

Hello, Ms. Tanner, your home is ready. You can pick up your keys at any time.

Jamal waited and the next message came on from a week prior. Ms. Tanner, this is Carlos Hernandez. I have completed the inspection on the 523 Dogswood Path property. You should be getting a call from the builders that you can move in by the weekend. If you need anything else, please let me know. I will be in my office Saturday morning for a moment but won't be answering the office phone. If you have any problems, my cell phone number is 717-272-6848. You can call that number at any time.

Chris jotted the mentioned information on the piece of paper.

"We can get directions from the internet," he told Jamal. They left Michelle's house after turning off the lights. Jamal pulled the door shut and caught up with Chris.

When they reached the Escalade, the rear tire was flat. Jamal didn't realize that he had backed up on a shard of glass. They changed the tire then returned to Chris' home.

Keesha was asleep on the sofa. She went to sleep tense and the lines that etched her forehead revealed her worry. This whole episode had her going through a lot. Not wanting to wake her, Jamal took the throw from Chris and placed it over her shoulders. He kissed her hair then went with Chris upstairs to his laptop.

They went to Mapquest and retrieved the directions. Chris turned to Jamal.

"Jamal, I really appreciate everything you have done for me, but maybe you should stay here with Keesha. I don't want you to get any more involved than you already are."

"We're family now. I'm going with you and we're going to get my niece. You understand me?"

Chris nodded. When he stood up, he and Jamal shook hands then shared a brotherly hug. This was going to be an uncertain battle. Chris only worried that his daughter was okay.

***

Michelle and Ashley were in the basement of their new home. Michelle prepared her shotgun for any intruders. Ashley watched her mother unveil her true personality. Her father told her that her mother was dangerous, but she hadn't believed him. She wanted and needed to know her mother so badly and now she wished that she had never met her.

Ashley held the wet towel her mother gave her against her nose. She refused to ask her mother for more ice. She could beat her, but she could not make her love her. Her cheek hurt badly, and the scrape on her thigh stung from when her mother dragged her down the stairs when she resisted. She wondered if her mother was going to kill her. She reasoned that the gun couldn't be for her father since he didn't know where they were.

When Michelle finished what she was doing, she moved over to her daughter and sat on the seat next to her.

"You know, none of this would have happened if you had only given us a chance. But instead, you had to sneak and call your father. Well, I want you to know that he is going to die and you are going to kill him."

Ashley turned away from her mother. Although the communication didn't come from her mouth, her defiance was noted.

"If you don't, I will shoot him with that tranquilizer and torture him first. You will watch every bit of it."

"Why are you so mean?" Ashley asked her mother. "My dad is a good man. Why do you want to hurt him? Why are you hurting me?" She glared at her mother with her penetrating stare.

"I like that fire in you. It reminds me so much of myself. You may not like me right now, but you are just like me. You'll see that soon. I'm not even mad at you, Ashley. Your defiance has only made me love you all the more. Your zeal to stand up for what you believe is just like mine."

"I'm like my father."

"Your father is a wimp because if it were me in that courtroom, there is no way he would have taken you from me without a fight. Look at you...loathing what you're made of. I'm your mother, Ashley, and there is nothing you can do to change that. You may have your dad's complexion, but that pretty, little face is all me."

"Liar. I look like my dad. Everyone says it."

"That's because they don't know me."

Michelle placed her hand on top of Ashley's. When Ashley tried to pull away from her, she held it firmly, but not enough to hurt her.

"I love you, Ashley, and I am not going to let you go. I will die first. I'm sorry that our relationship came to this, but you've got to give us a chance. I mean, a real chance and you will see that you've missed a lot. There's nothing I wouldn't do for you, Ashley."

"Then let me talk to my dad. Let me tell him that I love him."

Michelle shook her head no.

"I gave you to your dad for ten years, Ashley. He's seen you grow from a newborn baby into this adorable, young girl. He's done a fabulous job taking care of you; I will give him that. You're smart, well mannered and beautiful. I'm proud of what you've turned out to be. I don't want you to be angry, Ashley. You shouldn't be bitter toward me."

She pulled Ashley's hand to her lips and kissed it. Ashley turned and looked at her mother. It hurt her to see the tears in her eyes. Her mother did love her and her behavior was hurting her. Ashley didn't want to hurt her mother either. She wanted to reach out and love her, but all she could think about was her dad reaching out for her in the courtroom. She could hear the stories he would tell her at night just before she went to sleep.

Michelle pulled the towel away from Ashley's face. She was thankful that her eye didn't blacken behind the blow she gave her. She realized that Ashley had softened again.

"I don't want to make you cry, Ashley. All I'm asking is that you give me a fair chance. That's all. The court gave me two months to be with you without Chris' interference; then you will see him again. Can you at least give me that? Is that too much to ask for when I carried you for nine whole months?"

Ashley shook her head no as she considered what her mother was saying. She didn't want to hate her because she didn't like the way it felt. Two months wasn't a long time at all.

"You promise?" she asked.

"I promise. Ashley, the truth is I love your father. I never wanted to hurt him. That's why I wanted his child. I still want him."

"You do?"

"Yes. If you help me, I can still have him."

Ashley wanted to believe her.

"Wouldn't you rather have both of your real parents together than a make believe mommy?"

Ashley nodded to Michelle's delight.

"I love him, Ashley. I spent ten years in prison because I couldn't bear the fact that someone else was going to have him."

"You mean Aunt Keesha?"

"Is that what he told you to call her? She's not your aunt. She's the reason we are not together as a family now. He thought she loved him, but she married someone else."

"Uncle Jamal!" Ashley beamed.

"Come on, let's get you upstairs into the bath before your cupcake falls out."

Ashley laughed at her mother's description of her private part. She followed her upstairs from the basement. Michelle sat in the bathroom with Ashley talking to her. She could tell that her daughter felt a whole lot better than she did when she first took her from court.

***

Simone felt terrible about the events at court. She was tormented by the fact that it was her help that made it possible for Michelle to take Ashley from Chris. As much as she wanted to believe that it wasn't her fault, she knew that it was. How could she ever face him again? The fine line that separated her from doing the right thing and the wrong thing passed after being with him for seven years and only after realizing that Michelle was about to be released did she finally tell Chris of their ploy against him.

He had not returned any of her calls so calling him was out of the question. It was undeniable that she loved him because it was one o'clock in the morning and the only thing on her mind was he and Ashley. She got up and threw on some clothes. She wouldn't call first because she knew that he would not talk to her. Grateful that Chris didn't retrieve his keys from her, Simone drove over to Chris' house. She saw his car in the driveway so she knew that he was home. After taking in a deep breath, she turned the key in the lock and opened the door. Before she could close the door, a woman raced toward her calling, "Chris."

She spun around looking at the woman standing surprised in front of her.

"Who are you?" Simone asked curiously.

Keesha quickly gathered her senses.

"You must be Simone. I'm Keesha."

Simone had heard that name in the past. Her confusion was why Keesha was in Chris' house this time in the morning alone. She seemed just a little too comfortable there.

"Yes, I'm Simone. Where's Chris and why are you here?"

"I came to see if Chris was alright. I got news that he lost his daughter."

"I see. Well, where is he?"

"Ashley called him crying and he overheard Michelle strike her. He went to get his daughter."

Simone turned to leave, but Keesha grabbed her arm.

"Simone, they're not at Michelle's house. Chris left a note saying that he was going out to the Poconos where Michelle is."

"Did he leave an address?" Simone asked.

"No."

Simone raced upstairs hoping that Chris had left his laptop behind. To her delight, he had. She logged on to his computer and used his browser's history and found that the last thing he did was lookup an address in Mapquest. When she clicked on it, it pulled up Michelle's address and the directions. She printed a copy of it. When she turned around, Keesha was standing at the door.

"Are you seeing Chris?" Simone asked, worried that she might say yes.

"No. I'm married. My husband is with him."

Simone sighed.

"Look, if you are going out there, I'm going with you. I can't sit around here waiting to hear something."

Simone nodded. She and Keesha got into her Caravan and sped down the street until they turned onto the highway. The ride started off quiet, but the two women knew that the trip was a long one and there was no point being estranged.

"What happened between you and Chris? Why did you leave him?" Simone inquired.

Keesha smiled looking at the beautiful wedding ring on her finger that was a symbol of her and Jamal's love and commitment.

"I made a choice; a very difficult one too, because I loved Chris so much. When I see him, I get Goosebumps all over my body."

Simone frowned, but she didn't interrupt her revelation. She wanted to know so much about the Chris she didn't know.

"I should never have allowed our friendship to go to the next level, but I'm sure you've realized that Chris is very alluring. His seduction is majestic. He was more than I imagined. For a moment, he was enough for me to forget about his mother. She was my best friend. I loved Christine like a mother. Let me tell you, Christine was protective of her son. Anyway, in fear of losing my best friend, I started second guessing our relationship and had an affair with my husband. He wasn't my husband then, but we seemed destined to be together. He was special in every way a man could be. I hated hurting Chris. There isn't a day that goes by that he doesn't cross my mind."

She paused and turned to Simone who was still driving, but Keesha could tell that she had her best attention.

"When Chris made love to me, it was like I had left my body and entered this beautiful world. Every nerve of my body experienced his love. I don't know if it was his youth or if he just knew every spot to touch. My body sang when we made love. I can still remember falling asleep in his arms with his flesh still buried deep within me. Simone, I still love him. I love the special way he made me feel."

Simone nodded.

"I can imagine," she muttered.

"You don't have to worry about me. I will never leave Jamal and I will never do anything to jeopardize what we have. Although Jamal takes me to new heights, I still remember the innocent love of my best friend's son. When I left him, it hurt him more than I can ever explain. The chips are still falling for him and scattering about him. He remains plagued by his past relationship with Michelle. She was my friend, but she would have killed me over Chris. I know what he did to me; I can only imagine what he did to her to make her snap like that. She tried to kill me even though she knew that I was no longer with him."

Keesha stopped speaking and silently cried remembering her friend who died because of her.

"Michelle was unsuccessful in killing me, but she was successful in killing his mother. Chris hated me for that. He blamed me for losing his mother. If I could turn back the hands of time, I would. I might even have married him and given him the children he wanted."

Taking in all that Keesha revealed to her, Simone knew that Chris was going to kill Michelle if he had the chance. The only thing that could stop him was if Jamal had compassion for her and reasoned with him.

"Michelle is my cousin," Simone revealed shamefully. "When she told me of how Chris hurt her and left her pregnant, I wanted to help her punish him. I would do anything she had asked me to get back at him. I helped her get custody of Ashley, but that was before I fell in love with him. After keeping tabs on him as Ashley's social worker, we began doing things together. He was a wonderful father and I don't know what happened, but we became lovers. You're right about one thing; he is magical in the bed. All the anger that I had for him was replaced with pure lust and longing, but more than his body, I loved him. I loved being with him," she paused, "and with Ashley. She is a very well mannered little girl. He trained her to be not only respectful, but her heart is intact. She loved her mother because he taught her to love her. No matter how he felt about Michelle, he wouldn't rob her of a normal life. He was a real father. He held his hurt and disappointment so that she could enjoy her childhood. Even then, I didn't come clean. It took ten years for me to open up to him and tell him what I had done. I told him after he had asked me to marry him. He was serious about me. He wanted to be with me." She paused and looked to Keesha. "He wanted to marry me and Ashley wanted us to be together just as much. And me, I taught Ashley to keep secrets from her father. On our weekends together I snuck her to see her mother. I helped confuse her. I don't know why I did it, I mean, I loved Chris, but it didn't connect until he asked me to marry him."

"Why would Michelle want you sleeping with him? That doesn't make any sense for someone as jealous as she is."

"She didn't. Michelle was angry when she found out that I had fallen for Chris."

"What happened?"

"She caused terrible things to happen to me." Before Keesha could ask, Simone began with her heart stopping revelation. "She made someone force his way into my house and rape me. Now I'm pregnant and…"

"It's okay. You don't have to say."

Simone continued to drive at eighty miles an hour.

"Chris is a loving man. He will forgive you if you ask him. Make him believe that you're sorry. So much has happened to him regarding relationships, but he still harbors the desire to love."

"You say that with conviction."

"Because I know him. That bit of empathy that he has is what will keep him from killing Michelle. He may beat the crap out of her, but he won't kill her."

"Trust me, Keesha, he's going to kill her if he confirms that she has struck Ashley. He loves that girl more than himself and if he kills her, he will go to jail."

***

Michelle had put Ashley in the bed after sharing her heartfelt secret with her. She went into the living room and lay on the sofa. She had an uneasy feeling that Chris was nearby. For some strange reason, she felt his aura. She went to the basement and retrieved her small caliber handgun. She didn't want to shoot him, but she would if he acted hostile toward her.

By three thirty A.M., Michelle had fallen asleep. The gun had fallen from her hand onto the floor. Paranoia became distant and she trusted instinct to wake her if anything went wrong.

***

Chris and Jamal left the truck at the gate and walked the rest of the way, which was about a quarter mile, down a really dark road. Hissing and croaking echoed through the darkness as groups of deer roamed the properties. The low tapping of their sneakers on the pavement announced their presence and broke the silence. After about twenty minutes of walking, they were in Michelle's yard. There was one light on, which was on the first floor of the split-level ranch. The basement was ground level and could be easily looked into. Chris peered into the window for any sign of movement.

"Don't touch it. She may have an alarm attached to it," Jamal whispered to Chris. They moved around the house to the back where there was a set of wooden stairs leading up the back of the house to the first level just as the front of the house.

"Okay, I'll take the front of the house and you take the back," Chris orchestrated.

"Just wait there," Jamal nodded. "Don't come in until I see that everything is alright."

Chris shifted through the grass to the front of the house. He quietly mounted the steps and stood on the small porch where he peeped into the window scanning the small sitting room. However, he couldn't see into the adjoining room. "Ashley, I'm coming'" he whispered, preparing himself for the unexpected. He stood in front of the door, leaned back and with all the force he could muster, he rammed his shoulder into the door forcing it in.

The noise startled Michelle and she jumped up from her sleep. She looked around and moved toward the door with her .22 caliber pistol held straight in front of her. When she neared the sitting room, she found Chris on the floor holding his dislocated shoulder howling from the pain. She turned the light on so that she could see him better. The sight of him rolling around like that amused her.

"What the hell is wrong with you, Chris? You've been watching too many superhero movies. Now look at you," she teased still holding the gun toward him.

"Where's Ashley?" he asked through grunts. He finally sat up.

"If I killed you right now there would be no jury that could convict me. Breaking in an entering, I feared for my life. How did you find me?"

"Your answering machine. Where is my daughter?"

"Our daughter is upstairs sleeping. I know you didn't travel all this way to tuck her in. You're getting yourself all twisted up for nothing."

"Cut the crap, Michelle. Why did you hit Ashley?"

"You're too protective of her, Chris. Ashley is fine, but you're not going to see her. The court said that -"

"I don't care what they said. I want my daughter."

Michelle turned from Chris.

"I'm calling the police."

Chris fought to pull himself up.

"You know I loved you, Chris. All I've ever wanted was you and you still spit on me. We can be a family. Why must we continue to fight? Don't you ever think about us? Right now, as much as I would love to put a bullet in your head, all I can think about is riding you."

"Well, I assure you that you won't be riding me tonight or any other night. Is that all you think a relationship is about? Fucking? Is that all I meant to you, someone to seduce and control? That's why we parted. You don't love me, Michelle, you love the idea of us. I abandoned that idea a long time ago. There is nothing left of us for me to rekindle. Everything you have done up to this point has only hurt me and those around me. Now you're hurting our daughter, someone you claim you love. How can you love her and do what you did to her? Maybe the court couldn't see through you, but I know you for the monster that you are and the evil you are capable of. You dragged Ashley from the court kicking and screaming. I wouldn't have kept you from her, Michelle. I just wanted Ashley to be happy. I knew that you would try to turn her against me.

He surged toward Michelle surprising her. Without thinking, Michelle accidentally fired the gun striking Chris in the chest.

Jamal heard the gunfire and forced his way into the house just in time to grab Ashley who had stepped from the last step.

"Daddy," she screamed pulling away from Jamal, but he held her more firmly when he caught her arm again.

Michelle spun around to face Jamal.

"I know you. What are you doing here?"

"Put the gun down, Michelle," he said, moving toward her with Ashley held behind him.

"Chris!" Jamal called, but got no response.

She held the gun toward Jamal warning him not to get any closer.

Simone raced into the house through the door Chris had broken into. She screamed when she saw the blood spilling from Chris' chest.

"Oh my God, Michelle. How could you do this?"

"I didn't mean to. I didn't mean to kill him."

Simone knelt down next to him and lifted his eyelids. He stared up at her. Keesha then entered the house.

"Jesus, Chris!" She raced toward Michelle to attack her and Jamal quickly darted to Michelle and caught hold of the gun before she could fire on Keesha. He punched her knocking her out.

Keesha ran to Jamal.

"Honey, do something!" Keesha demanded through her panicked tears.

Jamal moved toward Chris to look at his injury. The blood prevented him from seeing anything. Simone continued to fill his lungs with oxygen while blowing into his mouth.

"Don't you dare die, Chris. Don't you dare leave me now."

Jamal told Keesha to drive down the road to the truck to get his medical kit. While she was gone, he hurried upstairs and hurried back with two towels, which he wet with cold water. He lifted Chris' arm to see what kind of damage might have been done. The bullet rested beneath the skin in his back. Once Keesha returned with his medical kit, he shinned a light on the impact to detect any bleeding beneath the skin. When he saw none, he used the scalpel to carefully open the skin and retrieve the bullet.

Keesha dialed Emergency giving them the address. She conveyed Chris' conditions to the attendant until paramedics arrived.

Ashley moved toward her father after he was lifted onto the gurney.

"I love you, Daddy," she told him in a quivering, raspy tone. Jamal held her shoulders.

The police arrived and entered the house. Jamal gave his account of the details as he knew them. Michelle had now become conscious with the help of the paramedics. After answering the questions the police asked, she was taken to the hospital for observation. An officer accompanied her in the ambulance.

Simone had gone with Chris to the hospital. He was still unconscious when they took him.

"Jamal, is he going to be okay?" Keesha asked him.

He opened his hand holding the bullet that failed to open.

"I don't know, sweetheart. Come on, let's get to the hospital."

He took Ashley over to the sofa and sat her down. She shivered and sobbed hysterically.

"It's going to be okay, sweetie. Can I take a look at you? Your face is a little swollen."

Ashley nodded.

"You're uncle Jamal?"

He smiled.

"Yes."

She turned to Keesha.

"And you're my aunt Keesha, right? I know you from your pictures. Where are Keona and Christian?"

"They're home," Keesha responded. "We'll take you with us to meet them."

Jamal gently felt her nose and cheeks. He looked into her eyes and felt her scalp for any lumps.

"Ashley, are you hurting anywhere else?"

She indicated her leg. Jamal looked at the scrape on her leg and felt to see if there were any other injuries.

"Did your mom put anything on it?"

She shook her head.

"Well, let me see what I have in my medical kit. I'm going to make it all better."

"Uncle Jamal, will my daddy die?"

He held her.

"He'll be fine, Ashley. Let's go see him."

After Jamal tended to Ashley's scrape, Keesha hugged her as though she was her own daughter. She then held Jamal.

"You don't know what you put me through tonight."

"I know, honey, and I'm sorry."

"But, I'm proud of the way you stepped in. I love you so much."

"Can I offer you a ride to the hospital?" the officer offered?"

"No. But my car is at the gate. Can you give us a lift there and we will follow you from that point?"

"Sure."

They got into the car

.

***

When they arrived at the hospital, Simone was sitting in the waiting room for word about Chris. When Ashley saw her, she ran into her arms.

"Hey, sweetie," she greeted while trying to hide her tears.

"Where is my dad?"

"They have him in surgery now," she truthfully told Ashley. "They're going to fix him up like new."

"What's going to happen to my mom?"

"She did a very bad thing, Ashley. Your mom will be gone for a very long time."

Tears streamed down her face.

"You mean she's going back to jail?"

Simone stifled her sniffling.

"Yes."

"Will I ever see her again?"

"I don't know. That's not for me to decide."

Keesha joined them in the seat next to Ashley.

"You'll have all of us in the meantime. Simone will be your new mommy and she will love and care for you and your dad."

Simone squeezed her hand for reassurance. This was tough on Ashley and it was necessary that Simone be strong for her. She deserved to be her mother. Chris would be proud of the way she held things together for his daughter.

***

Jamal had been allowed into the surgical ward to check on Chris because of his surgical background. He observed as they worked on Chris. His heart raced in anticipation of the outcome. A passage from the bible came to mind, which read Vengeance Is Mine. He didn't think about that when they raced into the night to this terrible doom. He went to a quiet corner and prayed for their forgiveness and that Chris would come through this with all of his organs and limbs intact. He prayed that whatever malice Chris and Michelle held toward each other would become a thing of the past and that they could get along for the sake of their beautiful daughter. He asked that a stable wife be given to Chris so that he would have someone to truly love, cherish and enjoy as a companion. He closed by asking that God bestow on Ashley the courage to be strong and wise against the enemy and to fortify her mind so that she could go on in the way of God. All this was asked in Jesus' name.

He returned to the door and peeked in. Chris was being moved to a monitoring room while he pulled through the anesthesia. Jamal spoke briefly with the surgeon for the details of the surgery. He firmly shook the surgeon's hand then went to see Chris. He entered the room and pulled a seat next to him. Chris was groggy, but was beginning to return from the deep sleep he had been put under. He struggled with his restraints when he became aware of his surroundings.

"Take it easy, buddy. The anesthesia is wearing off. How do you feel?"

Chris mumbled something to Jamal that couldn't be made out.

"I guess this isn't heaven," he teased when he realized that Jamal was there. "Where's Ashley?"

"She is in the waiting room with Keesha and Simone."

"How about Michelle?"

"She's also here. I knocked her out."

Chris let out a coughing laugh. Then his face became serious.

"Am I going to have to let my daughter go?"

"The authorities will be taking Michelle back to prison. This event broke her parole and will probably extend her time. I don't know what you've done to these women, but they fall madly in love with you," Jamal teased to make light of the situation.

"You're right about that," Chris retorted.

"Simone is outside. She is really upset about all of this. You think that you might go light on her this time?"

Chris could vaguely remember her blowing into his mouth and begging him not to die.

"I think she will make a wonderful mother for Ashley and a great wife for you."

"I know. I just need some time with my daughter alone. I can only imagine what all of this has done to her mentally."

"Ashley is holding up just fine. Simone is probably the fortitude she needs. If you're feeling up to it, I will see if I can get her in here to see you."

Chris shook his head with a great deal of effort.

"No. Let me rest. I will talk to Simone tomorrow."

"Okay. I'm going to see if I can get a room for the night. I will be back first thing in the morning."

"Jamal, thanks for everything. You know the last time I saw you, I would have never thought we would become friends."

"God works in mysterious ways."

He turned and left Chris to sleep.

Chapter Eighteen

Jamal rented a two-bedroom suite for all of them, located only ten minutes from the hospital. Ashley went into one room with Simone and Jamal and Keesha went into the other.

"I think I'm going to write a book," Jamal teased Keesha.

Her tense face broke into a wide grin.

"You have given me enough drama over the past ten years to write an entire best selling novel."

"You wouldn't dare."

"Are you kidding? We will be worth millions."

"We're already worth millions."

"More millions. We can never have enough money."

"You're silly. Come give me a kiss."

Jamal pulled Keesha close to him and planted a long, passionate kiss on her lips.

"I bet Chris can't kiss like that, can he?"

"No way, baby. Nobody kisses like you. Now be quiet and…"

"Enough said," he told her covering her mouth again with his.

***

Simone watched as Ashley slept soundly. Her chest rose and fell like the waves coming in and out of shore. She loved this child like her own and would do anything to have a second chance. There was too much mayhem for such a short space of time. Michelle had really upset their lives. She couldn't blame Chris if he didn't forgive her, but then Simone reasoned that he wouldn't have had Ashley if it weren't for her. Who else would have carried out Michelle's plot? She felt horrible and evil.

Simone felt something terrible, a pain greater than any she had known. She staggered out of the bed falling to the floor. She pulled herself up using the chair and doorknob as support. Jamal heard the noise and came out to see what was happening. Blood spilled down Simone's legs and onto the floor. Keesha came out also when she saw Jamal helping Simone up.

"Oh, God, Jamal, she's pregnant. She told me that earlier."

Jamal was in his boxers. Keesha brought his jeans out to him and he pulled them on. Simone was now hovered over the chair holding her stomach. Jamal pulled the card out of his pocket with the hospital's number and dialed it. He explained Simone's condition to the nurse and told her that he was on his way with the patient.

Keesha took some towels and handed them to Simone so that she could catch the blood with it.

"How far are you?" Jamal asked. Concerned that the child wouldn't be saved.

Losing so much blood, Simone only smiled at him. He lifted her up and hurried her out to his truck. He placed her onto the seat then hurried to the driver's seat. Once the car was started, he sped down the street. It was only six o'clock in the morning. He felt as if he had just lain down. Keesha remained at the hotel with Ashley who was still asleep.

At the hospital, a male nurse helped Jamal bring Simone into the emergency area. He told them that she was pregnant and that he was a gynecological surgeon.

"I need a room to examine her right now."

Simone was taken into a room where Jamal took a sonogram to see where the baby was positioned and what condition it was in. It was not in her uterus as he had hoped; it had attached itself within the lining of her right fallopian tube. A general surgeon entered the room to see the patient. Jamal showed him the rupture and pregnancy. She was then rushed to the surgical ward.

"Thank you, Dr. Warner. We will take over from here."

"Not this one. This is my field of medicine. I specialize in this."

"You are not authorized to perform surgery in this hospital."

"I am authorized to operate on call at any given time and we're wasting it right now."

The surgeon nodded and allowed Jamal to enter the surgical room. They used gas anesthesia to quickly put Simone under. Jamal had already put on a sterile garment and entered the room prepared to do what he was trained to do.

He made his first incision vertically in the abdominal wall below the navel and near the midline: it exposed the pelvic organs. The swollen tube became visible. He was grateful that the tube hadn't ruptured. He was then able to gently squeeze the embryonic tissue out of the outer end of the tube. He inserted a wide needle into the back wall of her vagina to drain out the blood that had accumulated in the pelvic region. The opening he had made was then closed with a single stitch.

Simone was taken to a recovery room and an antibiotic was administered intravenously. Jamal requested that Simone be taken to the room with another patient, Chris Walker. They agreed. He cleaned up and returned to the hotel.

Keesha didn't sleep as she had wanted to, but she lay across the bed with Ashley so that she wouldn't wake up frightened.

When Jamal entered, he took a quick shower and got into the bed. He knew that Keesha was in the room with Ashley. There was no reason for him to interrupt their sleep.

Chapter Nineteen

Chris woke up when the nurse began checking his vitals. He still felt weak from surgery. He thought about all that had happened in his life and what Jamal had told him before leaving him. He didn't want to spend his life being bitter all the time. He felt his mother's presence. She sat next to him on the bed then leaned down and kissed him like she used to when he was a young boy. He cried out all of his woes to her and she listened just as she always had.

"Chris," she spoke. "Son it's time for you to take control of your life. This is not what I had planned for you. You have a child and you have to be strong for her. Stop living in the past. I'm gone from this existence, but I am not suffering. You let go of that anger and let God fight your battle. Michelle will get what is coming to her in her own time and you won't have to worry about that. You just live your own life and take care of my grandchild." She smiled at him and whispered, "And my daughter-in-law too. Forgive and forget, Chris. Everyone makes mistakes."

Christine vanished from him. Dawn had arrived and the bright sun beamed into the room fully waking him from his sleep. He pulled his curtain back so that he could let in more light. He turned to look out the window and noticed Simone in the bed across from him. He tried to sit up, but pain warned him to stay down. His vocal cords were sore from the tubes they ran down his throat during surgery. He called her in a raspy tone. He found the button on his bed that helped lift him into a reclined position.

Simone heard the humming from the bed's motor and turned to see Chris across from her. She longed to hold him and tell him how sorry she was and to beg his forgiveness.

"How are you?" she asked weakly.

"I'm going to be fine. How are you? I didn't know that you were hurt."

"I lost the baby, Chris. I started hemorrhaging this morning and Jamal brought me to the hospital. I can't remember anything after that."

"I'm sorry, Simone. Are you going to be okay?"

"I don't know, are we?"

Understanding what she said, he nodded then managed to respond, "Yes."

The nurse entered the room and checked Simone's vitals.

"How are you today, Ms. Grey?"

"I'm a little sore, but I'll be fine."

"The doctor will be in shortly to talk to you."

Simone nodded.

The nurse left the room leaving them alone. Chris realized that Simone really did care about him and she went the distance to be there for him when he needed her. After considering all that they had been through as a couple, the only right answer would be to marry her. She was his wife in spirit already and also a mother to Ashley. There was nothing left in his mind to argue against her. He understood that she made a mistake and the most important part of a relationship is forgiveness. He had to bury his reservations and give love a chance; a real chance.

Although Chris hurt like hell, he used the button to help sit him up entirely then shifted himself off of the bed. A chill shot up his feet and sent a frigid sensation to his brain as he stood on the cold hospital floor with his bare feet. When he had steadied himself, he began his shuffle over to Simone. When she realized his plight, she did the same and pulled her sore abdominal muscles until she was also standing on the cold floor. The two of them moved like mummies until they were close enough to hold each other. They then kissed gently.

"I love you, Simone Grey."

"And I love you, Chris Walker."

"I know this isn't the proper place, but will you marry me and become my wife and the mother of my children? Not now of course. You need time to heal, but when you're feeling up to it?"

"Of course, I will marry you, Chris. Nothing could make me

more happy."

His pain became intense.

"Can you help me back to my bed now?"

She laughed and aided him back to bed. When he was back on the bed, she leaned over to him and placed another kiss on his lips.

"I was so afraid that I had lost you."

"Not this time. I'm going to be around for you for a long time to come. Besides, we've got babies to make."

She laughed and returned to her bed. Jamal, Keesha and Ashley entered the room clapping and congratulating them on their proposal.

"How are you two doing this morning?" Jamal beamed. "I'm tired and haven't gotten any sleep last night."

Keesha nudged him and told him to stop teasing them.

Ashley went to her father's bedside and he held her close to him then backed her away so that he could look at her. A tiny blue mark remained on her cheek, but other than that, she was as good as new.

"I bought you something," she told him holding a teddy forward for him.

He took it and held it close.

"Just what I needed."

He looked from one to the other.

"Are you guys all okay?" Chris asked referring to Jamal and Keesha.

Keesha moved toward Chris and placed a friendly kiss on his cheek.

"We thought we lost you for a moment." She then walked over to Simone and held her hand.

"How are you feeling?"

Simone nodded.

"Better now? Some things work out for the best."

She hugged her and told her, "Welcome to the family."

Ashley handed Simone a teddy just like the one she gave her father.

"I love you, Simone."

She held her close. The moment was touching for all of them. With all that had happened, their friendships and relationships heightened.

An officer entered the room looking for Chris. He wrote down the details of the account that landed Chris in the hospital. Chris explained why he was there and how his daughter had called him and what he had heard. For the sake of Ashley and remembering what his mother had told him, he didn't press charges. He told the officer that it was an accident and that the gun had went off when he surprised her.

His testimony lessened her charge, but Michelle got five years added to her sentence just for possession of a weapon. Of course, another ten years was still a long time to be locked up.

Chapter Twenty

Chris, Ashley, Simone, Jamal, Keesha, Keona and Christian were at the hearing concerning the weapon charge. Chris looked across at Michelle and something about her seemed at peace. She turned to meet his stare and what she felt for him could not be explained with words. She loved him. That was the best and only explanation for how she felt. Chris sat with Ashley by his side and her hand was interlocked with his. Michelle could tell that Ashley loved her father dearly. They had connected far greater than she would ever be able to. She was daddy's little girl.

Chris was called to the stand. He whispered to Ashley that he would be right back. Ashley felt a moment of trepidation since the last time they sat in a courtroom when she was taken away from her father. He assured her that everything was going to be just fine. Simone tucked Ashley within the circle of her arms and kissed her.

"Nothing is going to separate us ever again."

Ashley watched her mother fearing what surprise she had for all of them. When Chris was sworn in and seated, questions were asked of him concerning Michelle's intent with the gun. He began with a heartfelt statement.

"Love can make a person do crazy things. It can make someone irrational, even violent. I realized after this episode that she had deeper feelings for me than I harbored for her and my resistance to her continued petition made her vigilant. She was angry and hurt. I understand now what she felt and I'm sorry that I put her through that kind of hurt. I can wholeheartedly say that Michelle Tanner didn't fire that gun with intentions of killing me or even hurting me. With everything she has done, it has always been directed toward the people who she felt stood in her way. It was a mistake and if I had not surprised her, this error would never have happened. She was protecting her home and her daughter in an environment she was not accustomed to.

I believe that today she understands her error and is truly repenting of it. I have no desire or wanting of this court to take action against her on my account. She has lost so much time being punished for her past error. To answer the question posed. No, I do not believe that Michelle Tanner made an attempt to murder me and, no, I can not agree that she wanted to harm me. She was merely protecting her home from what she believed to be an intruder.

Chris met Michelle's stare and he quickly winked at her. What he wanted to say to her is that he forgave her and that he hoped that she could not only forgive him, but move on with her life. He stepped down from the stand. He could hear sniffling in the background. Keesha smiled at him as he returned to his seat. She knew that it took a lot of courage to say what he had. Jamal had a great deal of respect for him. He became not only a good man, but an honorable man. He believed if Chris' mother was looking down on him at that moment, she would be proud of the young, outstanding man he had become. He took his seat, and for the first time, felt at peace. Today he used the right head to make his decisions. The smaller had created this horrible circus he had been in.

Michelle was called to testify. Her legs felt weak as she sashayed to the stand. Everyone fell silent. You couldn't even hear the movements of bodies shifting in their seats or the hum of listeners taking a breath. It was a tense moment. She took her oath and was seated. Upon direction of the district attorney, she stated the facts as she recalled them. Before she could speak, tears streamed down her face. The judge handed her a tissue so that she could dry her eyes. She began…

"I won the custody case for my daughter, Ashley Tanner. This marked a victory for me. It was the first time I felt that I was victorious over Christine's prodigy son, Chris Walker. Somewhere inside, I wanted to hate him, to punish him. I wanted him to know the hurt and pain that he had caused me when he decided that I was no longer good enough for him. He used me like a toilet for his needs then discarded me like soiled toilet paper. Ashley is the aftermath of one of our episodes and, even then, he refused to rekindle our relationship. I thought of him as the worst kind of man. His entire world was against me including his mother. I really shouldn't have taken it personal; she didn't think anyone was good enough for her son."

Chris' heart raced with anticipation. Michelle confused him with her heartfelt revelation. Michelle continued.

"When I explained to her that I was pregnant, she told me that he would do the right thing and take care of the child's needs, but she would not encourage him to entertain a relationship with me. I started for the door but something inside me exploded. I was mad for just that second and before I knew it, I had taken a towel and wrapped it around her neck."

Michelle acted out the way she had done it. Her face twisted with the motion of her hands and she reenacted the events that took Christine Walker's life ten years ago.

"I wanted to stop, but I couldn't. I couldn't afford to let her get in the way of Chris and I possibly getting back together. She kicked and thrashed until she stopped breathing. She was gone."

Everyone sighed when she concluded the story. Her horrifying visual was unbearable.

"Ashley came home with me, crying and screaming. No matter what I said to her, she wouldn't listen. She raced to her room and remained there until she cried herself to sleep. She had no idea how much I cared for her. She was the only thing I had to remind me of the beauty her father and I shared. I thought that if I had left her alone that night she would wake up the next morning feeling better. The situation was tense and I understood that, but it wasn't. I had to take control of the situation. I sent her to take a bath because we were going to do fun things like we had done before, but things got ugly and out of hand really quickly. I heard her on the phone talking with her father and before I could think, I struck her. I didn't want to, but…"

She looked at her daughter now safely in her father's arms.

"There was so much blood. Her nose was bleeding. I gave her a towel and quickly left the house. I knew that Chris was on his way and that he would be very angry. He loved his daughter and he wouldn't have given me a chance to explain. We were going to move this weekend anyway, so I went to my newly built home in the Poconos. This would give Ashley and I the right setting and time to get to know and love each other. She would learn to love me as she did with her father. When we got to the house, I had the eerie feeling that Chris was going to show up. There was no reason to believe that because I hadn't told a soul about my new house, but I just felt that he was going to come and take my child away from me. For precaution, I kept a small caliber .22 nearby. I didn't intend to shoot him. I loved him. He barged in early in the morning while it was still dark outside. I saw him when he entered and I held him at gunpoint just to talk to him. I wanted to scare him long enough to tell him how I felt and what had happened. He didn't want to hear what I had to say, he just wanted his daughter, our Ashley. He raced toward me and before I knew it, I had shot him. When the blood started flowing, I was afraid; afraid that I had killed him and afraid that I would never be able to see him alive again. I panicked. People were entering my home from every direction."

She turned to Chris.

"I never wanted to hurt you, Chris. Never! And I am so sorry about all that I have done to harm you. Today, this is the end of our battle. I will not pursue you again. Ashley, you love your father always. He is a wonderful man. If he marries Simone, I want you to call her mommy and look to her as your mommy."

Ashley cried at her mother's statement. She got the feeling that she would never see her again.

She was allowed to leave the stand and return to her seat. Everyone in the courtroom felt her pain and sympathized with her allegations, but justice was justice and after a brief recess the jury returned with the verdict.

At the hearing, Michelle did not plead innocent. She apologized for everything she had done to Chris. She made it public that she understood her wrongs and felt that she should be punished for them. What surprised Chris was that she confessed to the court that she had killed Christine Walker. For these crimes, Michelle Tanner was sentenced to life imprisonment without the possibility of parole. Chris told her at the hearing that he forgave her and that he would encourage Ashley to write her on occasion and send her pictures. She waved goodbye to Ashley as they escorted her from the courtroom. Michelle looked at her daughter for the last time.

A month later, Michelle had released her entire estate to Chris and Ashley to be divided equally. Simone was named guardian over Ashley's share. She stipulated that she wanted monies set aside for her daughter's college education and for her future marriage. She knew that Simone would see to it that Ashley got every cent she left her.

When everything was finalized and in order, Michelle hung herself in her cell.

Some of the inmates said they heard her talking to someone just before she died, but that was only hearsay. Michelle was alone in her cell. There was one thing written on the cell wall that could not be explained... 'Vengeance is mine.'

Chris and Simone buried Michelle after a quiet service. Keesha and Jamal also attended with their twins Keona and Christian. Ashley said goodbye to her mother for the last time. She turned to her father with tears in her eyes.

"Will my mom go to hell?"

"I don't know, baby. That's not for you or me to know. We can only hope that God has mercy on her soul."

Chapter Twenty-One

Chris resigned from Goldman, Thurman & Sacs. He told Mr. Thurman that he was moving out of state and appreciated all that he had done for him.

"Chris, you know, you would have made an excellent partner and I am sorry to see you go. If you ever need anything, please don't hesitate to call."

Ashley gave him a hug. He was special to her. He came to all of her birthday parties and her plays at school, and always gave her wonderful presents when she came in to work with her father.

Chris sold the two properties that Michelle had. He didn't see any reason to keep them because they only harbored bad memories. He also sold Christine's old home. He was letting go of his past.

Simone didn't have any bad memories about her home. She rented it to a new family with a child and gave them an option to buy after two years.

Chris married Simone three months after everything closed. Their wedding was small, but everyone important was there to celebrate with them. Simone didn't get pregnant for two years. She gave birth to a handsome, little boy. Chris was proud of Chris Jr. and Ashley adored her little brother.

While sitting on their porch in Richmond, Virginia, Chris reflected on his past. He was glad that things turned out the way they did because if it had gone another way he wouldn't be here with the people important to him today. He understood that vengeance was not his and that everyone had to pay in their own time.

Inside the book Shadow Lover

Chapter One

The door swung open fiercely, almost coming off its hinges. Heavy thumping sounded on the floor as angry footsteps entered the house. An immense shadow cast its silhouette against the wall and floor. Backing away from the door, Angelica awaits her dark half. She had been in the kitchen preparing dinner, praying that she could make up for lost time and finish cooking prior to 6:00. With apprehension, she looked at the clock hanging adjacently to the door. Although the dew of perspiration stung her eyes, and she had difficulty seeing, her blurred vision noted that the clock read 5:59 with the second hand rapidly racing toward the twelve. Tick tock, tick tock, tick tock the red hand raced. It seemed to synchronize with the throb of her heart. In what seemed like five seconds was sixty and the clock now read 6:00…simultaneously, she turned off the burners…dinner was ready to be served. Just in time she murmured with a sigh of relief. Her life revolved around punctuality and schedule and late dinner was unacceptable. She hurriedly placed the dishes on the table, making certain that the utensils were in their proper place.

Dinner is ready, she said, in a voice so faint not even the sensitive ears of a trained canine could hear. Of course this was not the utterance of a secret jamboree but a plea for mercy. Today was the first time in a long time that dinner was not ready at least fifteen minutes before it was due. Towered by his formidable size, Angelica is struck to the floor!

"Noooo, please, somebody help me."

Her voice went unheard for there was no one around to hear her. Living in the country had its advantages and disadvantages. Privacy was one of the disadvantages for these impetuous beatings went unheard and unnoticed most of the time. On a rare occasion, a nosey neighbor over heard her perilous screams or caught a glimpse of her horrid beatings to no avail because people simply minded their own business.

Continuing to crouch in the corner while using her hands to shield her face, a series of blows descended upon her one after the other.

"Please stop," she cried through the cave created by her arms encircling her head.

Again and again the blows came, crashing down with immense pressure to the top and back of her head. On occasion when she came up for air, a blow would catch her already battered face. When he realized that she was protected from his fury, he snatched her up from her security position and flung her into the stove. The metal bit into her flesh and she let out a yelp. He raced toward her with one of his hands reaching out for her and the other clasped angrily in the air preparing to render a powerful blow. Angelica realizing the impact that this blow would carry, tried to flee but he caught her dress from behind and caused her to fall backward and strike the right upper portion of her head. A loud blunt sound followed and she lay lifeless on the floor. Angry eyes watched her, with fury and rage, while his anger diminished. His God given weapons had once again rained with hatred. Angelica lay unconscious on the floor with speckles of blood staining her blouse, the floor and the oven.

He now sat at the table, swallowing the bitter liquid which had become the epitome of his destruction. His boss had just laid him off and there was no way he could feed his family. His job let him down and so did his wife. Every day he slaved for her, earning a living so that she wouldn't have to work. Most women would appreciate that, but not Angelica; she needed that sense of independence. Thinking over the events, he considered himself a reasonable man. He allowed her to have a job and mingle with her friends. His dad told him a long time ago that a woman's place was at home and the sooner you let her join the harlot gang, the sooner you'll lose her. A woman with friends can't be trusted. He had always been faithful to her and knew that she had dark secrets. For the past few weeks, she has been getting home late and not having dinner ready. Her routine has changed and her preoccupation with the soaps has definitely altered her personality. She was looking and he knew it.

Angelica remained on the floor. Her eyelids blackened and shut by the impact of his fists. Her body lay motionless on the floor. Ivan loathed what he had just done. Another day like many brought him home to terrorize his wife. His fists marked his strength and the emblem of his power. The voice he hadn't the guts to use in the workplace, he used to succumb the gentle, loving lamb that lie before him. No matter how hard he tried to justify to himself what he had just done, the outcome remained the same … she was a good woman and his mind was over reacting. His jealousy was making him crazy and his obsession to control her had become inherent. He wondered why he hadn't just punched his boss. Instead, as always he came home and punished his wife for sticking by his side when he needed her the most. His fury subsided and the rage that had once again taken possession of him faded. He noticed the foil-covered pan on the stove along with two smoking pots. Ivan wondered what she had prepared for dinner. He walked over to the stove to take a look. He lifted the cover to smell the pleasant aroma of freshly steamed vegetables; nicely browned ribs in a roasting pan were coated with homemade hickory smoked barbecue sauce… He could feel his stomach churning. Angelica knew her way around the kitchen and one thing she loved other than him was cooking. Dinner was never late and definitely not burned. Ivan hated burnt spots in his meals. When the smell of his home cooked meal filled his lungs, Ivan looked to see why Angelica hadn't come to fix his plate. Normally she would bounce back into action, but this time she didn't even stir. He returned his attention to where his wife remained. He knelt to the floor and slid his hands underneath her back and thighs then raised her from her from the floor. He carried her to the bedroom and placed her on the bed. Looking at her face, he became troubled at the blood clogging her nostrils. He hurried to the bathroom and wet a towel with cold water then returned to where Angelica was lying. Gingerly, he wiped at it until he had removed all traces of his ugly act. He didn't mean to hurt her. He had just become so enraged at his boss and needed to vent out. It just happened. As usual, the memory was vague. He really didn't remember doing it, he just knew that he did. It was as though someone or something had taken over his body and caused him to commit such an ugly act. Guilt ridden, he called her name…

Angelica. Angelica. Come on honey, I'm sorry; I didn't mean to hurt you. I promise I won't do it again."

Her lips remained shut. Not even a quiver was to be seen. Ivan became concerned. He raised her swollen eye lid and she stared through him with a blank, unknowing stare. He placed his hand under her nose to see if she was breathing. A very faint wisp of air escaped her nostrils. Fear stricken… "No," he cried and snatched her up from the bed then hurried her off to the hospital.

After being summoned to the emergency room, Dr. Painkin hurried to see the incoming patient.

"What happened here?" He questioned noticing the woman's right eye was swollen and blue. He also immediately recognized the broken nose bridge which was twisted irreparably on her face. There was a slow trickle of blood escaping from her nostril. The doctor pulled his penlight from his pocket shining it into her eyes. Immediately he noticed the imbalanced pupils. A secretion oozed from her right ear which didn't appear to be blood but when he carefully moped it up, a pink halo immediately formed around it.

"Shit, cerebrospinal fluid!"

His angry eyes looked up at her husband who stood there biting his nails wondering if he had struck her one time too many.

"Did you do this?" He questioned him. Before Ivan could answer, the doctor ordered the patient be rushed to radiology for X-rays. "I don't want any time wasted."

The two nurses at his side hurried the body down the corridor. The other summoned radiology to the operating room. A scan was performed revealing an acute subdural hematoma caused by a remote fracture which shattered under the surface of the cranium creating multiple brain lacerations and arterial tears.

"This is going to be a tough one. I want my team summoned

right now." Dr. Frank said while examining the film. "She must have received a pretty hard blow for this type of injury. Take her to Trauma One and make certain she's prepped for surgery. I want her ready five minutes ago!"

Angelica was rushed to the first trauma room without delay. Her hair had been removed from the surgical area by the nurse prior to arriving to the surgical ward. The area had been cleansed and it was now the responsibility of the cardiologist and anesthesiologist to make certain the monitors are attached, and anesthesia administered.

In less than five minutes, Dr. Painkin entered the room with a trauma surgeon at his side. Because he specialized in neurosurgery, it was understood that this was his show and not trauma's. Also standing by for assistance was two surgical residents and a fourth year medical student. Nurse Green, the circulating nurse and best friend of Painkin looked on, alert for supply requests. There were five doctors surrounding Angelica's helpless body. A briefing was given to the other surgeons by Dr. Painkin and the incision spot was marked and opened. A thin incision was made to each layer cautiously until the swollen flesh was revealed.

"Look at the size of that thing," exclaimed Sherry Aredt. She had worked side by side with Dr. Painkin on three major brain operations since being on his staff over the past six months. As a resident, her surgical experience had heightened, but nothing could have prepared her for what she was seeing this very moment. Inside this woman's head was a hematoma the size of a golf ball, complicated by irreparable arterial tears. The increased swelling of the hematoma didn't make things easier as it continued to severely force the brain down into the brain stem. She was no expert but realized the desperate need for a miracle. If repair was at all possible, the patient would more than likely remain dysfunctional after the procedure. Sherry imagined that being a vegetable for the rest of your life was definitely worse than dying on an operating table.

"Damn, what am I going to do for this young lady? There is no help for her. She needs an angel of God to help her," exclaimed Dr. Painkin. He could feel anxiety and failure taunting him. He felt the acid building, racing to his throat. This beautiful woman was going to die and there was nothing he could do about it. There was a time he felt he could save the world and there was no problem he couldn't solve, and now a young woman would die on his table under his knife-his knife he thought again. The others looked at him for direction feeling the shared concern. No amount of study could have prepared them for this. Not one of them anticipated the disaster that lay before them. There would be six saviors going home with the same blood on their hands. A life lost who was beyond revival.

While the six stood around Angelica's head, deciding how to proceed, there was a seventh person in their midst. Although they could not see him, he was there, looking and observing what was transpiring before him. "You men have little faith-prayer without belief is useless." Looking from one to the other, he willed one of them to beseech his help. Without the summoning of the heart, his presence was void.

"What's this?" He questioned in disbelief. There was a despondent cry in the room. Someone loved this woman and was asking for help. Looking across the table, he spotted the unheard voice... Dr. Painkin had believed. He was asking that a higher power manifest its power and give this young woman another chance at life. He wanted to save one life from the hands of death and become her protector. Painkin had never seen her before but he felt an obligation and longing for her.

In hearing this, the power was granted. The unseen visitor's existence in this time would be short and his abilities limited, but he had sat long enough, watching this woman suffer at the hands of her husband. He didn't deserve her and certainly should not get away with it.

As the hand of the lead surgeon began the procedure, a miracle happened. His impotent hands made an attempt to stop the bleeding-it was remarkably easy. The clot was cleared and the pregnant tissue settled intact, in its proper place. Wondering eyes looked on in disbelief with renewed faith. Dr. Painkin could see the praise of his understudies. But what they didn't realize is that this is not a miracle by his hands but someone even higher who heard the covetous cries of his heart.

Her temporal readings were stable and signs of recovery which had been bleak were now promising. "Okay, everything looks good, let's close her up. Looks to me like another success story." Dr. Painkin said while his amazed eyes stared at the woman before him. Certainly, this must not have been her time. He knew that there was a greater power in the room with them watching over her because she was destined to die in surgery. When he saw that things were in place and his guidance was no longer required, he turned to leave the room and thought he saw a shadow walking ahead of him. He turned to look back at the others to see if they had noticed it. When he realized that they were diligently at work, he discarded the apparition as his imagination and figured he'd better keep it to himself.

Dr. Painkin cleaned up while staring at his reflection in the mirror, wondering if he was losing his mind. A tingle raced up his spine as his sixth sense told him that there was someone behind him. He spun around…

"Who's there?" He demanded looking wildly around the tiny scrub room—no one. Again he felt the dicey breath it was in his ear this time. A soft whisper spoke in his ear…

"Take care of her. Take care of this angel. She is now your responsibility."

Dr. Painkin searched again, he saw no one.

"Who are you? What do you mean take care of her? What about her husband?"

"Your request has been granted. Show yourself approved!"

Dr. Painkin waited for another response but received none. He beheld the shadow figure walking away from him. He left the room using a door which only he could see. He waited for something else or for a revelation but got none. The room was silent and no one else heard it.

***

Ivan paced the waiting room floor for hours waiting for the

results. Signing the permission slip to allow them to operate on his wife was like signing her over to judgment. He looked at his watch and wondered if this nightmare would have a positive ending.

"How could I have allowed my drinking to destroy my life and the life of my wife," he cried?

The nurse only listened. He didn't deserve any kindness for what he had done. He should be punished; no one should get away with hurting someone like that. When he opened his mouth to say something else to her, she walked away and started pulling files from the cabinet. He would not find comfort from her. He would realize that what he had done was wrong.

After ten long hours, Ivan was notified by Dr. Painkin that the surgery was over and his wife was now in recovery.

"Your wife will be taken to intensive care where a close eye will be kept on her for about six to eight weeks."

Ivan listened intently as the doctor explained her remaining condition.

"Can I see her now?" Ivan petitioned in a whisper of a voice. He knew that everyone despised him but she was his wife and they had no right to keep him from her. The doctor sighed as he fell into thought. As much as he wanted to protect his patient from this vicious man, the law was against him. Ivan was apparently a clever man and was able to satisfy the questions of the police and evade an immediate arrest. Unless his wife confirmed their suspicions and pressed charges, there was nothing he could do about keeping him from his wife.

"All right you can see her, but only for a moment. She must remain at complete rest. She will not be able to respond to you, so don't expect one. Any sudden movements can cause her to go into shock and she may begin to hemorrhage. Do you understand?"

"Yes, I understand. I really didn't mean to hurt her, I was just so angry and…"

"Please, don't finish, I know exactly what happened next. It should never have happened." After that he walked over to the nurse's station and instructed her to show him to recovery.

"Come with me Mr. Carty." She escorted him down a very dimly lit corridor which seemed to have no end, he wondered if she was escorting him to hell.

"Are you sure this is the way?" he asked the nurse with apprehension. Ivan felt a chill he had never felt before. There was something cold lurking at his heels, breathing down his neck, taunting him, loathing him. He tried to shake the thought but couldn't. He looked behind him, but saw nothing. It was there-something was there letting him know that he was hated and would not go unpunished-watching his every move. Even when he cheated on his wife, it was there threatening him. Of course nothing is said but he knew that something did not approve of him or his behavior.

The nurse looked back at him then continued in the direction she was going without answering him. Finally at the end of the hall, was a dimly lit room. Ivan slowly stepped into the room observing his surroundings as he entered. To the left of the room was a curtain pulled around what he presumed to be a bed. He heard a beeping noise coming from behind it. Cautiously he moved closer to the curtain wondering if his wife was really behind it. Then a thought flashed into his mind, he wondered if the hospital was plotting to kill him. Why would the curtains be pulled so tight? He wondered. He turned to look back at the nurse still standing at the door watching him.

"Look, do you want to see your wife or not? I don't have all day!" she said in an annoyed tone.

"Yes, I'm sorry, I'm just afraid of what I will see."

"What do you expect to see, you just bashed you wife's head in, do you think a miracle occurred during the past ten hours?"

Ivan felt a chill behind the nurse's statement. He finally stepped up to the head of the bed and pulled the curtain.

"Aaaaaah!" he shrieked. "Oh my God," he said backing away, almost running. The nurse watched him trembling like a sufferer of Parkinson's disease.

"What the hell is wrong with you Mr. Carty?" Her voice was strong admonishing him for almost knocking her down.

"What happened to her?" He stammered, demanding answers.

"That's none of your damned business."

"It is my business. That's not how she looked when I brought her here."

"How the hell would you know what she looked like when she got here? You don't even know her! Your wife's in the next bed!"

The woman was so heavily sedated that she didn't hear any of the ruckus going on.

"Oh, I'm sorry." Ivan said as he sheepishly re-entered the room bypassing the first bed avoiding any contact. He hurried over to the next bed where his wife lay with her head bandaged. The nurse fought hard to keep from laughing. He did exactly what she expected. She knew that he would look for his wife in the first bed. That patient scared her the first time she saw her. He's lucky he didn't defecate on himself! That patient has severe nerve damage which caused her face to puff up and twist in a horrifying way. Anyone would have responded that way if they didn't expect to see that.

Ivan had a lovely wife behind all those bruises but of course no one could see it because five long years had passed and not a week went by that she didn't suffer at his hands. And now, her beauty was concealed by white bandages. He held her hand, wishing that he could wipe away her pain. A tear found its way to his eye as he lowered his face to hers to give her a kiss.

"Mr. Carty, you're going to have to leave now." Dr. Painkin interrupted him with his sudden appearance and abrupt order. Loathing him, he remained in the doorway.

"All right, please take care of her. She's all I've got."

The doctor scrutinized him expressionlessly. "We'll do our best; of course you know it will take some time."

"How much time are you talking about?"

"As I said before, it will take at least a month. It all depends on her recovery and how she fights to get through this."

Ivan thanked the doctor and walked out the room. The nurse stepped aside to allow him to pass. The doctor checked her chart and told the nurse that it was time to administer her medication again.

Angelica, in her sleeping state heard a voice speaking to her…

"I have come to save you!"

"Who are you?"

"That isn't important right now; the only thing that matters is that you recover."

She squinted and strained her eyes to see the figure that stood in the shadows.

"If you are here to help me, why are you hiding from me?"

"Now is not the time for me to reveal myself. In time I will tell you who I am and why I am here, but for now, I want you to focus on getting better. Will you do that for me?"

"Yes. Are you some sort of angel or something?"

"No, not really, but if it makes you more comfortable, you can say that."

She started to ask him another question but he turned and walked away. In a whisper he responded…

"Your love-your savior is before you and he will protect you."

First, I would like to thank you for continuing to support me and my work. If you are reading this letter, I am talking to you. Your word of mouth has become my greatest asset. I hope that after having read this book as well as my other titles (listed at the front of this book) that you will be encouraged to sign my guest book and share your thoughts with me and others. More important, your comments at Amazon.com helps let readers know what you think about my book. All of your comments are important and appreciated. If you find that you enjoy my writing and story lines, please tell your friends and others browsing at stores so that they too can join the fan club.

Every quarter, I put up new short stories for your enjoyment at my website—www.anewhopepublishing.com as well as listing short stories by others who may be like yourself, who have written a story and not yet ready to publish it, but desire to share it with someone else.

If you are a member of a book club, I would love to hear your views on my book and be invited to either an in-person discussion or telephone/chatroom discussion. Although I can not make it to every book club, I do make every effort to answer interview questions or schedule time to discuss the book via other means. All of my titles make great club topics and there is an enormous amount of subject matter and issues that are concerns for both men and women. Encourage your club members and friends to make my titles a choice to read and discuss. By the way, some of your most cutting edge novels are written by self-published authors. Make special efforts to try self-published novels that you may not have heard about, I assure you that you will be pleasantly surprised that the variety you are seeking is already out there.

I love all of you. Continue to read and support our authors.

Hope C. Clarke